THE MIS-ARRANGEMENT OF SANA SAEED

THE MIS-ARRANGEMENT OF SANA SAEED

A Novel

NOREEN MUGHEES

This is a work of fiction. All of the names, characters, organizations, places and events portrayed in this novel are either products of the author's imagination or are used fictitiously. Any resemblance to real or actual events, locales, or persons, living or dead, is entirely coincidental.

Published in the United States by Alcove Press, an imprint of The Quick Brown Fox & Company LLC.

Alcove Press and its logo are trademarks of The Quick Brown Fox & Company LLC.

Library of Congress Catalog-in-Publication data available upon request.

ISBN (paperback): 978-1-63910-511-3
ISBN (ebook): 978-1-63910-512-0

Cover illustration by Samya Arif
Cover typography by Heather VenHuizen

Printed in the United States.

www.alcovepress.com

Alcove Press
34 West 27th St., 10th Floor
New York, NY 10001

First Edition: October 2023

10 9 8 7 6 5 4 3 2 1

For A, H-Z

All I know about Ishq is because of you.

CHAPTER ONE

SANA

It is a truth universally acknowledged that a single desi woman, in want of getting her nagging mom off her back, must eventually settle for the most boringly eligible rishta alive.

—Ammi

Okay, my mother didn't really say that. She has never read Jane Austen, while I have read *Pride and Prejudice* and *Persuasion* at least as many times as Ammi has tried to set me up with an arranged suitor.

And that's a lot.

A click-clack of heels reverberates down the hall.

"Oooh, you brought me laddus. You *are* a bestie," Ainee squeals.

I swivel to face her, my chair's squeak cutting through the drone of the copier next to my cubicle. "Ammi asked me to bring laddus tonight. I spent my whole lunch hour finding them and they cost a fortune, because this place makes them fresh. Now scram." I wave a dismissive hand at her.

Ainee and I have known each other all our lives, so of course she doesn't retreat but moves right next to the box and hitches herself up to sit on the long desk. Then she creeps her fingers toward the sweet chickpea mounds flour-fried in ghee.

I smack her hand. "Let me concentrate. I have to finish a few emails, then scramble to Ammi's before they arrive." I bite my tongue, but too late.

"They?" Ainee's expression clicks in understanding. "Got a hot rishta date tonight, habibti?"

A shudder runs up my spine as I recall the last rishta. Junaid. He wanted me to marry him and his twin daughters in a hurry. I was able to overlook the recently deceased wife and the canary-yellow teeth; what I couldn't ignore was how he hightailed it out of there the second I mentioned Zia. My brother is all things good in the world, encapsulated into an adorable seventeen-year-old boy. So what if he's on the spectrum? He is perfect to me. To hell with whoever thinks otherwise.

If I have to pick between Zia and marriage, is there really a choice? He and I are a package deal.

However, Ammi often mentions Zia's impending guardianship trust and my being married in the same sentence. In her mind, marriage and security are interlinked. For so long, my father was the provider for our family, at least while he still had his nine-to-five. Ammi never even learned how to drive because he drove her everywhere. He treated her like a queen—not that she deserved anything less. But now, every time she mentions marriage and Z's future together, it's a not-so-thinly veiled hint: if I don't settle down soon, I won't be named as Zia's primary caretaker in the guardianship trust she's putting together for him now that he's seventeen.

I know she's right. But I just can't let go of the idea that one of these days, my very own Captain Wentworth—someone so perfect he's practically fictional—will sweep me off my feet.

There are reasons I hide rishta setups from Ainee. One, because she thinks the antiquated matchmaking ritual should have retired with our parents. Two, because she wants hourly updates when she knows about the rishta meetings.

Ainee quirks an eyebrow. "You're still doing that, are you?" This single eyebrow raise is more impressive than a fresh mango lassi. No matter how many times I've tried, I haven't even come close to the amount of condescension she packs into this single gesture.

But Ainee is good at a lot of things. Dressing impeccably is one—right now she's wearing a dark-maroon sweater dress and riding boots. She's ready for a meeting with the new deputy attorney general assigned to my case, or to go to an after-work party. Unlike me, in my mismatched hijab and long, loose shirt over corduroy pants. Ainee is also engaged to a swoon-worthy, successful desi man, while I'm still meeting with arranged suitors at my mother's house.

I let out a cleansing breath and click on my email. "Yeah, not everyone finds their person in high school. Even though you did give poor Haroon quite the run-around . . ."

"Haroon needed to grow up from being a coddled mama's boy before he could convince me to spend eternity with him. And can you blame me? It's not like my parents had a perfect marriage like yours. Some people settle, and others chase ghosts." She points her perfectly manicured finger in my direction. "Who's the poor suitor this time? A green-card hunter fresh off the boat?"

"Gawd, I hope not! The matchmaker from the masjid chased my sister down. And apparently, he's a good catch."

"Pfft . . . heard that before." Ainee shakes her head in a manner reminiscent of my mother when she's eaten anything I've cooked.

I glance at the clock, which reads twenty after five, and then at my task list. "Ainee, seriously, I have to finish up and leave. If you want, we can walk out to the parking garage in half an hour, and you can grill me then."

She lets out a frustrated huff and slips off the desk. "Be ready to dish the deets."

As she click-clacks away, her comment about chasing ghosts nags at me. Is it true? Am I chasing a ghost?

I have often wondered, if I were to piece together my own Captain Wentworth, how he would look? What he would be like? And every time I close my eyes, all I see is him. His stark gray eyes. His rare but gorgeous smile.

Shahri.

How is it possible that even after eighteen years, I've stood where he left me? Watching everyone else around me fall in love, while I can't move from that one place where only he and I exist. Like that tree in Ainee's backyard in Scarsdale where Shahri and my names are carved.

Ainee's my best friend, but she's never filled that void. Shahri knew things I needed even before I did. He spoke to me without words.

I dislodge these thoughts from my brain and open an email from Marc, my supervisor:

Make sure to have all the ExGen files reviewed by Monday—you're taking over the case.

What? No! I cover my face with my hands. This just ruined my weekend. I have a caseload of two people already, and Marc just added the most litigious permit to my pile.

I spend the next half hour reviewing the documents on the server, trying to remind myself why I work here. *Because you care about disadvantaged communities that are at risk of poor environmental conditions.*

I stare at the slogan in my email signature: *Department of Environmental Conservation: Clean air and water should be free, because nature intended it that way.*

My phone beeps with my little brother's ringtone: "You Are My Sunshine." Cheesy, I know . . . but he really is my reprieve in so many ways. My sunshine on dark days.

When the phone connects, his image fills my screen. He stares at the carpet, a curl dropping on his forehead as he rocks and rubs the hairbrush in a self-soothing rhythm.

My forehead wrinkles. "What's going on, Z? Did Ammi and Rana baji say something? What's worrying my little brother?"

Zia rocks more now—clearly, something has him agitated. "Ammi wants me to go to Lata's house. I don't want to. I want to stay in my pajamas and play on my iPad. And I was good, Sana baji. I did all my chores and behaved in school today."

Lata Auntie is a neighborhood auntie who watched Zia when he was younger. Ammi sometimes has him go over there if she has to go to an appointment . . . or if she wants to avoid having potential rishta proposals families see him.

I fume. But I calm myself so as not to rouse Zia any further. "I'll talk to Ammi and Rana baji, don't worry."

"Okay." He hangs up.

It's bad enough I have to fight everyone else outside the house for him; it's the fights with my own that are the hardest.

I type a text to Rana, knowing well she might not respond. It's dinner prep time for her and the family.

Please tell Ammi not to send Zia anywhere. I want him to meet the rishta family.

* * *

When Ainee knocks on my cubicle wall, I realize it's already six. I hit save, grab my bag, laddus, and coat, and walk out with her.

We say good-bye to the security guard and step outside. A chilly breeze hits us like a wave as we turn the corner. Her teeth chatter as she asks, "Why do you agree to this torture?"

I chuckle. "Because I want to get married. If you'd paid attention in Sunday school, you'd know it is half my deen, part of being a Muslim. I mean, you're on your way to do the same with Haroon."

Ainee slows down and glares. "Yeah, that's the answer you give to the rishta auntie who's interrogating her potential daughter-in-law. But Sana, you could try muslimshaadi.com or something. There's nothing wrong with getting to know someone without the pressure of the family."

Her words remind me of a Bollywood movie in which Ranbir Kapoor, tells Deepika, while he's proposing marriage to her, "I'm not the marrying kind, but for someone as amazing as you, I want to settle down."

I have struggled with this notion of how much expectation is put on Deepika's character. Like, now she has to be amazing every day for the rest of her life—the way he wants her to be. Instead of going into marriage with the mindset of *'I want to marry this person because I want to have an eternity with them, no matter how amazing they are or aren't.'*

Marriage isn't just tinkling bells and rose petals; it's a lifelong commitment to weather the bad days with the good. It's sometimes being amazing, and sometimes not even being ordinary.

But telling Ainee all that means getting into the whole argument over whether one type of marriage is better than the other, and it's not.

I take in a long breath of the cool air. "My family means a lot to me. Plus I want to be in Zia's life. I can't do that if Ammi and I are at odds, or if I choose someone she hates." I envelop Ainee's cold hand in mine and shiver. "And no, I'm not putting my mug on any website. What's online dating anyway, if not rishtas matched by algorithms? I trust my family a bit more than artificial intelligence."

She presses the parking garage elevator button with her free hand. "So you're expecting love at first sight at this rishta meeting tonight? Fawad Khan and his mother will sweep you off your feet?"

I let go of her hand and shrug. The heater in the elevator feels nice and toasty. "If he's a decent guy, we can talk and see where it takes us. I'm thirty-three. Ammi is losing her patience with me. When she's upset with me, that means being away from Zia. I can't disappoint my little brother. As for Fawad," I say, referring to the famous movie star, "I heard he's happily married with kids, and I'm no home-wrecker."

"Well, he's allowed four wives, you know," she says with a mischievous glint in her eyes.

I ignore that. "I agree to these meetings because it makes Ammi happy. She's talking about Z and a plan for his future, and she may not include me in Z's guardianship trust if I'm still single. But it's not the only reason. I also want what Rana has, what Ammi and Abba had," I tell her in a low voice. My older sister Rana's happy marriage gives me hope in the matchmaking process, no matter how much I dread it.

Ainee smiles. "I get that. And I know my halal/haram ratio is way below yours. I don't wear a hijab like you. And Haroon and I are a love match." Ainee shrugs. "But I suppose arranged marriages do work. They can't all be as bad as my parents'."

"It couldn't have been that bad if you and Reema came out of it. And Haroon is great. Count your blessings."

The door dings open, and we step outside. I wave good-bye to Ainee and rush to my car.

I hope you're on your way. Ammi's text pings.

Mirchi, my 1972 Honda Civic, hisses as I turn on the heat. She's named after the hottest pepper and still has the bite of one, even though she's old. But she's my only remnant from our happy days as a family. I touch my father's prayer beads hanging from the rearview mirror. Mirchi was Abba's darling. We had some great memories in this car, and I cling to them like I do to her.

Mirchi screeches an expletive as I drag her gears into drive. It's Friday, and the sounds of tires on concrete are more pronounced as people leave for the weekend.

I puff out my frozen breath; it condenses on my glasses. I wipe my lenses on my woolen hijab, muttering all the supplications I know. "Ya Allah! Please. I don't want any more delays. Ammi will hurl galiyaan at you and me both, Mirchi."

Mirchi's voice replies in my head. *I don't care for your mother's curses, and I'm half-dead, anyway.*

I press the FM radio button. Bollywood music fills the air. It's a song about lost love. An ache spreads through me. *Chasing ghosts . . .* I twist the radio tuner to change the song, but Mirchi rebukes me with static. "Have it your way, saali," I curse.

* * *

Ammi's modest townhouse is as cookie-cutter as all the other off-white, vinyl-lined duplexes in Yonkers. This neighborhood is one you'd see in a panoramic shot in a family movie. As I pull into my mother's driveway and park, the familiar waft of fried onions makes my mouth water.

Most windows are closed to shut out gossip as much as the chilly air, but not Ammi's. As much as she loves desi food, the smell of spices tends to settle if we don't air the kitchen. Of course, leaving the windows open also prevents the fire alarms from beeping and announcing to the world we'll have company later.

From the other side of the duplex, a door opens and a curious gaze burns my back. Mrs. Sharma, our neighbor, waves and approaches. "Back again for the weekend, Sana? I like that you're here like a good daughter every weekend, even when you have an apartment of your own."

I nod, taking hurried strides to the front door. Better not to engage with her.

She gathers her sari to the side and follows. "Arrey, are special guests coming for dinner? Your mother's been cooking all day." She closes her eyes, inhaling a long breath, and continues. "I smell spicy cutlets, rice kheer, and chicken biryani." With a hand to her chest, she ambles toward me.

That she can recognize all those dishes with a single inhale is not a surprise; that she can tell it's for special guests is a bit unexpected. Ammi cooks up a storm at the mention of anyone stopping by.

I climb the steps two at a time to Ammi's front door. "I'm sure she's cooking for us. Hope everyone in your family is okay. It was nice to catch up—"

She follows me to the doorstep, and we awkwardly stand there for a minute, her mouth opening and closing. I'm not about to volunteer. But if I were to guess, she probably wants to find out who's invited. I can't be mean to her because she's my mother's regular ride to the grocery store. If only my mother would learn to drive or get an Uber. But she's too stubborn and technology averse.

As Mrs. Sharma stands there swallowing her saliva, I'm forced to ask, "Would you like to come in?"

She beats me to the doorknob, but as she's about to step in, a male voice booms from the other half of the duplex. "Arrey, sunti ho? Listen! Where is my evening tea, dear?"

She mutters some galiyaan, or what I think are bad words under her breath and retreats. "Tell your mother to save me a few cutlets and biryani. I'll stop by later."

I dig my keys out and unlock the front door. I didn't grow up in this duplex. We had a nice house once, before the bankruptcy and my father's death.

Shahri was not only my childhood best friend; he was the son Abba never had. My father was a kind, patient man with a big heart. He and Shahri were so alike. In Abba, Shahri found a father figure, unlike his own uncle, Sibte, who was supposed to be his adoptive father—but adoptive father he was not. Not even close.

When Abba and Sibte went into business together, Ammi warned Abba about Sibte and how he always put money first. But Abba paid no heed. He thought he knew Sibte, but until you deal with money, do you ever really know someone? The signs were there. Sibte was not a chef, and Abba was not good with books. Sibte was a ruthless penny pincher and Abba would let people eat for free. At first, they were the only halal restaurant in town. But after a slew of modern eateries offering halal options opened up, the business went downhill. My father never recovered from that loss. None of us did.

Sibte and his family—including Shahri—left town for California, but the ramifications of the failed business were far from over. The following year was consumed by bankruptcy, legal battles, and more stress than Abba could handle. Even though he'd already had a minor heart attack years prior and his own father had died of heart disease, he gave up his health insurance to save money after the bankruptcy. He didn't survive the second heart attack.

I was sixteen. Zia was just a few months old. At seventeen, my sister Rana became our babysitter, and to this day she acts like one.

My mother drowned herself in work to make ends meet. Worked in the school cafeteria during the day and as a seamstress, caterer, and cleaner at night. After Abba's death, I never saw her sleep for more than five hours at a time.

She opens the door. "Salaam alaikum, Ammi."

The aroma of gravy is pronounced in the small foyer. The crackling of mustard seeds popping in the kitchen leaks into the living room. She waves the big frying spatula and mutters, "Make sure you wear the clothes I laid out." She swings on her heel and yells over her shoulder before heading into the kitchen, "And try some lipstick, for a change." Of course picking my clothes wasn't enough. She has to emphasize the importance of putting on my best face, again.

I put a hand on my chest to calm my racing heart. Something is missing. Usually, Zia greets me with a bear hug as soon as I enter. But not today. I draw a long, cleansing breath as I head to the stairs.

The living room is spotless, as it always is before these rishta meetups. The custard-yellow paint makes the room brighter. The sofas pushed against the wall provide more space. You never know how many family members will attend rishta meetups. The sequin throw pillows that Ammi's kept for special occasions add some sparkle to the older slip-covered sofas. The Arabic calligraphy framed with *La Ilaha Illa lah* in beautiful loops and curls decorates the otherwise bare walls. The declaration in Arabic has been engraved in my memory longer than anything else: *There is no God but Allah, and Prophet Muhammad (PBUH) is His Messenger.*

Our guests have been invited for seven PM. But by Desi Standard Time, we shouldn't expect them until eight. I dash to my room in Ammi's house.

After showering, I hear a commotion downstairs and the footfalls of young kids running about. The arrival of my sister and her crew. Maybe Zia is with her.

A little after seven, my sister's voice booms, "They're here. Hurry down."

They're on time? It makes me want to revoke their desi card so fast. But then a glimmer of hope rises. Maybe he's not like all the other guys and their ammis. In hopes of impressing this one, I lay aside my beloved glasses aside for contacts. Several frustrating minutes later my eyes settle into the discomfort. I finish my makeup and slide on a painful pair of heels, another item that I seldom don. My curly long hair falls to the side. A bunch of hairpins later, it's all tucked away. The blue silk of the hijab glides smoothly against my skin. Embroidered with gold flecks, it glitters in the mirror as I pin it up. The peacock-blue Anarkali gown swirls as I sway from side to side and reflect on the unspectacled, prettier version of me. Maybe it's time to leave my daydreams and heartbreak aside and try to be practical about finding someone to assume this partnership with me. Maybe love will come after.

CHAPTER TWO

SANA

With sweaty palms and a heart thumping wild, I make my way to the living room. I say a little prayer, a dua that Rana comes through with this setup. I take a tentative step down the stairs. Unfamiliar with heels, I descend slowly. Midstep, I stop to survey the room. My sister sits next to Ammi on the couch. The prospective rishta and his father sit on the sofa facing me. With that distraction, I wobble. The room spins for a second; I'm about to stumble in front of a rishta suitor and company.

The room falls silent as they await my crash.

I catch myself on the banister and remain upright. I truly don't want to blow my chances with this rishta even before we say a word to each other.

The rishta uncle and his son exhale in relief. This is different. Usually, I see aunties and their obedient sons in tow. This one is here with his dad.

Zia is not here. Damn Rana. And of course, now I can't even say anything until they all leave.

Just based on that, I should reject the match and go back upstairs—if these people aren't accepting of my brother, I'm not accepting of them. But then I look at Ammi's face. She's smiling—the kind of smile that's full of hope—and my heart melts. I set my grudge aside and pull out my mental rishta checklist.

Graceful entrance: uncheck.

I exhale. "Salaam alaikum."

The rishta is a chestnut-complexioned man with a warm smile. His hair is in a ponytail, and he is dressed impeccably in an off-white dress shirt and khakis. His socks are a solid brown with geometrical patterns running zigzag. He seems familiar, but I can't quite figure out where I've seen him.

Ammi boy: uncheck.

Quirky sense of fashion: check.

Whoa. My sister is maybe getting somewhere?

My brother-in-law introduces us, and the rishta gives me a smile.

Ammi slides over so I can slip between her and Rana. "This is my younger daughter, Sana. She works in law but also goes to college on the computer." My mother tries hard to sell me.

The rishta uncle's face lines with confusion. Then it finally dawns on him that she's referring to online classes. He smiles and introduces his son. "This is Adam. He's my only son and runs a successful café in Long Island City."

LIC is where I work; maybe that's why he seems familiar. I flick a gaze in his direction and notice his wrist tattoo as he fixes a strand that has come loose from his pulled-back hair. He is clearly an independent man, yet his being here shows that he respects tradition. Maybe he thinks like me, that an arranged match with the blessing of our families will be the best thing for us.

Rana's husband, Farooq, tells Adam that I work in the same area, and he smiles and nods.

Rana offers, "Would you like some chai?"

Instead of giving me a gentle nudge to fetch tea, my mother lodges her elbow right in my abdomen.

I bite my lip to stifle a yelp.

As I scamper to the kitchen I overhear the older man talking, "It's so nice you've raised her to be a good cook like yourself. All this lovely aroma of food that your daughter prepared must've been your influence. Cooking is so important in our household, being that my son is a chef and I love to cook myself."

Ammi's voice hitches higher in surprise. "MashAllah, you cook? Your wife is lucky."

The uncle replies in a low, wistful tone. "When she is around. Adam's mom has a thriving business, which keeps her very busy. My daughters are abroad. This is why I want Adam to settle down and give me some grandkids to keep me busy. Life's too short; you never know."

"MashAllah, he is so wonderful to think about his parents' wishes. May Allah reward him." Ammi beams as she compliments Adam.

An awkward silence fills the room, and I am glad to escape to the kitchen.

Ammi's kitchen is a medley of smells, sweet and spicy mingled with the pungent odor of caramelized onions. The cracked window brings in a tiny breeze. I shiver and approach the food.

Ammi's already set the tea tray on our small kitchen table—porcelain cups and matching teapot, with a tea cozy on top to keep in the warmth. My mother is nothing if not a stickler for tradition. The oven opens with a thump as I pull out the baking sheet with pea- and potato-filled pastries and samosas. The steam from the hot samosas condenses on the plate as I heap the triangular-shaped pastries to the side. A tiny bowl of mint chutney sits between the cups and matching plates. The assortment of smells, from fresh mint to baked samosas, fills the kitchen.

As I set the samosas on the table, my sister's voice spills over to the kitchen. "Sure. You both can talk in the kitchen."

Uff Allah! This is a new development. Usually the rishta party is limited to the living room; it's seldom gone beyond devouring my mother's samosas and tea and skedaddling right after. Adam actually wants to talk.

A sudden shuffle of heavy footsteps frightens me. I put a hand to my racing heart.

Adam's face colors in embarrassment, and he takes a tentative step toward where I've arranged the tea tray. "Sorry. Didn't mean to scare you." he says.

I avoid his gaze and busy myself with reaching for a tray from the kitchen cabinet. He sees me struggle and slips next to me to help. "Let me get that for you." He smells of musk and a spicy aftershave.

No BO: check.

He feels me ogling him and smiles, his hazel eyes shining with a mischievous glint. "Uff. Anken chaar abhi say?"

He speaks Urdu with a thick accent, and his suggestion of locking gazes like we're in love is the kind of banter I don't expect at such a setup. Usually it's the elders talking and rishta aunties grilling me on my cooking skills and how many times a day I pray. Adam is totally not what I expected.

Cultured desi: check.

I lift the right hand to slide my glasses up, then realize I don't have glasses on today. Awkward. I reply with a sheepish grin. "You know, I got called *four eyes* a lot by my friends when I was young, because I wear glasses."

"And here I was trying to impress you with Shah Rukh Khan–level banter. That happens when I'm nervous." He places the tray on the round kitchen table and purses his lips to suppress a laugh.

Bollywood fan: check.

That he's nervous somewhat surprises me. He seems calm for someone nervous. I'm not nervous; I've had so many of these meetings that I know not to get too invested in them. Maybe he's new to this?

For a few awkward moments, neither of us talks. My hands shiver as I place the triangular samosas on the tray and fill small bowls with chutney. Him being so close is getting to me.

"Let's give them the food so they will stop eavesdropping on our conversation." He tips his head in the direction of our families, who are so quiet it's as if they're holding their breath for the big finale.

I like him already. A little bit. Maybe. In a nonromantic sort of way. Not that he's not handsome. He is average height and lean, though his eyes are sad. I don't pry, because he's here and seems interested in the process and is better than any prospect I've ever met. And we have a common ground to build on, and his father and my family are getting on so well.

Adam glances through the open kitchen window into our small backyard. "Hey, do you mind if we take a quick walk? I don't want to ask in front of your family if you're not comfortable. No pressure." He steps next to me with the tray of tea.

I can tell from his face that he's being sincere. Maybe I should keep an open mind? It blows me away that my conservative family would agree to a rishta proposal from him. Yeah, he's desi, but not in a Junaid sort of way where I am his last option and hence his ammi dear finds the oldest spinster on the block for a sure-shot yes.

I hesitate, then nod. "I don't see why not."

We carry the trays of samosas, laddus, and tea into the living room.

Adam asks Ammi, "Auntie, do you mind if Sana and I take a quick walk in your backyard?"

Rana's hand, reaching for the laddus, halts. She raises an eyebrow suggestively. "What could you two possibly have to talk about that we can't hear?"

"I want to give you something to talk about, Rana baji," Adam teases her.

Ammi lifts her teacup and nods. "Let the kids talk, Rana."

Adam follows me to the backyard through our galley kitchen. He opens the screen door onto the concrete steps leading to the patch of green. Our small backyard is enclosed with chain-link fencing that offers little privacy. I'm sure Mrs. Sharma is peeking from her second-floor bedroom right into our backyard.

He admires the rosebush and the potted plants lining the sides. He crosses his arms and says, "Sorry to put you in a bind. I wanted to chat with you because I don't want you to feel pressured, you know. I'm a believer in tradition when it comes to marriage and family, but I do want someone who is like-minded."

The sun is setting, and the last of the rays bathe the sky in an apricot tint. The sweet smell of roses fills the air as we stroll. I shiver in the cool breeze.

He takes off his jacket and offers it to me. It still smells of him, and it feels very intimate for a first meeting. I steal a glance at him, trying to figure him out. Adam looks away, as if he's searching for words. He's a handsome, charming man with perfect teeth and a calm personality. But despite his sweet gesture, there's something distant about him.

I don't know about him, but I'm here because of Zia. Maybe he has a reason like Zia? Or his father does?

I decline his jacket and stride in step with him, hoping to warm up. "I believe in arranged marriages," I tell him. "But I have to ask you something. I hope you don't mind." I avoid his eyes and mentally smack myself for having absolutely no chill.

"Uh-oh. This must be a loaded question. Whenever I've been pulled aside with the preface of *I hope you don't mind*, it is almost always about something I'm supposed to mind."

I cross my arms and say, "I'm not a rishta skeptic. It worked for my mother and sister, so I have faith in this somewhat creaky, fickle system. It's a hit-or-miss, you know. But my question is . . . why does the rishta process appeal to someone like you? You are not exactly who I think fits the bill. And you seem so familiar. Have I seen you in Long Island City?"

"You're worse than aunties judging the contents by my cover . . ." He runs a hand through his hair. A long strand slips free from his ponytail. Adam pushes it back and kicks a pebble. "About being familiar, I own the café Tease. You may have seen me there. I'm usually in the kitchen, but once in a while I help out in the front."

The lightbulb in my brain goes off—yes, he's the barista at Tease! I smile.

"As for my reasons for being here, that's more complicated. One is that Abba is getting old and I'm his only son. My sisters are married and living in Dubai. Abba recently survived a stroke, and I promised him I will settle down with a nice desi girl. The older I get, the more I realize that having kids and a family is what I've always wanted. I want a partner who thinks the same and is committed to family and religion."

I nod. "So why me?"

He trades a glance with me. "Your biodata was smuggled to me by a desi auntie who was peddling them in the masjid office, which my sister frequents when she's in town visiting her in-laws. We reached out to the auntie from the masjid again, and she connected us to Rana."

Biodata is a desi version of an online dating profile, except it's managed by a middle-aged desi matchmaker with lots of family connections and an office in the masjid. It has my family history and made-up hobbies that make me an attractive potential daughter-in-law, with interests like cooking and sewing, all in a doomed file sitting in her huge filing cabinet collecting dust.

He smiles, and the corners of his eyes crinkle. "I heard you have quite the rishta reputation. Your biodata came with all the look-before-you-leap warnings. The rishta auntie said, I kid you not, 'This one is a chronic rishta refuser. You'd be better off with Sadia, who just graduated'"—he drops his voice for the drumroll effect—"'high school.' So you know I had to try my luck."

"Is this why you're here? You had to see the un-rishta-able girl?"

He senses my hesitation but continues to stride in step. "I don't have time to be matched online and then go on dates to convince someone to marry me. I'd rather have someone who wants to get married and find a common ground to build a relationship on. Everything else I'm sure will follow."

A rustle on the other side of the fence alerts me to Mrs. Sharma. She is parallel-walking with us now, leaning closer to the fence, hoping to catch snippets of our conversation. The beauty of chain-link fences is that they offer no privacy on either side.

I drop my voice, and he moves an inch closer. It makes me nervous, the closeness. I keep my eyes to the ground and say, "Sorry about the nosy neighbors; not much happens here without Mrs. Sharma knowing. Hello, Mrs. Sharma!" I raise my voice clear enough for her to hear.

Mrs. Sharma waves at us, embarrassed. She nods in acknowledgment, then beelines to her house.

Once she's out of earshot, I tell him, "Marriage is a big decision and affects not just the two of us, but our families. I've always thought families meeting and getting along is a great first step. And if I am not rushed into a decision, it can work. I do have to think about my responsibilities to . . ." I pause, wondering if I should bring up Z.

Maybe don't bring up my being caretaker for my brother on our first rishta talk. But this is why I'm here doing this. For Z. Only for him will I endure this.

I finish my thought: "Them."

Adam swings around to lock gazes with me. His hazel eyes are softer than my own skeptical ones. "Look. I'll be honest. I did a lot of asking around before I agreed to come here. I asked my employees about you, because my first two rishta meetups were, to say the least, interesting."

I widen my eyes. It's good to hear that girls aren't the only ones enduring these horrible setups. "Tell me more."

He chuckles, then jams his hands in his pockets. "Well, one girl needed a quick marriage to prevent being deported for shoplifting. And the second was looking for someone to rescue her from her parents—she looked like a teenager. I honestly thought I was on *To Catch a Predator*." He wipes a bead of sweat from his forehead.

I snort-laugh. "Uff . . . Allah! I'm surprised you didn't give up on arranged marriages then and there."

He shrugs. "I've seen what love marriages are like as well, starting with my parents'." He scratches his chin, then continues matching my short strides. "So no method is perfect. And there's a reason why arranged marriages are more successful, right?" He glances up, looking into my eyes sincerely. "If you want to think more about it, I'm okay with that. You can always visit me with your friends at the café, and we can talk and get to know each other a little more."

I'm surprised at his nonchalance in talking about marriage with no mention of love. Part of me wants to ask, *What trajectory in life did you take to be so cynical of all things love?* But then he could ask me the same. And what would I say? *My heart is half agony, half hope*? That's just bakwas, as Ammi would say—nonsense, and not rooted in any practicality. Practical and romance never go hand in hand.

"I agree. Marriage is a coalition, an alliance formed by a common goal. My parents did that and love followed, from understanding, patience, and time. Ammi and Abba fought but made up. In the end, everything they did was for us, you know? There was no *I* but *we*. And that takes a lot of patience." I flick him a gaze and find that he's nodding and paying attention to what I'm saying.

Good listener: check.

We want the same things, yet my heart is not leaping with joy. But maybe this is the kind of love that lasts, the one that grows to a flame from kindling and not the sweeping love in movies. Maybe the slow burn is more constant than insta love—after all, it took Wentworth years to convince Anne. Twice.

"The pressure that comes with being in this kind of arrangement, will you able to handle it?" I ask. "What if Ammi wants us engaged tomorrow?" I shake my head. "What am I saying? Ammi wants us engaged *tonight*. Are you ready for that level of commitment?" I avoid his gaze and scuff my shoe against the dirt.

"I am ready. I mean, that's how it's done, right? We agree to make it work." He says it with a flat tone, as if he's presenting a business proposal and not talking about a relationship that's supposed to be for this life and hereafter. But maybe, logically, this is how it's done? Less focus on butterflies and more a willingness to commit. It took Ammi and Abba time and patience; I need to do the same.

I chew my lip. "Maybe? I've never had this before. A rishta that I can ponder over is new to me. I need a bit to process all this."

Adam stares at my face for clues while I stay silent, then says in a quiet tone, "Unless there's another suitor lurking, of course. Take your time. You know where I work."

Another suitor? Why would he say that? My heartbeat ticks up, but I keep my face neutral. He cannot possibly know. I need to put an end to this stupid childish fantasy. Adam is a good match, and I should really think about him, Zia, and our future together. I need to wake up from this daydream.

"For sure. I hope to hear more soon."

CHAPTER THREE

SANA

Sunlight peeks through my semi-open blinds. The time on my wall clock is blurry, but I know it's late. I groan and reach for my glasses.

The purple walls calm the dread rising in my chest. Part of me wants to hide here among my Austens and Brontës and not face the music. My small room is made even smaller because of overflowing bookshelves—mostly classics, romance novels, and some environmental law texts, though most of my work books are at the apartment I share with Ainee. The shag lavender carpet and matching sari curtains have been my companions since high school, just like my beloved books.

In the corner, above my desk, is my photo nook. In the middle there was once a picture of Shahri and my family, together. Now it's a weird blank space, with pictures of my high school and college graduation surrounding it. I took it down after Abba's death, because it would pain Ammi to see it.

Ammi knocks on my door with her distinctive faint rap, then a rustle of feet. I know she's leaning on the door, listening, deciding whether I'm awake.

I yell, "Come in!"

"Come downstairs. We have to talk." Her footsteps fade before I can make an excuse. Last night I avoided sharing the details of my conversation with Adam with her because I wanted to think it over first. Lying is not something I excel in, especially to my mother, who can smell my bullshit like burnt onions.

I follow the hushed sounds downstairs. The pungent scent of zeera seeds and onions from last night lingers in the air. Ammi sits at the kitchen table, drinking tea. Her grim face is cradled in her hands.

"Salaam alaikum, Ammi. Why the glum face? Did someone die?" I tease her.

Ammi shakes her head. "Allah na karey. Stop talking nonsense."

I avoid her glare. "Is Zia home?"

She sips from her cup. "No. I can't drive all alone to get him, and you've decided to sleep in again. Did you and Adam talk about anything useful, ya phir just bakwas? When I saw the tattoos, I was going to show them the door." Her lips thin in a straight line, and she heaves a sigh. "Talking to his father changed my mind. His father seems mild mannered and a decent man. MashAllah! He shared his dum pukht recipe. Adam is from a respectable family, from what Rana and the masjid matchmaker tell me. So just this time, I'm glad I was proven wrong."

I slide into the chair next to her at the round kitchen table. "A tattooed half-desi is a contender? Just wanna make sure you're not running a fever, Ammi." I touch her forehead in a mock temperature check.

Ammi smacks my hand, then points her index finger to her heart for emphasis. "Outside is deceptive, beti. Rana told me she'll find a good match you'd like, and I was skeptical, but you should be happy. He's what you girls are into, right? You should be happy. He belongs to a good Syed family."

Syeds are the direct descendants of the Prophet; the cultural importance that's given to Syeds is that of blue bloods. Ammi is all about pedigree and shajras and where the boy's family originated from instead of the people they have become.

Ammi, meanwhile, counts all Adam's qualities like she's counting socks in a BOGO sale. Carefully dismantling all my defenses. Uff Allah! What is it about him that makes me hesitant? Maybe because he talks of marriage as a contract. To me, spending your life with someone and having a family is more than that. I want my kids to grow up surrounded by love, like I did. We didn't have much else, but we had heaps of love.

This is an arranged marriage, I remind myself. *The point is the commitment. The love will come with time, as it did for Rana and Ammi.*

I swallow and try to digress. "But you sent Zia away. I wanted them to meet him and, more importantly, Zia to meet them. I wanted to gauge how they get along . . . Please, Ammi," I plead. "I am not saying no to him. I agree that he is a good man. I just don't want to rush into a marriage after meeting him once."

"Why would Zia dislike him? Z has the purest heart. I would not let them enter my house if I thought Z is not going to be happy with them. Zia is my child and responsibility. So are you. I am answerable for his future and yours."

She cradles her face and says in a dejected tone, one I've heard multiple times, after every rishta debacle, "You're thirty-three, going to be thirty-four soon, then forty. All the girls your age are married; some have a couple kids. Even Ainee, your best friend who is younger than you, is engaged. I'm trying, Sana. But you can't be so picky about every single rishta. There are so few left to begin with."

She leans back on her chair. "Look at your sister. She has four kids, mashAllah."

I do a big mental eye roll. Rana hasn't made it any easier by setting the standards so high. The perfect desi daughter. Married at the right age of twenty-one to a religious and successful desi man. In my mother's eyes, Rana has it all: a mother-in-law who adores her, four children, and a big custom-built home in a nice part of town a few minutes from here.

I lean forward to squeeze her steepled hand on the table, but she retreats as if to say, *Nope, you're not going to win this one.* I smile, then say, "Ammi, I'm only thirty-three, not forty. And you're the one who says Allah plans destinies. If it's in my qismet, I will get married. If not, I'm happy being with you and Zia."

"Sana, beti . . . you have found faults with every single proposal. Is there someone you're holding out for? Don't lie to me." She looks at me with hooded eyes, as if she's trying to uncover a mystery.

There's something to be said for how Ammi goes for the jugular. My face heats, so I avoid her gaze and collect her empty teacup and move it to the sink. I try to convince myself she cannot possibly know my feelings for Shahri. But maybe her mother's instincts are stronger than my deception.

A memory strikes me, from when Shahri and I were about eleven.

He came over, dressed in cricket gear, and waved the bat. "Zayn Uncle promised to play cricket with me, since my uncle never has time." He swung his bat around for practice.

"Come inside and wait. Ammi's making lassi," I told him. I was a little jealous that he'd been spending so much time with Abba lately and not as much with me.

"Where is he?" He stepped inside but remained close to the door, as if he couldn't wait.

"Don't be rude. You could ask me how I am and stuff, instead of running away to the backyard with Abba for hours." I huffed and jabbed my finger at him.

He smiled and leaned the bat close to the door. "I don't want to take my shoes off, and I know Zayn uncle takes a break for the prayers. I want to get some time playing. I promise we'll hang out after."

Before I could retort, Abba's voice interrupted our conversation. "C'mon, beta. Let me teach you how to bat." He squeezed Shahri's shoulder.

He'd called him *son*. Ya Allah!

And yet, once Shahri's family left town, after nearly destroying my family, I never heard from him again.

This baggage of not being able to confront him has plagued me for eighteen years. A part of me still lives there, in that time, so long ago.

Ammi taps my shoulder. "Kahan gum ho? If there is someone, tell me, please . . ."

I straighten up. "There is no one. You know I won't do that to you, Ammi. Don't you trust me?"

"Then why don't you understand that marriage is half your deen? It's what the Prophet of Allah told us; it's what I want and what your father would've wanted. I have to think not just about you but Zia as well. He's turning eighteen; he needs to have a guardianship trust. I want to tell your father, when I meet him in the afterlife, that I fulfilled all my responsibilities. For you, and whatever I can for Z to make sure he's taken care of when I am gone." She says it in a tone that is condescending and guilt inducing at the same time.

Ammi knows Zia is my weakness. She knows I would never engage in rishta talk if it weren't for him. This is why she uses him. But whatever. She is our mother. Zia's *and* mine.

"Don't worry about me, Ammi. Once I finish law school, I'll get a better job. We'll get Zia into a good private school. Ainee was telling me about this wonderful school in New York City. I *am* considering Adam, and that is the only thing I can commit for now."

Ammi cups my face, forcing me to look right at her, and gives me that look, the one that means *warning.* "I'm tired of fighting with you. Will you please pick up Zia from Rana's house and bring him home?"

"I will. Anything else, my sweet ammi?" I engulf her with my arms and kiss her cheek. She smells of jasmine oil and cardamom. A lifetime smell I associate with her.

"I want you to agree to meet with Adam again, and his family. You will not get any better than him. I want you to stop flailing and decide. What is more important—your foolish, childish crushes or your brother's future?"

Ammi's drawn the line in sand. This is my test. A test of how far I'll go for my brother.

It's time to really show her.

* * *

Mirchi makes a choking sound as I turn the ignition, as if she's acknowledging the gaping hole left in my life by my father's death—and the ultimatum I just received from my living parent. I touch Abba's prayer beads hanging from the dashboard mirror.

I turn into my sister's long driveway leading up to her expansive property spanning a couple of acres. One of her kids—Rayhan, my oldest nephew—is outside with the sitter. He waves and calls out, "Sana Khala!" and sprints in my direction.

Mirchi scoffs when I shift the gears to park. *You'd better put on your armor and sharpen your knives if you want to get out of here alive*, she seems to say.

"Mind your business, old lady," I tell her through gritted teeth.

Part of me wants to try to enter through the back door, find Zia, and escape.

A knock on the car window startles me. At seven, Rayhan is still in the adorable phase, so I smile and step outside.

He scrunches his nose. "Khala, your car is old. Why do you still drive it?"

I ruffle his hair and pinch his cheeks. "This is your nana's car; she's not old, she's family. And shh . . . Mirchi gets mad if you badmouth her."

He slaps his forehead and says, "Don't you know cars don't have feelings? My ammi is right about you, Khala."

"How so?"

Without batting a single eyelash, he blurts, "That you're turning into a senile spinster. You look really old. How old are you? And just so you know, I can only count five hundred."

"Gee, thanks. Remind me of this the next time you want an Eid present from me." I narrow my eyes.

He runs inside and announces my arrival while I brace myself for damnation. My sister appears in the doorway.

"Salaam, Rana baji." I stay outside, hoping she'll get the message.

"Walaikum salaam. Come on in." She steps to the side and leaves the door ajar.

"Um, maybe next time. I need to drop Zia home." I stand at the threshold.

She gives me a look I've seen so many times before. A look that says, *You're not getting out of this easily.*

I step inside but stay close to the door.

Rana looks over her shoulder and says, "My mother-in-law has been asking about you nonstop. You know Adam's mom is a famous designer. We're all so excited . . ."

Excited? What am I missing?

"Why the excitement? I'm not engaged to him yet."

Her face starts to color. "Sana, he's not waiting forever. Men like him—Syed, handsome, and well-to-do—have a line of possible rishtas. You know his mother has stores in Dubai, New York, and all the major cities. He is a catch. And he has expressed an interest in you. The matchmaker was telling me he didn't even look at another biodata."

Why should I resist something that could have the potential to help me stay in Zia's life? Adam seems like a good guy, patient and soft-spoken. He is educated and loves his family, his father and my mother get along . . . maybe I'm resisting it too much. Maybe this is as good as it gets, unless I'm ready to fight my family and be away from Zia. "Can we not rush to the mosque quite yet? I think Adam is a decent guy, and I consider him a good prospect. But give me some time to think. Adam has already agreed to that. Can I ask the same from you? Please? And now I really have to pick up Zia and bring him home. I have a long drive home to Queens after."

Thankfully, Zia comes bounding down the stairs two at a time, his iPad clutched under one arm. As soon as he sees me, his face illuminates with a handsome smile and he yells, "Sana baji! You're here. Can we go home, please?"

"Sure, teddy bear. You have everything?" I avoid looking at my sister.

"Yes." He points to his backpack on his shoulder and slides on his sneakers.

"Go sit in Mirchi. I'll be right out," I tell Zia with a smile.

After Zia is out of sight, Rana crosses her arms and slumps her shoulders. "Ammi is excited about Adam, Sana. Ammi's old, and her diabetes and age are not getting any better. Think about her and Zia. She lets you get away with things I never did. I wasn't allowed to live away from home—one, because we couldn't afford it, and two, she just didn't feel comfortable. But you . . ." She flits her gaze at me, then chides, "Ammi gives you all this freedom, and all she wants from you is to settle down; once she's gone, it's just me and you left for Zia. It's better to have a partner to help you navigate. I need you to give me an answer for the matchmaker. Should I tell her it's a yes?"

This is it. The moment of truth.

Rana's right—no more notions of love or thoughts of falling and swooning. I will be practical, like my sister, and everything else will fall into place.

I nod my agreement.

She grins. "You're doing the right thing."

* * *

Zia sits in the back seat, his fingers stroking the plastic-coated bristles of his hairbrush. He hums a tuneless song. His short, curly hair is the same inky black as the beginnings of a beard on his tan cheeks. His face is serene, though his body rocks in a self-soothing rhythm.

As though sensing my hesitation—because we've always had that kind of connection—Zia smiles at me. "McDonald's?"

"Sure." I smile back and start the drive to a McDonald's that Zia likes.

As we drive under the big yellow arches a short while later, I realize I've made the right choice. Going out for a quick bite is fun for Zia. His needs are simple: a Happy Meal with a fish fillet and a hot-fudge sundae. A treat at his favorite happy place besides home.

I park the car, and we go inside. The unmistakable greasy smell of french fries hits us as we swing the door open.

The saltiness of the fried food brings back memories. Ammi used to bring us McDonald's after long shifts of working overtime here.

I'm glad Ammi and Rana were relieved I've agreed to give things a go with Adam. They have sacrificed a lot for me, and doing something for them felt good.

Zia darts into the restaurant and goes over his order like a mantra. "I want a fish fillet. Happy Meal and a hot-fudge sundae." Once we're at the front of the line, he repeats it to the teenager behind the register.

We pick up our order and settle into a booth in the dining area. A lady walking by gazes at my hijab and my brother's flailing arms and keeps walking. No one sits in the booth next to ours. Zia loves to sit tucked away, staring out the window, oblivious to the judgmental stares of people who don't appreciate his uniqueness as I do. If only the people who judge him could see inside his mind. They would see that he is a warrior, to sit here among all the sensory overload and be able to function. To survive among us neurotypicals who are immune to so many sounds that Zia finds disconcerting. He rocks in a stim while I set the food on the table.

We're both anomalies. But today, like Zia, I don't let it get to me.

"Baji, will you get married to him?" he asks with his mouth full, tartar sauce dripping from his sandwich onto the papered tray. "Rana said, 'Adam is coming to see Sana. You should stay here; we don't want him to run away.'"

My heart breaks into a million pieces. I kiss his forehead, then tear open the packet of crushed peanuts to sprinkle over his hot-fudge sundae. "No one's running away because of you. And if they are, they mean nothing to me. But Adam seems like a nice guy; I can't wait for you to meet him. And if you don't like him, guess what? I don't either."

I dunk my fries in the ketchup and let the savory and sweet flavors dissolve the bitterness coursing through me.

A snicker and collective laughter from a group of teenagers sitting a few seats across from us hits my ears. The way their eyes dart between me and Zia lets me know this is more than just curiosity about us. It's not a we're-perplexed-as-to-what-zoo-let-you-loose look but a we-know-you're-weird-and-so-we-will-make-you-uncomfortable look.

I glare at them. They have a portable speaker on the table blasting music. They turn it up. The pimpliest kid shouts, "Hey, dot-head weirdos! Go back to where you came from."

Where did *that* slur come from? I don't have a dot on my head.

Does he know that Muslims don't wear bindis on their heads like Hindus? Maybe that's a nuance that's lost on him—maybe he sees all browns as one, without any diversity.

I retort, "That's not nice," and simultaneously think of how I sound like an auntie rebuking me for refusing to be a green-card bride.

"You wanna fight us, brownie? Show us some curry-te chops?" the oldest snickers. He's slightly taller than me, and I'm not sure I could take him down in a tussle. Should've worn my combat boots.

At five feet nothing, I don't intimidate those brats. Ignoring them will make them bolder. Is there an employee . . . ? Yes, a cashier who just finished taking an order.

I hate leaving Zia alone for even a second, but we need help.

That is why you need a rishta. As usual, I remember Ammi's wisdom at the worst times.

Once I'm up front, I pound the counter to catch the attention of the cashier texting on her phone.

"Welcome to McDonald's. May I help you?" Her eyes are still lowered, fingers flying over the phone.

"Can I have a word with the manager, please?"

"Tania!" she yells. "Lady here wants to talk." She signals for me to move aside.

When Tania arrives, I'm surprised. She looks desi. She mutters in a thick accent, "If you're here about the coupon system or the ice cream machine, they're both down."

Coupons and ice cream? Now that's a combination I wouldn't have thought of together. And why is she attributing both of them to me? "No, I'm here because those teenagers are bothering us."

"What?" She cups an ear with her hand.

I raise my voice. "Those teenagers are saying mean things to my brother. Can you talk to them?"

"I can't leave the register, but I'll send someone over." She swings around and leaves. I wait for a few minutes, but there's no follow-up from her.

I'd expected to be treated better by a fellow desi. Then I realize—if she interferes, the teens will have another target.

I head back to Zia. Sometimes you have to do things yourself.

But before I can get back to the table, a stern voice demands of the teenagers, "Then apologize."

I glance over to find a tall, athletic guy with back muscles stretching out his gray T-shirt. His tone is commanding but not loud.

"Sorry," one of the miscreants mutters.

A couple of his friends scamper toward the exit, but one stops close to me. A whiff of greasy fries, Axe body spray, and sweat hits me. Then my foot catches on something, and I pitch forward.

I wish we had stayed home.

CHAPTER FOUR

DANIEL

Dammit, I'm being ghosted.

I tap my watch for the umpteenth time. And, yeah, he is way beyond fashionably late. An hour and a half late.

'America has become home,' the pro bono client said when he begged for my help to stay in this country. No matter what has gone right or wrong since he's been here, this is his home now, away from poverty and war.

But I'm less irritated at the client, who has apparently decided to not show up, and more because I don't want to be surrounded by high school kids let loose.

Being back in New York is bittersweet. Growing up here wasn't easy, especially for a fresh-off-the-boat like me. In high school, I was the "Paki" with an accent. I missed my narrow, dusty streets, my siblings, and all things Islamabad. I missed my birth mother sometimes too, but forgiveness is hard. In her defense, she had an asshole for a husband. All his money was spent on alcohol and get-rich schemes to compete with his rich in-laws. My mother left a life of privilege, and my father died trying to achieve one.

Every place I've lived has a part of me, every house a piece. That's a lot of missing pieces if you've been uprooted and replanted several times. I've changed homes, countries, names. The ache and the sense of loss are part of my DNA.

And I've never stopped missing *her*—my childhood and teenage best friend, the one I left at sixteen when the strife between her father and my uncle drove my family out of town. The one I always think of the second I set foot in New York.

If Ammi—my aunt and adoptive mother—weren't in the fourth stage of colorectal cancer, we'd probably never have come back here. But she wanted to make things right, as a promise to her late husband, my uncle. To her, old matters still need closure in this town.

In my view, closure is a double-edged sword: digging into wounds that haven't healed only makes them bleed more. But when you love someone, all you want is for them to happy, even when it's not the easiest thing to do, nor the most rational. And I love Ammi, the only real parent I've ever known. So here we are, after selling the house in California, packing up, and uprooting, back to my best-friend-turned-stranger's town.

When I circle around to make sure I haven't missed my client, this kid in a booth near the window catches my eye. He's a teenager but looks like he could be on the autism spectrum. He's covered his ears to shut out the noise and is rocking back and forth. Some asshat teenagers across the dining area are taunting him.

He looks like he's about to cry.

He looks like he's all alone.

Who'd walk off and leave a defenseless kid by himself?

I approach the group. "What's going on?"

The tallest of the group replies, "Mind your own business."

I pull out my deputy attorney general badge and watch the color drain from this obnoxious boy's face. He puts up a hand and retreats. "We were just trying to be friendly, sir."

I jab my finger at him. "Then apologize."

These are the kind of jerks I've dealt with all my life; part of me wants to really teach him a lesson. My jaw tenses, and I curl my fists in order to keep myself from hurting him.

The miscreant mutters, "Sorry." All that fake bravado sheds off him like fall leaves.

A shuffle of feet close by makes me glance up. It's a woman. Her face is flushed, and she watches the bullied boy like she knows him.

The idiotic teenager I forced to apologize flips me the bird, then before I can stop him, sticks a foot out and trips her.

I lunge for her, trying to catch her before her head hits the corner of the booth.

The instant my hands touch her, I freeze. Maybe it's the sugar rush—I shouldn't have had that McFlurry—or I'm just having a lucid dream. She smells of jasmine and coconut. Her eyes are the color of sandalwood and bright as the summer sun. She matches every outline of the face that's haunted my memories since adolescence. I've stored that outline where I keep all my precious dreams and, above all, my hope.

But *she* didn't have a brother. My mind tells me to grow the hell up and stop daydreaming about my childhood crush.

Must not stare at her like the hormone-fueled teenager I just dealt with.

She pushes her glasses up on her cute-as-a-button nose. For a few seconds, our gazes lock and her face softens.

My fingers graze her back and linger. There's something palpable between us.

She must feel something as well, because her face colors, now a darker shade of burnished copper.

She bolts upright and darts to the boy. “You okay, Zia?”

“Yes, baji.”

She’s his sister. *Phew.* I don’t know why I’m relieved, though she looks too young to be his mother. No matter how flustered I am, I can’t lose my shit over her.

I cross my arms over my chest, trying to put up the impenetrable wall that has kept me safe. “Miss, he was terrified.” I point at the poor boy. “You can’t leave him alone to be bullied like this.”

“And you are?” She doesn’t return my glance. Rude.

But she’s smoothing his hair; it’s clear she cares about him. Maybe I jumped to conclusions about her.

Irritated, I ignore the woman and smile at the boy. “Hey, bud, here’s my business card. Call me if anyone ever gives you trouble. If I don’t pick up, leave a message, and I’ll call you back, I promise.”

The boy smiles and tells her, “He talked to those meanies, and they left me alone.”

She rips my card from Zia’s hand, half glances at it, then tosses it on the table. “We don’t need your help.” She turns to the boy, wipes his chin, then helps him out of the booth. He grabs my card on his way out, but she’s too busy swearing at me to notice. She mutters loud enough for me to hear, “These goras have such a savior complex. Man na maan main tera mehmaan. Not like I asked for his help.”

Gora? Does she not realize that I am a desi? Fair-skinned desis like me exist, and for her to dismiss me so easily is intriguing and annoying at the same time.

“Try again. I’m as desi as you.” I give her a wry smile. “This should teach you not to judge. And *thanks* is the word you’re looking for, right?”

Her eyes widen, but she doesn't back down. "I stepped away to get the managers. I had it under control. Let's go, Z." She nudges her brother to leave, then huffs, "And you judged me too."

"Baji, he is a nice man. Don't be mad." Zia flicks his gaze at me and smiles.

She chews her bottom lip and flushes. It makes her look even prettier. She is messing with my system, making me feel things I have no right to feel for this hauntingly beautiful stranger.

She twists the corner of her hijab and says in a low voice, "I am sorry, and thank you for helping my brother. I don't leave him alone, ever, but I had to ask them to intervene. I didn't want to argue with those jerks."

She's apologizing, even though her anger toward me hasn't completely dissipated. All this for her brother. It's the kind of unselfish, unadulterated love that has the power to melt even someone as cynical as me.

But why do her eyes remind me of *her*? The one person I've been trying to forget since the day I left this wretched state.

CHAPTER FIVE

SANA

As I drive Zia home, all he can talk about is his new superhero—the man that rescued him. Daniel Malik, according to his business card.

I drop my brother at Ammi's, then spend the drive to my Queens apartment fuming and thinking of all the comebacks I should've said to that asshole. I'd never leave Zia alone unless it was important. Who the hell does that privileged jerk think he is?

And why did his touch send such a spark through me?

This is what I've been wanting to feel with Adam, with the other suitors. Maybe I'm going senile, because when he touched my arm, my back, I couldn't decide whether to slap him silly or swoon.

I park Mirchi and take a long, cleansing breath before climbing the stairs.

Before I open the door to our apartment, the lock unclicks and Ainee sticks her hand out. "Where's the biryani your ammi made?"

I swat her hand. "Ammi served me some deep-guilt curry. Want that?"

Her shoulders droop, and she moves to one side to let me in. "Dammit. Should've ordered pizza." Her pink pajamas rustle as she sinks into the leather couch in the living room. "So what was wrong with this rishta? Or does he not match this image in your head from eighteen years ago?" She fiddles with the remote and puts on the *Real Housewives* of somewhere.

I sling my keys on the key hook and wash my hands before putting the teakettle on the stove. "Nothing was wrong with him, which is why I am considering him. He's an attractive guy, cultured, and seems like he's from a good family. He has tattoos and a ponytail, and yet Ammi likes him."

Ainee narrows her eyes at me. "He seems amazing. I'm waiting for your *but*."

"I don't know; I kind of gave up on this idea of falling for someone before I marry, and then as soon as I agree to move forward with Adam, I meet this guy at the McDonald's . . ." I glance at her face. "And I felt something."

She scoffs and shakes her head. "No! You don't really believe in this bullshit, do you? As your best friend, I must stop this bakwas about some stranger at McDonald's making you all roohani. This soul mate stuff is rubbish. I'm marrying Haroon after being with him for so many years, but I swear if he were to disappear without contact for more than a month, I'd move on."

As I pour the tea in the ceramic mug, her voice is clear over the sound of hot water splashing in the cup. "I'm hungry. Did you eat dinner?"

"Not yet." Thanks to those kids and that intrusive man. Something about him seemed so familiar . . . but I'm sure it was just my imagination.

I hand Ainee a steaming mug and flop back on the sofa, taking a sip of my own milky tea. Adam's nice, charming, cute, and we can talk about our families. He's part desi, so we have a lot in common culturally. But do I like him enough to commit to a marriage?

I gulp down the tea and stare into the cup. "I told Ammi and Rana I like Adam and that I want to talk to him a bit more. They seemed happy about that, at least."

Ainee shrugs. "What's the deal, though, really? Do you never want to get married? I mean, it's worked for my older sister so far. She's avoided the rishta aunties and marriage. So hey, all the power to you."

"I do want to get married. You took years to commit to Haroon—it might take me a few weeks to commit to Adam, okay?" I pick up the mugs and head to the kitchen. "It's not like I don't have enough on my plate, especially with ExGen now being my headache."

Ainee keeps her eyes glued to the TV but asks, "ExGen? I got an email with a huge attachment, but I didn't read it." Ainee is in IT—she's no expert in environmental lawsuits. But sometimes she's asked to pull old records. "What is the short version? Emphasis on short." Ainee is the only person I know who can talk and watch TV with equal concentration.

I smirk. "We've had complaints about ExGen for years; apparently Brian and Marc were sweeping it under the rug. One of the groups sued, so Marc had to pull Brian away. And since I'm not a lawyer yet, we had to get the deputy attorney general involved. Lawsuits are a lot of work, especially if it's a company as big as ExGen. I'm scared of the scrutiny, but I also want to make sure I'm doing what is in the best interest of this community."

I let out a long breath as I wash the teacups and put them on the dish rack to dry. The suds from the dish soap pop as I rinse out the sink.

"You're screwed," Ainee yells over the running water. "No wonder Marc passed this problem child to you. Maybe the DAG is a nice old lawyer who will take mercy on you and not be mean and condescending. Or maybe he's as expected: a rigid khadoos."

"Khadoos is one word for it. Old, stuffy bureaucrat is another." I wipe my hands on the kitchen towel. "I am still flabbergasted as to why the hell Marc would assign me to this absolute nightmare of a permit; he could've picked anyone. In all these years working for him, he's never wanted me to have any responsibilities. And now, all of a sudden, he shoves me into the limelight with a permit and a big fat lawsuit." I slide onto the sofa next to her.

"What better way for him to prove that he cares about minorities than put a visibly Muslim person in charge? Marc didn't get to where he is by not being strategic," Ainee says without shifting her gaze from the screen, where Raquel's throwing a glass of champagne in Paige's face. "Yes, get that witch!" Ainee screams at the screen.

"I thought you didn't like Raquel."

"I hate her," she admits. "Are you going to tell Marc you don't want to be on the case, then?"

I avoid her gaze and play with the loose thread on the throw pillow. "And get demoted or fired? I need this job, at least until I finish school. I promised Ammi to help with Zia's tuition if we get him into a private school."

She lowers the volume on the TV. "Sana, you work so hard, and you're the only one in that unit who's not white. He is not firing you. But he knows he can dump this on you, and you would rather deal with this shit than confront him. You're such a middle child."

"And you're such a baby, always speaking your mind. Ainee, I can't say no, because next time he won't give me a big project, saying,

'Oh, I tried, but you didn't want it.'" I draw a long breath in. "Anyway, I've had a long day. I'm going to turn in."

"Night," she says, before going back to her show.

I head to my room. After a shower, I sit in front of the mirror, untangling my long tresses. My curls bounce, refusing to be tamed by my thick brush. Ammi's words ring in my ear: *Your father and I got married in two weeks.*

It was after Abba graduated from Caltech and before he returned to India to visit his parents. They insisted he not go back alone, so they looked far and wide and zeroed in on three potential girls. When he recalled this story one night, Rana and I demanded he tell us why he'd chosen Ammi. He said it was her smile. I wish it were that simple for me. I want to feel how I felt earlier with that beardo. Something electric. But he was a stranger, and infuriating, and I'll never see him again.

I dry my hair and hang the wet towel on the hook on my closet door. The sliding door creaks, and I kneel to see if it's gone off its tracks. From inside the closet, something angular pokes my back. It's my keepsake box. My childhood, my life's most precious possessions, are all collected in this chest. I open the latch.

As my hand glides through the pictures, a gold locket gleams in the light. It's my Soni locket. My last gift from Shahri. It's heart shaped, with *Soni* inlaid in Arabic script. It's subtle, and the calligraphy loops make it even more gorgeous. A single emerald is set in the middle.

When Shahri gave it to me, I rubbed on the gorgeous green gem and asked with a quirked eyebrow, "My name is spelled *S-A-N-A*. Are you sure this is for me?"

He smiled and explained, "*Soni* means *pretty girl* in Punjabi. It's the only thing I have left of my mother's. My grandmother had a ring that matched."

He told me the ring was now in his aunt's possession, and she was keeping it safe until he was ready to give it to the girl he'd marry. I'm sure he's married by now; did he give her that ring? I wonder if she knows there's a matching locket.

I pick up the locket and walk to the mirror. Touching the Arabic letters, I put it around my neck. I want to be back in that time when we were friends. I must've been fifteen, Shahri sixteen, when we last saw each other.

Sometimes it feels like it was a different life, or that I've made him up in my head—that I've been chasing this fantasy most of my adulthood.

When night comes, I dream of Ainee's wedding. Shahri is there, but before I can see his face, a fight breaks out between our families.

CHAPTER SIX

SANA

My choice of hijab Monday morning gets an appreciative glance from Ainee. "Whoa, you're serious about making an impression on this poor old man today, aren't you?"

I scoff at her description of the deputy attorney general. "Poor he isn't. Old, probably. I'm picturing a balding, fast-talking man, worse than Marc, who probably drinks Metamucil and crosses all his *t*'s with emphasis."

"Habibti, why bother, then? You're better off saving that peach lip gloss for Adam."

One elevator ride later, we walk toward our cubicles. The corridor leading to mine is empty. Peering over my cubicle wall, I glimpse Marc trying to open my filing cabinet. My heartbeat hikes up. One, he usually sends a litany of emails before paying an actual visit. Two, I'm early today, so he probably assumed I wouldn't be in my office.

I clear my throat. "Good morning."

Marc's face pales as if he's gotten caught with his hands in a cookie jar. Then he tips his head in the direction of my file cabinet. "I needed to check the older ExGen files—I didn't review them. Stupid Brian was supposed to leaf through it before he went on vacation, but of course he didn't. Incompetent nincompoops are what I have to work with every day." He darts a gaze at me as if to classify me as one. Then he lets out an exasperated breath and points to the file cabinet. "Also, why's this locked? What if I need something?"

I look him in the eye. "I'm just following the protocol. ExGen is in litigation, so everything has to be documented. You can email me, and I will give you anything you need. I can't leave the file cabinets unlocked."

Take that, Ainee. I can put Marc in his place.

His face flushes bright red.

Marc tucks back a long strand of his combed-over hair. He stumbles over the recycling bin as he tries to give me a death glare and retreat simultaneously. He doesn't intimidate me as much as when I was a novice ten long years ago, though that doesn't mean he doesn't try.

When he walks away, I turn on my computer and log in to find three unread messages. Two are from Eileen, Mr. Malik's secretary, and the other is from DAG Malik. His name rings a bell—maybe I've seen it in the file somewhere?

Ms. Saeed,

Can you please prepare a short summary of the ExGen case and leave a copy of the old permit in my office?

Rude. No pleasantries, I get. But not even a freaking *Regards* in the sign-off? I type a reply.

Mr. Malik:

I am the newest reviewer for the permit for ExGen. Nadine Velez, who lives close to the plant, is suing our department because she thinks the last permit should have had stricter limits on air emissions from the plant. She's suing us and ExGen because she believes her son died from complications due to the harmful air emissions and poor water quality. I will have all the reports and data we used for our permit last time around, as well as the data they're submitting with the renewal permit, compiled and analyzed for you in a memo.

I prepare the memo, copy the old permits, and head to the C-office designated for the DAG.

I knock.

No answer.

I peek inside. The desk light and the computer screen are on, but he's not there. I bet he's a lazy bureaucrat like Marc—after making me slog, he's nowhere to be found. I rub my temples to ease the beginning of a caffeine headache. I need a coffee break. I leave the files on the desk and dart out.

Grabbing my wallet, I hurry through the corridor. It's early, and the usual din of the cafeteria aside, things seem quiet this morning. That is until I see a familiar face—Beardo from McDonald's.

His high cheekbones and broad shoulders are unmistakable. He's paying for his drink, so I'm sure he doesn't see me. Why, Allah? Not today—not two days in a row.

I'm a mature, confident woman . . . usually. Right now I duck behind a pillar and wait for him to leave. This is what I've come to—a chronic avoider of conflict, behaving like a cat scared of a bath, shuddering at the mere sight of a deliciously handsome but surly-as-hell stranger. With the stealth of a burglar, I retreat. Right before I step out, a tap on my shoulder stops me in my tracks.

Holy shit.

"There she is." Melissa, my secretary, is right behind me; he is right next to her.

Panic and something else—a flutter of butterfly wings—fill my stomach.

When he looks at me, Ainee's words ring in my ear: *Habibti, get yourself someone who looks at you the same way Shahrukh Khan looks at Kajol in* Kuch Kuch Hota Hai. Now I know what she was talking about. It's not just how he looks at me. It's the way his eyes change when he does. Dark and a little intense. His beard is neatly trimmed; his tailored suit fits him perfectly. Ya Allah! Have mercy on my innocent heart.

My face warms.

Melissa chirps in her upbeat, high-pitched nasally voice, "Sana, this is Mr. Daniel Malik, the new DAG." She smiles. "Mr. Malik, this is Sana Saeed, our legal analyst."

Dammit. Avoiding him is just not in my qismet. I'll have to assist him on ExGen.

Daniel's mouth opens and closes, and he adjusts his tie. He recovers from the shock as if this is the first time his gorgeous eyes have ever locked with mine. "Ms. Saeed, did you have the memo completed per my instructions?" The way he says *per my instructions* makes me feel like I'm in kindergarten. His aloof civility—so out of sync with his gaze—befuddles the hell out of me. Worse, he wants to talk shop in the middle of a busy cafeteria, whereas most people, including me, are here on their caffeine break.

"Yes. I dropped them off in your office a bit ago." I try to avoid his gaze, instead focusing on Melissa. She's busy texting; when her phone rings, she excuses herself, leaving me with him.

"Can we discuss the details in my office?" he asks, striding toward the door.

When I don't follow, he swings around and raises an eyebrow.

"Um . . ." I rack my brain to come up with an answer. "I'm on my break right now."

"Whenever you're done, then?" he says with such disdain in his voice, it's as if I just cut him out of my will. "And can you please bring the latest enforcement action report as well?" He slides his tortoiseshell glasses up his thin, aquiline nose. He looks older than when I saw him at McDonald's. It must be the glasses. He towers over me, and if he'd smile, he would look even more handsome.

Just when I think he's about to leave, his eyes linger on something. I look down. The Soni locket has caught his attention. The locket Shahri gave me eighteen years ago.

His mouth opens, but he doesn't say anything. It's like he's trying hard not to ask, but his face changes and all the lines from his forehead diminish. Something shifts between us when he says, "Sa—Ms. Saeed . . . thanks."

His gray eyes track me like a hawk, turning my insides warm and gooey. It's like a part of me is invigorated, almost charged. This is ridiculous. I'll be reporting to him on ExGen. I'm probably violating some HR manual rule right now: *Thou shalt not think sexy thoughts about your boss.*

I turn to move away. "Sure."

Before I leave his office, I mentally high-five myself for the peach lip gloss. Because he definitely did a double take.

Why does life always through a curve ball when I least expect it?

* * *

After gathering paperwork and checking my reflection on the computer screen, I make my way to his office and knock. Jazz is playing in the office. *Jazz.* How old is he?

"Come in."

I didn't pay much attention to his office earlier. But now I notice how bare it is—there isn't much to give me any hints about him. No sweet engagement photos or dog pictures on the wall. Not even a plant. Just degrees and diplomas. Law books fill a bookcase in the corner. Everything is neat and antiseptic, unlike my chaos.

"Have a seat," he says, without meeting my eyes.

Holding the file, I approach the chair; before I even place my butt on the seat, the chair swivels. I lose my balance and nearly fall. I am worse than the clumsy rom-com cliché—I am the ungraceful faller, like the ones in the *spoof* of a rom-com.

I grab the table for support with both hands before I become a dramedy. The papers fly all over, some landing in his lap. In those few seconds of clumsiness, he loses his cold civility and the creases on his forehead smooth out.

Daniel focuses on my locket, which has come untucked from my clothes again in this near tumble. Clearing his throat, he holds out his hand to steady me.

I ogle his wide hand with long fingers. Instead of taking his hand, I touch the raised lettering on the locket and swallow hard.

"Ms. Saeed—" He leans forward to collect the scattered leaflets, at the same time I do, and bangs his forehead on mine.

I see stars. And my tingling skin and drumming heart are unrelenting. I wish this were a bad dream.

It's not. He rubs his forehead, and a lock of hair falls forward. His minty breath, the spicy cologne, and that lock of hair are real. So are his gray eyes, shining bright like Ammi's antique silver. Mesmerizing. The only other person I've ever known with gray eyes is the one whose image stays in my head no matter how many times I try to forget him.

Shahri.

But that can't be. Shahri is not Daniel Malik. Shahri is on another coast, probably married to a rich desi girl who looks like Mahira Khan.

He hands me the scattered sheets and holds up his hands in an *It's okay* gesture. The pinched brow and his thinned lips tell me that whatever mask he let slip is back on, full force.

For the next few minutes, we leaf through the papers in silence, rearranging them in order. His face is relaxed now as he scans the documents. He doesn't wear a ring—a successful desi man like him being single surprises me. He doesn't seem like the kind who'd chase girls, and there's a quiet mystery about him, but how has he managed to avoid the rishta aunties?

"I'm a little surprised at what we see on paper versus the claims of what is happening to this community," he says. "Surely, one of them is fudging the truth."

"I've only recently been assigned to this case, but from what I've read from Brian's notes, they seem to be in compliance. The data on paper looks clean. I have requested the data the plaintiff, Nadine, has gathered from nonprofits in the area. If ExGen is supplying all the data, maybe we can't trust them completely."

Daniel scratches his forehead, and I can't quite decipher if it's because he's having a hard time believing what I just said or if somehow I'm irritating him. "This is insane. Right in the middle of an important case, someone decided to switch the permit over to a novice. What kind of idiots am I dealing with here?"

Part of me wants to snap back and ask what the hell he means by *novice*. And *idiots*. I grit my teeth and fail to keep the disdain from my voice when I say, "I have worked here for almost ten years now."

His eyes dart from the file to the locket again. He presses his lips in a straight line, as if he's raring to ask a question. I tuck the golden culprit underneath my hijab. "I was assigned to this project recently, yes. But I've tried to research the details as much as possible. The lawsuit was filed by Nadine, and she claims that the poor air quality was a major factor in her son's death from asthma complications. She and a few other residents think the permits we're issuing are not strict enough and there are issues in the groundwater and drinking water."

His focus on me is so intense, the large, airy office seems to shrink in size. "Interesting."

I shift in the leather chair, causing a rustle.

He grabs a pen and writes something before continuing his questioning. "What do you think of Marc's involvement? He is the section chief; he must've known that something was up. Was any of this discussed with you before assigning you this project?"

Marc is a socially inept, morally ambiguous ass, but I can't tell Mr. Malik that. "Marc wants to keep things smooth sailing, keep issuing permits without strict limits, because it means less opposition from ExGen. It's political, and of course, ExGen has deep pockets. They could sue us, and they have a legal team which has won lawsuits for them before. But I don't know if he'd actually go to the extent of putting the lives of people we're supposed to protect in jeopardy."

"There are limited reasons why people work in public policy—some are would-be politicians, some are genuinely interested in public health and safety, and some want power and of course the money that comes with it," he opines as he concentrates on the bullet points of the case I've highlighted for him.

"And you've already decided what categories to file everyone in, after meeting them a couple of times? That's fastidious and opinionated." I cross my arms. Even his baritone voice stirs something in me.

Dammit! I need to rein in my gaze, tape my ears and nose, and not let him bother me.

Then I remember how much Z loved him. My brother felt this man's pull. And I swear, I feel it too, sitting here with my face heating up by the second. Especially when he looks at me the way he is right now, eyes dark and narrowed, searching for something. Warming me like a hot chai on a rainy afternoon.

"My instincts have yet to betray me. And for your information, I would never put you in the same category as Marc." As he says *you*, his tone softens.

I swallow, because this is not a *you* that's condescending or a *you* that's aloof, it's a *you* that is a caress.

Even though part of me wants to trust him, I can't bad-mouth my boss to him. I have no idea where his loyalties lie. "I'm not sure I want to be in a category."

Mr. Malik leans back in his chair, and as his shoulders slacken, so does the tension between us. "I'll be honest. I believe the residents and the complaints—there's no way that kid's getting sick and missing school for so many days in a row isn't tied to this. It's not a random coincidence. Maybe someone is looking the other way, or maybe there's more to the story. I will get to the bottom of it, and by Allah, if I find out that those poor people have been suffering because some here are at fault, there will be consequences."

His moods are more difficult to interpret than Rumi's philosophy, but when he speaks in that voice with that edge, his passion about environmental and social justice for this community is obvious. There's something so incredibly attractive about a man who's willing to fight for those with no voice. Like he did for Zia; like he wants to do for the people of Hempstead.

I chose to go into public service for the same reason—to help immigrants like my parents, who worked hard and had no time to do much else. To fight for them and be there for them when no one else was.

I don't want to get sucked into his hot-and-cold ping-pong. It's best to get away from him; I don't like the way I react to him. "Is there anything else you need?" I ask.

"No. This will be all."

CHAPTER SEVEN

DANIEL

Soni.

That locket. She still has it. I scratch my head, because it baffles me. She baffles me.

I've thought of her often, despite not wanting to, wondering why she never answered the letters I wrote.

When I was seven, my birth mother decided to give me to my aunt—my mother was having trouble supporting us, and my aunt, her sister, desperately wanted a sibling for Saleem but had had a hysterectomy because of a cancerous cyst. My birth mother gave me this locket as she swiped tears from her eyes, and she wasn't the kind to get too sentimental. It was one of the only occasions in my life I remember her being this way. She said, "I know you're young. But I don't know if I will ever get to meet the girl you marry, so this is my gift for her. Your father gave this to me. This was his nickname for me. One day you'll have your own soni."

When Sana turned fifteen, I held out the long rectangular box for her. "You deserve something special. My mother gave this to me before I left Pakistan. I wanted you to have a piece of—" I couldn't say it. Couldn't say *me*. It would've been too much on her, especially with our families constantly bickering and our fates uncertain.

My throat closes. I swallow and pace the room. The way I'm angsting over this, you'd think it happened yesterday. I'm not supposed to care about this old history. I am much too old and way more cynical. I've moved on.

But something did happen yesterday.

Sana Saeed waltzed back into my life.

We've both always been passionate about the environment, so her working here makes sense. And becoming a lawyer was a dream I shared so many times with her. My nana was a well-known barrister in Islamabad before going into politics, and I wanted to follow in his footsteps.

I've never been a very religious man. I used to think destiny is what you make of it. The allure of qismet as a mystical concept was the kind of new-age bullshit that didn't exist for me. Leaving things to chance is akin to leaving a boat untethered in a storm, hoping and praying no harm comes to it.

But Sana and me working together now . . . it's qismet.

If I tell her who I am, it's going to ruin our professional relationship. I can't tell her yet. Not in an office setting, anyway. Working with Sana and pretending we're strangers will be a challenge, but as soon as this assignment wraps up in a few weeks, we can part as mere coworkers, and eventually we'll revert to being strangers.

Sana and I can never be reacquainted as we were. What if she's like the rest of her family now: too easily influenced, too judgmental, too untrustworthy?

C'mon, you secretly hoped to see her, my mind scoffs.

I loosen my tie and run a hand through my hair. I'm practically burning holes in this office carpet with my pacing. If I were home, I'd go for a run.

"Get a grip," I say aloud. "She's a coworker, nothing else."

I pick up the phone and dial my only confidant—Saleem, my brother.

It goes to voice mail, and I don't leave a message. I'm sure he'll call back when he has a minute.

I need to get out of here. My head is pounding; I can't help but think about her. Maybe caffeine can help.

The wide strip mall parking lot is buzzing with the lunch crowd. Most are dressed in business attire and walk in groups. A teenager on a bike whooshes past me; I sidestep in time. The restaurants are bursting with customers, and the opening and closing of doors fans the familiar smell of greasy fries and pizza.

I rub my temples to ease my headache. The name *Tease* gleams in gold letters above a small café. The waft of coffee grounds and sweet pastries tickles my nostrils as I get in line. At the register, a girl's hand hovers, ready to punch in my order. She doesn't look me in the eye. "Can I help you?"

"Coffee. To go, please."

When she looks up, her eyes linger on my face, and her lips curl into a smile. "How would you like it?" Then she wets her lips and says with a sultry voice, "Sugar."

I am unfazed by her attention. My reply is curt. "Black. No sugar."

When she hands me the coffee, her fingertips graze mine, lingering, so I know the touch isn't accidental. I cringe at the uninvited touch.

"Come back again, handsome."

It's not that I don't crave someone in my life. Or that I'm unaccustomed to attention. It's more that I miss having a loving touch in my life—not a random stranger but someone familiar. But every time I try, it's too hard. The wall I've built to protect my heart remains impenetrable.

I've never had a serious relationship.

I was the older son, and all the expectations rested on me. I had to work twice as hard. And when you're constantly trying to live up to your family's expectations, there isn't much time to pursue girls. And college was hard. Between fighting with my uncle for independence, constantly wanting to move out, and worrying what would happen to my aunt if I did. Plus Ammi never approved of casual dating; she wanted me to get married. Which was what Saleem did. Way before me. Right in the middle of college. That ended in a divorce, which further steeled me against all things love and marriage. Then Uncle got sick and died. Then Ammi's cancer came back . . . it's almost like there was a divine plan to keep me single

Or maybe, like Saleem says, I'm clinging to the past.

As I step outside, his name flashes on my cell phone screen. Speak of the devil.

"Salaam, bade bhai," my brother says. "How's your first day? I hope you've met someone hot and that's why you were calling me earlier."

"I work for the government, not a film studio. But you will never believe who works with me."

There's some shuffling, then I hear the car door close and a seat belt click.

My stomach knots. "Is everything okay?"

"Sorry, Ammi was feeling a little weak. But she's okay. Her nurse is sitting in the back with her. Who'd you run into? Sanam Saeed?" My brother's expectation of me running into Pakistani actresses amuses him more than me.

I pause. "Try another Saeed."

For several seconds, Saleem is utterly quiet. Then, "No shit! The ex–best friend turned enemy?"

"Yup. Should I tell her who I am?"

"She doesn't *know*?"

"I don't think so." And why would she? She knows me as Daniel Malik. And I look a lot different than I did in our early teen years.

"I mean, you changed your name to hide, but then alienated friends as a result. It's a shame, isn't it?" Saleem says softly. I know he means well. But he's still throwing this subtle jab to rouse me.

I take in the mild April air mixed with the scent of blooming cherry blossoms that line the street before I reply. "I don't regret anything," I say in an even tone. No anger or shame. I don't have to justify a decision I made years ago to protect myself.

After my uncle decided to sue Sana's father, the whole community turned against him. People we'd been friends with cut off relations—and rightfully so. But my aunt stuck with her husband. Staying in town proved too difficult for my narcissistic uncle. He had some connections in California. And of course, it was far enough for rumors not to travel. We packed up and left, and I was uprooted and transplanted again.

The only choice I had was to shed my name and not lug my past with me wherever I went. I hoped this move to California would be the last move ever. No one except Sana mattered then, and she hadn't returned any of my letters or responded to any of my attempts to stay connected. So the idea of becoming someone else was appealing—even Google couldn't find me if I was Daniel and not Shahri. I've been Daniel for over fifteen years now. It's what everyone calls me, including my family.

"Sorry. I shouldn't have said that," Saleem says. "You had your reasons. But maybe it's time to confront some of those issues. Ammi's doing that too, by being back."

Part of me wants to call him on his bullshit by asking him if he's confronting *his* demons. But I won't be petty. "Anyway, I've got to go. Is Ammi okay?"

"Yeah. She's sleeping in the back—the chemo tires her. And I won't mention anything about this to her."

I sweep through the sliding doors of my office building and mutter into the phone, "I appreciate it. I don't want her to worry."

* * *

When I enter the kitchen the next morning after my run, the smell of freshly pan-fried parathas and omelets assaults my senses.

Ammi and Saleem are at the breakfast table. The housekeeper brings them steaming cups of chai.

"Aa gaye, beta. Took you a while. Join us?" Ammi asks.

"Let me shower first. Why the constant texts?" I squeeze Saleem's shoulder.

My brother Saleem is sweet and soft, like the rice kheer pudding he's devouring. Any other sibling would be jealous of how an adoptee like me has always been given more attention by our mother. Not him. Even after his divorce, he hasn't become distant. Cynical, yes, but still generous.

He shoves a bite of the pudding into his mouth. "I was telling Ammi we should look for a SIL, because you're constantly surrounded by hot women who are interested in you. She wanted you to jog back as soon as possible to join this discussion."

"SIL?" I sit next to him.

"Sister-in-law, or bhabhi, if you prefer the desi version. I hear all the rishta aunties are eager to set you up," he says with a devilish glint in his eyes.

"Don't tell me rishta aunties are already paying us visits. Other things in life are more important than getting us married, Ammi.

I'm settling into this job. No rishtas for me, thank you. But if Saleem is so inclined, I'm sure we could find him someone." I slap the back of his arm.

"Yeah, no one wants damaged goods." He polishes off the rest of the kheer and stares at the wisp of steam rising from his cup of chai.

"Both my sons are wonderful; any woman would be lucky to have them." Ammi smiles and tousles his hair. "But Daniel, you're the older brother, and it's your turn. The East Coast friends here aren't as hostile as I'd thought they'd be; we've been invited to Ainee's house. It'll be a good chance to clear the air."

I squeeze Ammi's shoulder. "Are you sure? They're all going to be there. I don't want you to get disappointed if Soofia Auntie is still mad."

Ammi gives me a wry smile. "I *have* to face her and say my piece. If I had a way to get through to her or her daughters, it would be easier. But Soofia hates as she loves, with all that she is . . ."

Shit. If I tell her I work with Sana, she's going to want me to ask Sana to help plead Ammi's case to Soofia. And if I do, I become a liar to Sana, and our work life becomes hell. But with Ammi so determined to go to this party, Sana will find out the truth anyway. I scratch the back of my head and try to process. Maybe I need to find Sana and tell her before she can find out from anyone else.

Ammi pats my hand. "Sooner or later, we all have to face our fears. And maybe Soofia will forgive us and we can have some of the friendship we shared back, even though it'll never be as it was. You know how I've always felt about Sana . . ."

"Ammi, you *have* tried to reach out to her, when we were in California. Soofia Auntie refused to acknowledge any attempts at reconciliation. And Sana . . ." I flick my gaze to Saleem, who gestures *zip it* with his hands. I'm not sure why he does that, but I decide to let it go.

"What about her?" Ammi's eyes widen.

"Nothing. I'd better shower. See you in a bit."

After a shower, I dig out our old albums and find the picture I'm looking for: all of us together with Sana's family.

The Saeeds. There were many reasons for our estrangement, but the two big ones—Sana's dad and mine—are gone. Yet this stupid feud between the families persists.

On the day the photo was taken, Sana, Rana, Saleem, and I were playing carrom in our backyard under a brutal summer sun, shortly before everything blew up. In fact, that day contributed to the blowup. Sweat trickled down my back as Sana and I spread the board and rejoiced in beating Rana and Saleem.

"You guys cheat, with your secret signals to each other." Rana pointed an accusing finger at Sana.

"Stop being a sore loser," Sana scoffed. "We don't have secret signals."

Rana stood up with her hands on her hips. "Bullshit! He's helping you win. Are you blind?"

"We're sitting opposite each other; I'm not even talking to him. You're being ridiculous, baji, and I'll tell Ammi you swore," Sana defended me.

Trouble was, I was in fact helping Sana win. I could tell where she was going to strike from the slight way she leaned right when she focused on a piece and from the way she creased her forehead in concentration when she was frustrated. She said so much without a single word. And Rana had caught on to that—maybe she was jealous. We were always together, me and Sana. Sometimes we even finished each other's sentences.

"You *are* blind. And you"—Rana wagged her finger at me—"are her little puppet. Play with each other; I'm done." She flipped the board and walked away.

"What the hell?" Sana jumped up and followed her sister. "What is wrong with you? Apologize to Shahri."

"Get the hell away from me, both of you." Rana shoved her to the side.

Sana stumbled and hit her head on the side of a table. A trickle of blood streaked her pink shirt and hijab. Sana howled and touched her wound, bloodying her hands. The sight of blood made her pass out.

At all the commotion, the adults rushed to the backyard.

Sana came around, sobs racking her frame, as her father compressed the oozing wound. Soofia Auntie helped her inside.

My uncle—I'd never seen him as a parent the way I did Ammi—gripped my collar and demanded, "Did you do this?"

Rana shivered. Behind her father's back, she folded her hands in a plea. She wanted me to take the blame.

Zayn uncle stepped in. "Sibte bhai, he's just a kid. It probably was not his fault; I know these girls fight sometimes. Rana, did you fight with your sister?"

I swallowed and then lied. "No, Zayn uncle, it was my fault."

My uncle Sibte hit me across the face. I bit my cheek to keep from screaming in pain.

Zayn came between us when my uncle raised his hand again. And thus started the beginning of a cold war between them. Zayn had always had my back, a fact that my uncle could never fully digest. Every time my uncle would be mean to me to get back at Ammi for taking me in, Zayn called him out. It was another reason the relationship deteriorated.

The last time the two men spoke was that day, in that backyard. Their relationship had been doomed from the moment the business began to struggle. But the slap was the last straw. My uncle's reputation, as a calm, collected businessman never recovered.

CHAPTER EIGHT

SANA

My phone pings with Ainee's text: *Pls be on time for my engagement party.*

It's six AM on a Saturday. She couldn't have waited a couple more hours to text me? Ammi and Rana have been on my case about dressing to impress, on the mere suggestion that Adam's mother may grace us with her presence. But at this point, it's still a maybe. Rana and I are getting our makeup done at the salon later. I groan and flip the covers.

Desi events scare me—the relentless questions about my impending spinsterhood, the aunties avoiding Ammi because they fear she'll ask to arrange another suitor for me, the pitying looks that mean *Oh, look at her. You know, she's turning forty soon. She'll never get a rishta proposal then.*

There's a shuffle of feet outside, and then Ammi's voice booms, "Rana will be here in an hour. Come down for breakfast if you're hungry."

Even before I reach the kitchen, the smell of potato pancakes and cilantro hits my nostrils. Ammi's making aloo tikki. Yum.

"Come, help me make breakfast. What are you going to feed your family if you never learn?"

"Maybe my family will do fine on pizza and Coke." I tease her.

"Have I taught you nothing? Everyone will blame the way I've brought you up . . . uff Allah." She puts a hand to her chest.

I mash the potatoes and cut some cilantro and onions, my eyes watering as I chop vigorously.

Ammi teases me. "Ya Allah! You haven't even fried a single aloo tikki, and you're already in tears."

I sprinkle in crushed red pepper, salt, smoked and ground zeera seeds, and ground tamarind and knead it together. Ammi demonstrates how to shape the patties into circles before dipping them in egg, then into bread crumbs, and pan-frying them. The mustard oil crackles once the patties settle in the pan. A familiar aroma of sweet semolina halwa fills the air as Ammi warms up the tray of dessert in the oven.

Just as I set the table for breakfast, the doorbell rings. My sister and her crew of kids enter the kitchen, and the kids start gobbling the food.

I swat my little nephew's hand. "Wash your hands."

My nephew ignores me, fills his plate with curried chickpeas, potato patties, and semolina halwa. He runs to the living room to join his brother and sisters. They have already turned on the TV. Zia plays with them in the living room, and Ammi and Rana chat over tea. Ammi's quiet house is alive, and I want this for myself so much that my heart aches.

After breakfast, my sister takes me to the side, and her jaw clenches. "I have news. Shahida Auntie is going to be at Ainee's party."

Holy shit, Shahida Auntie is back in New York? I'm surprised Ainee didn't mention this to me. Maybe she didn't know? "Is Shahri going to be there?" I ask.

Of course Ammi enters the room in time to hear my question. She lowers her voice and talks through clenched teeth. "These are the people responsible for your father's death, and all you care about is your childhood crush?"

"Ammi, please, it's Ainee's party. Maybe for one night we can forget and ignore them? For Ainee and Haroon's sake, let's shelve the past away for one night."

Ammi points her accusing finger. "We were homeless in Ramadan. If it weren't for Ainee's mother, we wouldn't have a roof over our head. Your father never recovered from that. I can ignore them, but if Shahri comes near you . . . Allah kasam, I'll teach him a lesson."

I could argue with her about how unfair her treatment of Shahri is and how Abba loved him. But, I knew that would only lead to her suspicions about my feelings toward him and questions about my intentions with Adam. And I don't want this ancient argument clouding over the event tonight.

The part of me that hoped for a nice, calm evening crashes. Nothing is going to be calm about this party.

CHAPTER NINE

DANIEL

My fingers quiver as I pull on a crisp white shirt and charcoal-gray slacks for the party. I'm not sure if it's because I'm nervous or because my mind and emotions are not in tandem. At least it'll all be done today and I won't have to carry this burden of a lie. I just need to get to the party and ahold of Sana to spill the beans before she hears it from anyone else.

A knock on my door startles me.

Saleem waves and utters a quick "Assalamualaikum" before he enters, crossing his arms and tutting. "Not Hugo Boss, please, bade bhai."

"I like when you address me as your big brother, even though you're acting as Ammi's spy." I punch his shoulder. "She had to send the sherwani police."

"You've got to look the part, bro. If you do, all the rishta aunties will be lining up." He grabs the garment bag from my closet and pulls out the black sherwani and leaves it on my bed. "This will look good on you. Are you nervous?"

I rake a hand through my semi-wet hair and remove the white button-down. Even though I want rishta aunties to stay the hell away, I want to look good for the party—my first time seeing everyone in a long time. "I think I'm worried more than nervous. What if Sana gets mad when she sees me and thinks I should've told her everything earlier?"

Saleem helps me slide on the sherwani. "Well, it's not like you've known it that long. I might have Reema's number; I can call and see if Ainee can help? In any case, it's better in this setting than a scandal at work . . ."

"Ooh! You work fast—you got Ainee's sister's digits? Maybe I should tell Ammi about your crush? Yeah, if Ainee can help, that'll at least give me the peace of mind not to create a ruckus." I crane my neck to glance at him and find that his eyes, despite all his attempts at being lighthearted, have that faraway look. "You okay, Sal?"

He gives me a wry smile. "Why wouldn't I be? I'm just going to hang out by the door, away from the food, to avoid probing questions about my divorce. Hopefully, there are no bodies to clean up after you tell Sana, and Ammi talks to Soofia Auntie." He paces my room and settles on the chair behind me. "It's all so messed up. Abba was who he was. But Soofia Auntie has really nursed and nurtured that grudge."

"She has her reasons. And Ammi was always too afraid to reach out when Sibte uncle was alive." I try to suppress the disdain in my voice.

Saleem nods in agreement. "He did regret all this when he was about to pass. Too late, I know. And yes, Ammi should've done more. No one is perfect." He draws a long breath before he says, "But she was trying to protect you from him. Abba was just looking for excuses to throw you out—and Ammi standing up for Soofia would've been such a trigger."

My uncle hated me, and I know why. He was supposed to marry Zahida, my birth mother, and not my aunt, her sister, Shahida. I shake my head. "Poor Ammi. She shouldn't have had to make that choice. But she did keep quiet because of me; I don't doubt that. He thought you deserved all of Ammi's love, not to have to share it with a child that was picked up from his wife's sister's pound. What was our grandfather thinking, marrying the other sister to a pissed-off jilted groom at the altar? Like somehow it would save face."

My birth mother had eloped, against her father's wishes, with a poor teacher she'd met in college—my birth father. Foolishly, she'd ignored her arranged engagement to Sibte, because she'd thought her father would eventually give in and call the arrangement off. He didn't, so she ran away—the very day of her and Sibte's wedding. My aunt took her place to save her father from a big embarrassment.

After my alcoholic, abusive father drank himself to death, Amma had a hard time keeping a roof over us. So she gave me away, partially to give me a better life and partially because it meant one less mouth to feed.

"It did save face. He won the local election to be in Pakistani parliament. But anyway, here we are. Ready to face our father's demons." Saleem scratches his chin. "With Ammi's health being what it is, I'm worried about bringing her into this emotionally charged situation. I know she's sincere about wanting to apologize to Sana's mother, but I wouldn't blame Soofia Auntie if she questions Ammi's intentions."

"Neither one of them wanted to choose their friendship over their husband's wishes." I touch his shoulder.

He still stares into the distance. "This is all petty bullshit. I see so many parallels between my marriage and this falling-out. I wish forgiveness came easy, but it doesn't. And being the bigger person is hard as fuck . . ."

My heart breaks for my younger brother. I squeeze his hand.

After he leaves, I open the chest of drawers to look for my watch, and a small velvet box catches my eye. "Puttar," my birth mother said, pressing the box into my hand, "this is all I have of your nani. When you were born, she told me to give it to your future wife."

The sunlight from the window catches the emerald in the ring, and the stone glitters. I close my eyes and see Sana. The grown-up, knocking-heads-with-me Sana. The coconut-perfumed, almond-eyed Sana.

CHAPTER TEN

SANA

Rana brings the car to a stop in front of Ainee's house. "Let's go, we're late." She carries a box of Indian sweets and motions us forward. I hold a gift basket for Ainee's family in one hand and Zia's hand with the other.

As we make our way toward the front door of the old Victorian mansion, everyone carefully avoids the muddy puddles left over from the rain earlier. I pause and take in the house. It's fitting that the first big wedding in their family will be here. We've always had big parties in this backyard, with half of the local mosque invited for Eid and so many other gatherings.

It's the only house remaining from our childhood; mine was auctioned and Shahri's sold.

Ainee's mother, stepfather, and sister are standing together, greeting guests. Beyond, close families and friends I haven't seen for a while are gathered in the great room. Flowers occupy every corner of the room.

On the other side of the room is Ainee's fiancé, Haroon, and his family. His mother, father, and sister stand in a corner, talking to guests and offering them food. From the kitchen comes a garden of scents: the unmistakable whiff of basmati and thick korma curry. The sweet smells of rose water and cardamom fill the whole house. A stage has been set up with decorations that declare mubarak, and loud bhangra tunes play over the sound system.

At the noise, Zia clutches my hand in a death grip. He's already overwhelmed by all the visual and aural stimulation. He pulls on me with one hand while his other covers his ear. "Can we go home?" he shouts over the music.

"We can't leave yet, but let me take you upstairs to Ainee's room. She has it ready for you. I'll bring a plate of food later." I link his arm in mine and take him upstairs, where the sounds of the party are muted.

Ainee has placed noise-canceling headphones and DVDs of Zia's favorite Star Wars movies beside the TV stand. He picks a movie, slips his headphones over his ears, and settles on the recliner.

"If you need to, come get me," I remind him. "I'll be close. I promise we will leave as soon as we can."

I close the door behind me and return to the party, which is now in full dinner mode. Guests mingle and carry plates of food with steam rising from the fresh basmati rice.

I pivot around a few people to get to Ainee.

She screams. "Oh-em-gee, Sana! You look great. Come here, let me see." She grabs my hand and spins me around. My Anarkali gown shimmers in the bright overhead lights. She admires the jade-green bodice with silver beadwork.

Ainee lifts my chin and remarks, "You had your makeup done! I love the way they did your eyes. Watch it, habibti; don't steal my thunder. I can tell it's going to be a good night for you. Adam and his family are running a little late, but he's going to flip when he sees you. Also avoid nine o'clock—he's in search of a green-card bride. And make sure to go to your favorite spot in the backyard before dessert; there's a surprise for you."

I'm about to ask what kind of surprise when Haroon calls out, "Ainee! Your mom's looking for you."

Ainee flits away.

I stop by the kitchen and prep a plate with Zia's favorite desi foods—butter chicken and soft, buttery naan. In a small dessert bowl, I scoop the fluffy and milky ras malai covered in pistachios. I balance the plate and dessert bowl as I make my way through the crowd.

Upstairs, I set the plate on a table and grab a juice from the mini fridge in Ainee's room. Then I alert Zia by patting his shoulder.

"Thanks." He digs into his food.

From Ainee's big window facing the back, I glance into the dimly lit backyard. There's our tree—the one Shahri and I carved our names into when we were little.

I know Ainee said to wait until before dessert to head outside for whatever my surprise is, but suddenly there's nowhere else I want to be.

I'm drifting toward the tree when a silhouette appears by the trunk. I inhale sharply—those shoulders. I've known them. I've felt them. The silhouette touches our names. The *S+S* carved in crude letters.

Shivers run up my spine in anticipation. "Shahri?" I murmur over the sounds of crickets. And then I'm sprinting toward the dark figure while holding my long gown in one hand. My heels sink in the boggy mud, but I dig them out and keep going.

Is it Shahri? Surely he's the only one who cares about this tree—*our* tree. My chest tightens and my skin prickles as I approach him from behind and tap on his shoulder.

CHAPTER ELEVEN

DANIEL

My fingers brush over the jagged edges of our initials carved into the bark. My skin tingles from the anticipation of seeing her.

I accosted Ainee earlier and told her she needed to have Sana meet me out here—*before* Saleem brought Ammi to the party.

Ainee shook her head. "Dude, she's pissed at you for abandoning her."

"I know she is. That's why I want to talk to her. In my defense, I did try to connect with her, but never heard back."

There's a tap on my shoulder. Then I smell her jasmine perfume. Sana.

Her voice is high pitched. "Shahri?"

For a minute I am completely frozen, forgetting we stand here as adults. All the walls I've built around me start to crack. This is where I was my happiest self.

She may never forgive me. But whether I like it or not, this is the moment of my truth. Our truth.

My heart races as I swing around to look at her.

Sana's face loses color; she looks as if she's seen a ghost. "What are you . . ." Her eyes widen.

I hesitate and then whisper, "Soni meri Soni . . ." I sing the song we used to sing together from a popular Bollywood movie.

"Aur nahin koi honi soni," she completes the lyrics. Her face is a kaleidoscope of emotions, from surprise, to horror, to something new. Her jaw sets. "You knew. Of course you knew. You saw this—" She touches her locket. "Yet you said nothing. Shit! What kind of game are you playing? Why didn't you say something?" She takes a step back. "Here I was, thinking you are Daniel Malik. Mr. DAG with a conscience, the environmental warrior. But you are just like them—gain our trust and then stab us in the back—" Her voice catches.

"A game? No, Sana, when I saw you at the office, it wasn't appropriate to talk about this." I wave a hand between us. God, she looks so beautiful. Her eyes are bright, and she's flushed with anger and colors, and I can't decide if I should fight her or surrender.

Her maroon lips tremble. "We were friends. I thought you, of all your family, could be trusted, Shahri . . ." Her voice breaks. "To think, I wrote to you every week for months . . ."

She wrote to me?

"I wrote to *you* for months!" I say. "That day I came to see you, before leaving for California, I rode my bike for miles, but Zayn uncle didn't let me see you . . ." My voice is a higher pitch as I curl my fingers to stop myself from getting swept up in emotions. Does she know how it felt? To be shoved in the back seat of her father's car, with tears rolling down my face?

There was always that fear in my head, however irrational, that if I ever tried to see her, reach out to her, he would find a way to shove me in the back of that old car of his. So I stayed away.

"Rana and Ammi wouldn't let me out of the house." Sana crosses her arms.

So she wanted to see me too.

We stand there for a second. I am unsure what to say. Sana chews her bottom lip.

A faint breeze carries the smell of honeysuckle; my heart swells at the memories of us running around here. The honeysuckle bushes were always a fixture in this backyard. Does Sana remember these moments as I do? It was all so long ago; we were children then. Maybe the girl I used to know exists only in my memories and the person standing before me is nothing like her.

Before I can say anything, Saleem is running across the lawn toward us. He rests his hands on his knees to catch his breath. "Ammi and Soofia Auntie are having words."

The three of us rush inside.

The scene in the house is as chaotic as I was dreading. Ammi's face is pale, and Soofia points a finger at her. "After all you've put my family through, how dare you show up here!"

"Soofia, I come with a plea and ask you to forgive us. Tell me what I can do, but please don't shut me out. I was helpless. I wanted to reach out, but Sibte warned me. I had my son to worry about." Ammi leans on her walker and tries to take Soofia Auntie's hand.

Soofia jerks her hand back and points at me. "He is the cause, then?"

"Tell me my kaffara. I'll do anything for my penance." Ammi continues to plead, her voice breaking.

"Bring my husband back. Bring my house, my reputation back. Give me the time I spent working to pay off the debt plus interest your husband sued me for. Or the time I spent away from my children. Missing every milestone of their life, because I was too busy working?" Soofia scoffs. "Don't bother me again with this bakwas." She turns away from Ammi.

My mother is in tears. Ainee's mother steps up to console her, and Saleem and I rush to her side.

My gaze flicks to Soofia's face. She has aged gracefully, but she isn't the tall, cheerful woman I once knew. Her face is wizened. Soofia's cheerful, sunny disposition, which was once her essence, seems like a dream. But maybe this is what years of festering grudges does: it changes us into bitter versions of ourselves.

I square my shoulders and move to shield Ammi and raise my voice, because seeing my mother in tears makes me lose my cool. "Please, do not talk to my mother that way. She doesn't deserve this."

Soofia doesn't show any signs of empathy toward Ammi. Eighteen years have certainly changed things.

Sana tips her angry face in my direction. "And who says you have any right to talk to my mother that way? Shahida Auntie, it's best you leave now."

I tighten my fists and try to curb my anger. Fatima Auntie, Ainee's mother, squeezes my shoulder. "Beta, let's not go back to where we were. Your mother wants to reconcile. It's a step in a good direction. Why don't we all sit down and talk like adults?"

Soofia waves a dismissive hand and says, "Nahin. Bas. I've heard enough. Let's go, betiyon."

Like an obedient daughter, Sana rushes away at her mother's side. Ainee meets them by the car with Zia. I'm glad he missed the big blowout between our families.

* * *

SANA

Shahri has single-handedly ruined everything for me: my childhood memories, my best friend's engagement party, my job. Now would not be the best time to tell Ammi and Rana that I have to see him every weekday.

The second he looked at the Soni locket, he knew who I was. Why didn't he say anything? The Shahri I knew wouldn't lie.

But he is not Shahri anymore; he is another man whose eyes beguile me. A man called Daniel. Like Ammi always warned me: *Do not trust the ones with light eyes; they are bey-murawat.* And he is that—inconsiderate and cold.

Rana puts a hand to her chest. "Shahida Auntie could've waited until after chai and dessert. Talk about ruining a good party! Those kulfis were brought from that desi place I love too."

My sister's lament riles up Ammi even more. "The Khalil family has no shame, even after all they've put us through. Such a dutiful nephew, fighting with me to protect his aunt. But like Sibte, they all are snakes."

"Shahida Auntie considers Shahri her son," I interject. "And yes, while she never really did anything to help us, she did try to call and apologize afterward, except you and Abba wouldn't even talk to her." I don't know why I say that, knowing it'll only anger my mother. Maybe it's habit—I've always defended them when anyone doubted Shahida's love for Shahri, or vice versa.

Ammi stops. "He stood there and insulted me—insulted your dead father. You keep his junky car to prove your affection to your abba, yet you advocate for that family. They're all cut from the same cloth. If your love for your father were real, you'd forget about that family, especially Shahri."

"I'm not defending him. Just stating the facts." I open the passenger side door for her.

Rana and Zia slide into the back seats. Once everyone is settled, I jam the car keys in the ignition to start Mirchi, who groans and sputters in protest, as if to say, *Don't take your anger out on me!*

Ammi clicks on her seat belt and shakes her head disapprovingly. "I've had enough with this." She points an accusing finger in my direction. "I want you to commit to Adam's rishta." Ammi crosses her arms.

"What do you mean?" Knuckles white, I grab the steering wheel.

"You know what I mean." My mother is never this angry, like the-veins-in-her-neck-jutting-out angry. "I talked to Adam's dad and told him you and Ainee are allowed to visit him. Such decent people—he asked permission for the two of you to see each other with a chaperone. If you don't like Adam, fine. Just make sure you find someone before our meeting with the lawyer in two weeks. Because if you don't, I am leaving you out of Zia's guardianship. And my will."

CHAPTER TWELVE

SANA

I almost jab myself with a hijab pin Monday, as my thoughts drift back to yesterday. Saturday night was disastrous.

Daniel is Shahri—and completely off-limits. Our families ruined Ainee's engagement party.

Ammi wants me to commit to marrying Adam soon, or I lose out on being in Zia's life and Ammi's will. I have to go see Adam today, now that Ammi's ultimatum is already a couple days old.

Please, do not talk to my mother that way. It's not just the words he said, but also the way he said them, with such bitterness, that makes my heart ache. Despite what Ammi thinks, I have no hard feelings toward Shahida Auntie. And I know Daniel cares about us. How am I supposed to ignore all of our history and pretend we're strangers? Or worse, enemies.

My pulse kicks up a notch. *Daniel.* I've moved on from calling him Shahri.

Doesn't matter; they're both jerks.

I have to show him I'm not stuck in the past—and more importantly, not stuck on him.

An arranged marriage to Adam is the way to go. No messy feelings, no expectations, a pact and a life similar to all the other women in my family. Maybe love isn't my qismet.

I manage to avoid Daniel all morning, but then I get an email from Marc asking me and Ainee to attend a meeting. When Daniel walks inside the conference room where Ainee and I are waiting for the meeting to start, a sense of dread constricts my neck muscles. His athletic build fills his navy-blue suit, and he's as irritatingly good-looking as he was when I last saw him, suit or shalwar kameez, he can rock them both.

Annoying. His perfectly sculpted jaw hardens as he and Marc settle in the chairs across from us. They begin talking, heatedly, about the most recent permit and the need for more public involvement.

I dart my gaze to my notepad and scribble to keep myself from ogling him.

My father used to tease my mother with a poem by Amir Khusrau: *Chap tilak sab cheen li toh say naina mila key.*

You've bewitched me by a single glance, and once I lock my eyes with you, I forget who I am.

My phone flashes with Ainee's text. Thank Allah my phone's on silent.

Ainee: *There's your haughty-hottie.*

My fingers fly: *He's not mine and I pity whoever calls him theirs.*

I look up, and his eyes, gray and icy, meet mine for a microsecond. A shiver runs up my spine.

Ainee: *You sure ogle him like he's your BF.*

Me: *BF? I hope by that you mean a bad friend.*

Marc clears his throat in that gratingly crisp way of his and shoots a glance in my direction. "DAG Malik has a lot of concerns about the way we're handling the case. I think we've done a great job in the past with community engagement and our permits."

Daniel's eyes search mine, like he did in his office the other day—as if he wants to dig deeper, as if he's trying to determine whose side I'm actually on. "Ms. Saeed, what do you think?"

For years I've been to these meetings, and no one has ever asked my opinion. I shift in my seat and scramble to come up with a straight answer that doesn't implicate Marc or make him look incompetent.

Way to put me on the spot, dammit. I'll show him. I look him right in the eye. "There definitely needs to be more of a dialogue between the community leaders and us. What we do here affects their daily lives. I can look into arranging a public forum; I've already gathered the names. I can't comment on the last permit or the efficacy of the limits, as I wasn't involved. But yes, there's definitely a need for more transparency on our end."

Ainee smiles and mouths, *Brava*.

Marc looks at me as if he's never heard me talk before. His face is flushed deep red, and his right eye twitches.

"Interesting. Do you have any correspondence from these residents, Ms. Saeed?" Daniel's grays search my browns with an unblinking gaze.

I avert my eyes and stare at my file. "I have emails from concerned citizens and calls to the hotline, some from before Nadine's case—"

Marc puts his hand up and interrupts. "Mr. Malik, I don't know why you're questioning my staff. This is ridiculous."

"Your staff, Mr. Bukowski, was not finished speaking." Daniel's jaw clenches.

Silence.

Daniel tips his chin at me. "Continue."

"I'd like to do more outreach and make a case that we should deny any expansion until we know for sure. That's all." As I mutter this, I realize why I like to fade into the background—because that's my safe place. But Daniel gave me the spotlight, and it wasn't that bad. I suppose that's what a good lawyer does: dissects and puts unwilling people on the stand. But it turns out that speaking my mind, being heard, is empowering. I can do this—like Daniel, I can feel passionately about work *and* voice my disapproval in order to succeed.

Daniel asks Ainee a few questions about reports on the database and whether her team in the IT department can help us collect some archived reports and data. But for the rest of the time, he pretends to ignore me. The problem is, it's hard for me to ignore him. Every time I steal a glance at him, my breath catches. His high cheekbones and that perfect jawline are so distracting. His voice has that baritone that sounds like sweet jalebi syrup in my ears.

Marc drones on until his phone beeps. He points to his watch and announces, "I have a lunch meeting, so unless there's anything else, let's wrap up?"

Daniel shrugs but stays put. These two are not getting along, and I'm in the middle because of ExGen. In Daniel's defense, he asked all the right questions. And he's certainly looking to help the residents. I'm not sure Marc agrees.

I pick up my files, ready to bolt.

Ainee grabs my wrist and says out loud, "Let's go see your Adam."

I wiggle out of her grip and put a finger on my lips to shush her. "Stop. *Please.*"

Daniel's eyes meet mine for a second, and a thousand butterflies swirl in my belly. *Grow up, Sana.*

Grown-up me is still looking for the Shahri I knew, that crease on his forehead when he concentrated, that smile that crept up from the corner that illuminated his lips like a sun peeking through the cloud. If I found it, I could look at his eyes all day and it'd all feel like a measly minute.

Marc taps his shoulder, so he looks away, and the spell is broken.

Ainee shakes her head, then whispers in my ear, "I wonder what made him turn into such a grouch. And I did him the favor of arranging for you to meet him yesterday, before the war of words between the Saeeds and the Khalils. And way to ruin my party, you two."

"You know, you could have told me he'd be there last night." I punch her arm.

"Like you would have ever met him if I did." She shakes her head. "He was really pleading to talk to you the night of my engagement party, I guess he still cares. Plus, Shahida auntie's not doing well, so I wanted to be nice to old family friends."

I think about how different Shahida Auntie looked last night and say in a lowered voice, "Shahida Auntie has lost a lot of weight—she looks so different from when I last saw her. She's beautiful still, but that light in her eyes, it's so diminished. It seemed like she really wanted to talk to us, before Ammi shut her down."

Ainee gives me a wry smile. "Remember their parties? She was the best host ever."

I nod. I miss that time, when all was well. That one Eid is so fresh in my mind, when she had an open house for the whole community. She entertained us in her backyard with biryani, sweet syrupy vermicelli, and so many other treats. She brought out a big tandoor oven and served us fresh naan with every type of filling possible. I don't think I remember a more perfect Eid. Shahri and I spent the whole day together, helping her, and afterward all the kids watched a movie on the big projector screen. There were even loot bags to take home. But the main reason it'll forever be my best Eid memory is because our families really enjoyed each other's company.

Rather than thinking about the perfect memories from the past that only revive this ache, I should create new ones. I smile at Ainee and say, "Let's go see Adam."

* * *

On the drive to Tease, I glance at the early spring sky and marvel at the trees beginning to look alive again. Maybe this is a new beginning for me as well.

I park Mirchi, and my door thuds closed when I step outside.

The smell of tea and fresh coffee grounds along with the sweet smell of cherry pastries make my stomach growl. Haroon and Adam are waiting for us at the corner table. They get up when they see us.

"There he is." Ainee's taupe lip gloss shines as she waves at Haroon.

Haroon stands to receive Ainee. It's a sweet gesture, and she rewards him with a generous hug. After that, she forgets all about me.

A nudge on my shoulder and a waft of cardamom alert me to Adam.

"Hungry?" He carries a tray of food and leads me to a corner booth away from Ainee and Haroon. Adam places the tray to the side and arranges small plates with all my favorites on the table. He must've asked his staff about what I order most often.

My stomach growls at the assortment, from creamy rice pudding to flaky ground beef pastries and a steaming cup of ginger tea. I clench my fingers to avoid grabbing the warm pastries.

He pushes the empty tray aside. "I hope this is all right. I assumed you're here because of my culinary skills and not my rugged good looks."

His eyes shine with laughter. I feel the weight of his kindness. He doesn't fill my stomach with butterflies, but his sweet concern warms my soul. He went through all this on the chance I'd show up today. Maybe I can grow to love him. He's handsome, successful, and a charmer. Maybe I should accept what he has to offer and keep my fingers crossed to fall into something deeper with him.

I take a sip of chai for warm liquid courage.

He raises an eyebrow. "What's bothering the lovely lady today? Chai confessional time? I promise your secrets will be safe with me." His hand hovers over the cup, like he is swearing by it. "Even though I never heard back from you. I was looking forward to seeing you at Ainee's party, but you'd left by the time we arrived."

I twist my fingers and say, "Ammi wants us to do baat pakki or engagement as soon as possible. She's done all the inquiries. And the auntie brigade passed you with flying colors."

The cogs in my brain are in motion—he may be what Allah has sent as an answer to my ammi's prayers. Adam would be the perfect choice. If not perfect, then the safest choice, perhaps.

Adam shifts and locks his gaze with mine. "We can have the nikah this weekend if you want." He purses his lips to conceal a smile.

I twist my fingers and say, "My family has given me a deadline to commit to having someone in my life. It's two weeks from now."

A sweet smile illuminates his face. He lowers his voice and leans close. "Wallahi, I didn't go on any more rishta searches. I don't need to. I believe in arranged marriages. Don't you?"

I gulp. I don't have to look at him to know he's serious. The leather seat crinkles as I move to the end of the booth.

"I do," I say, because this is what I'm going to believe in now. I'm going to listen to my sane self instead of my heart.

He slides next to me and moves his hand close to mine but halts when I pull mine back a bit.

His shoulders slump. "As long as you promise to give this a chance"—he waves his wrist between us—"I'm ready to take this arrangement seriously. Abba talked to your mother this morning and accepted an invitation to come over next weekend. He was so happy when he called earlier. I've not seen him so happy in years. But please honor our arrangement. And I will do the same. You have my word."

My heart sends me all the signals that I'm making a grave mistake. I feel the same unease I do when I've hopped on the wrong train and now I've to figure out how to get off in a hurry. But I shut it all down and tell myself I've finally grown up and am making the right decision. After all, Adam is what Daniel could never be: my family's choice. A good man who will stick around and care for my brother as much as I do.

"I'm all in," he says.

I try to lighten things up by cracking an awkward joke. "Adam, is it possible for you to meet the other man in my life? Someone I love more than anyone else in the world? I bet you're going to love him too." Adam's face goes from confused to a smile when it dawns on him that I'm not serious. "You will find me a very patient man, Sana, with anyone and everyone in your life. I'll be delighted to meet your little brother, whom I've heard so much about."

I arch an eyebrow. "Ammi told your abba about Zia?"

"Yes. And I'll be honored to have him in my life." He cuts a piece of baklava for me. "To new beginnings."

I swallow and plaster on a smile. "To new beginnings."

CHAPTER THIRTEEN

SANA

When I get back to the office, a familiar face appears on the other side of the glass door. Daniel, on his way out of the building.

Our gazes meet as he pushes the door forward. He doesn't nod in acknowledgment, yet his eyes linger on my face. All it would take is a friendly little movement of the head, but apparently, for Daniel, warmth doesn't exist.

Forget him.

I ignore my racing heartbeats and break our staring contest. The air from the heater warms me even more as I flash my badge to Kevin, and he nods.

A text pings. It's Adam: *Hope it's okay to text, and can't wait to see you and Zia soon.*

I break into a smile and hum a tuneless song all the way to my cubicle. Adam makes me forget about Daniel, and that's a very good thing. I step into my cubicle a little giddy; things are finally going according to plan.

But when I look at my computer, all the breath leaves my body. A note is Scotch-taped to the screen. Its bold letters scream at me.

STOP THE KILLING, BITCH. TURN TO JESUS.

I feel a sinking feeling in the pit of my stomach. My hand flies to my mouth. Sweat forms on my forehead, and I wipe it with the back of my sleeve. I look over my shoulder—is someone watching me?

I throw the note into my top desk drawer and slam it shut, hoping to contain the hatred in that small space, then I run to the bathroom and hide in a stall. I sink to the floor, the white tiled floor cold against my warm palms, and let the flood of tears escape. All I want to do is curl up in a ball.

Light footsteps in the stall next to mine break my trance. My secretary's familiar voice saying "talk later" reverberates over the toilet flushing. I wipe away the tears and step out of the stall.

My pale reflection in the mirror stares back at me.

Melissa washes her hands vigorously in the sink. "Are you okay?" she asks.

Everything feels surreal, like things aren't happening in real time. It's like I'm in a fever dream.

The cold water from the tap awakens me from the trance. I wipe my face, hoping Melissa didn't catch that I was crying. "I, um—there was a note."

She narrows her gaze. "What note? Show me."

We return to my cubicle. I open my drawer and hand the note to Melissa.

She scowls and looks around to see if anything else has been disturbed, then she waves her hand in the air and yells out, "I can't believe this nonsense!"

Ainee hears the commotion and comes over. Melissa hands her the note. She's aghast when she reads it. "Call the state police, Melissa."

Holding my head in my hands, I rub my throbbing temples. "I don't know who . . . why . . ." My voice breaks, but I push my tears back. I will not break down in the middle of my office.

Melissa pivots behind me to grab the desk phone and instructs me, "You need to stay until the police get here. They'll want to talk to you."

While Melissa talks to the police, I touch my face, stopping short of pinching myself. Is this really happening? Is whoever wrote this note watching us?

Life changes in a flash. Lunch was so good, and then this . . .

The questions in my head scare me, so I quiet my mind and focus on controlling my rapid breathing and accelerated pulse. My colleagues returning after late lunches glance quizzically in our direction, but no one approaches us. One of them must have done it—but who? Is it Debbie, who showcases her MAGA merchandise with pride, or Brian, who sports a giant crucifix around his neck, or Kelly, who always stares at my hijab and never says hello? It could be anyone in the small crowd of people looking in our direction. Another shudder runs up my spine—this person must really hate me, and yet they work possibly a few feet from me. Will I ever stop looking at all of them differently?

When Brian tries to approach us, Ainee tells him to buzz off.

The state police arrive, and Melissa rubs my arm, tipping her head in the direction of the hallway. "We have to go to the conference room. They're ready for you."

The cop, an older, heavyset white man with salt-and-pepper hair and a thick black mustache, signals for me to sit. The radio on his belt chatters, interrupting the silence I've felt since seeing that note. His name tag reads *J. O'Brien*. "Ma'am, I'm going to ask you a few questions."

My hands shake as I nod.

"When were you last in your cubicle?"

"Around noon. Maybe a little before."

"Can you give me a timeline?"

"It was right after, um, a meeting. And then we went to lunch."

"We?" he echoes.

"Me and Ainee . . . my friend Ainee, who works here. She and I went out to lunch."

"Where did you go?"

Is this standard questioning procedure? Maybe it is, and I'm still reeling and my mind isn't ready for the probing or the push to remember details.

He looks at me, tapping his pencil against his notepad, waiting for my response.

Knowing he's here to help me, I close my eyes and shake away my jitters and try to soothe my fears about him and his intentions. "I was at the Tease café downtown."

"Do you go there often?"

I know that his questions are all pertinent and he's asking them for a reason, but I can't wait to be away from this room and this questioning. "Sometimes," I reply.

"Has this happened before?"

"No."

"Are you sure?" He cocks an eyebrow.

My pulse thunders in my ears as I whisper, "Yes."

He lets out an exasperated exhale and cups his ear. "Pardon?"

I swallow and say, "Yes, I'm sure."

"How long have you worked here?" he continues.

"Ten years."

At this, Officer O'Brien looks up. Was he expecting this complaint to come from a newer employee? Does he doubt me? I can't tell. His face shows no sign of empathy or emotion. Maybe he wants to hear a different story than the one I'm giving.

The conference room is so quiet I can hear myself breathe. The overhead lights reflect on Officer O'Brien's glasses as he moves. I shiver, partly from the vent blowing cold air above me and partly because his icy stare rattles me.

He leans on the long mahogany table and busily writes on his forms. Finally, he fixes his intense gaze on me. "Did anything unusual happen with any of your coworkers this morning? Would anyone have a reason to write this note? Could it be a prank?"

His disbelief makes me feel like I'm in a nurse's office complaining about a fake illness to get out of school. I shake my head. "Prank? I don't think anyone would use such harsh words if they were playing. And I've always gotten along well with my coworkers. I don't think anyone has a reason to leave me a note like this."

Officer O'Brien peers over his glasses at me. "It's hard to see how someone could get in and out of your cubicle unnoticed."

It's not his disbelief or that he has a hard time believing me that irks me; it's that he feels like this whole thing is a big waste of his time and he'd rather be out there solving big crimes.

I clear my throat and reply with a steady voice, trying to summon up all my poise. "I'm not sure either. But I'm next to Melissa, the secretary. People come and go from her area all the time. No one would pay any attention to a person walking by."

He writes in his notepad in quick scribbles, asks me a few more questions, and then gathers his papers and the file. His radio chirps again as he hands me his card. "Ms. Saeed, call me if you remember anything else."

Debra, the human resources manager, walks in. Her short blond hair stays put even when she moves. Her red lipstick matches her manicured nails. Chagrined, she says robotically, "Ms. Saeed, we need to check your cubicle and make sure nothing else was left in there. We have to do a sweep on everything: your computer, the files, your phone. This is a state building, so it's a security concern. Here's a release form saying the state police were called for your safety and they checked to ensure there were no imminent threats to your life."

Suddenly, the thought of sitting in my office scares me. My mouth goes dry. What if this happens again?

"Can I temporarily sit elsewhere?" I look at her, hoping for some empathy—a softening face or a squeeze of the hand.

Nothing.

"We'll see what we can do. I'll talk to Marc." She shuffles the papers and then taps the stack. "The places I need your signature are marked." She points to the pile in front of her and hands them to me.

I sign with quivering fingers and return them.

As I stand, Debra holds up her hand to assist me. "Take the rest of the day off. And more if you need time off. Do you want someone to walk you to your car?"

"No. I should be okay." I walk out of there and stop by Ainee's cubicle to let her know I'm heading home.

Ainee looks at me, concerned. "I'll drive you home."

"No, thanks. I'm going to Ammi's. I'll call you tomorrow." To reassure her I'm okay, I pat her arm.

"At least let me walk you to your car." Ainee doesn't wait for my answer; she just falls into step beside me. She breathes heavily, her jaw set. "Why are you so calm, Sana? If it were me, I'd be screaming and shouting. Stop accepting this bullshit—"

I stop and look her in the eye. "What is that going to accomplish, besides gaining me more attention? As if people don't already notice me. As if I don't get stared at and harassed all the time already. If I become angry, I become 'one of them,' and that's never going to stop this vicious cycle of hate."

It's not that I don't feel her rage. I do, but anger is not the solution. I have to trust the system to catch the culprit and hope it's not someone I work with every day.

Ainee shakes my arm. "Sana, you're working on a high-profile case—maybe you're a target because of that? That's what I want to believe, anyway; the alternative is scary as shit. Either way, HR should move you—you shouldn't have to work in that cubicle." She squeezes my arm. "Take some time off—you never do, but time away can be great for your mental health. And I'm here for you if you want to talk."

"I will. Thanks for being here." I give Ainee a quick hug and climb into Mirchi.

"Get me home quick, Mirchi." I slide the key into the ignition. She starts without a fuss and even lets me switch to my favorite radio station and crank up the heat. "Thanks," I say, and run my fingers on the steering wheel. Who says she doesn't know how I feel and what I need? She's just testy because she's old. Reminds me of my abba when he got tired.

On my hour-long drive to Ammi's, I think about Debra, Officer O'Brien, Ainee, and my coworkers. About their perceptions of me, my reality, and the ultimate irony of my intention to be inconspicuous. How I was so happy earlier after my conversation with Adam.

This isn't the first time that I—a visibly Muslim woman—have been subject to a hate crime. Every single time we travel, our bags get chosen to be searched for a "random" check. The invasive pats and screenings are just the price I pay to wear my religion on my head. The incidents have made me resilient; they've also made me retreat.

Identity is hard. No wonder our cousins in India call us ABCD—American Born Confused Desis. Where do I belong? India? I'd be a minority there as well. What would my abba think of today? He left his family, close friends, everyone behind to give us a better future.

Yes, our lives are better, but they aren't free of prejudice. I wonder if he'd think it was all worth the emotional and physical isolation from all that he held dear.

My mother has told me stories of riots in India where Muslim-majority neighborhoods were targeted, the women raped and the men hanged. One such night, before I was born, my father escaped the riots with the help of his neighbors. Once my parents had Rana and me, they decided to move to the U.S.—to a better life, one they hoped would be sans prejudice and fear. Sometimes I wonder how, if he were alive, my father would react to the uptick in hate crimes here. This isn't why he left the place of his birth and his thriving family business.

I can't tell my mother what happened. She'll worry, and maybe there's nothing to worry about. I think happy thoughts, and about how Adam and I agreed to being arranged.

I knock on the door of Ammi's house, then step inside and call out, "Salaam and surprise!"

Zia squeals in delight and rushes down the stairs to hug me. I hold on to him for so long I begin to sob. He wiggles away.

Ammi fixes her dupatta over her head and asks, concern lining her forehead, "Jani, everything okay?"

"I'm okay. I was just missing everyone, so I took some time off to spend with my favorite people." I plaster on a smile and avoid her direct gaze.

She cradles my face, forcing me to look at her. One look and she knows. "I'll bring you something to eat, and then you will tell me what is really going on. Because you never take more than a day off, even for Eid."

When Zia is back in his room and Ammi has fed me samosas and masala tea, she presses me on what happened. I give her all the details, leaving out the part about the cop's probing questions.

"You should quit and find something closer," Ammi tells me with hooded eyes.

I let out a long breath. "And give them exactly what they want? No, Ammi. Plus I still have a semester of school left before I get my JD. Maybe after I graduate."

"Uff . . . always excuses. How long are you home for?"

A knock at the door comes even before I can reply, and I'm grateful for it.

Ammi is so happy when she greets Adam at the door—and a little upset that I didn't tell her beforehand.

Adam comes to my rescue and tells Ammi, "I didn't want you to go through any trouble, so I asked Sana to keep it a surprise."

I mouth "Thank you" when Ammi goes to the kitchen to get started on tea.

Adam wins half the battle because he shows up with potted plants and fruit baskets. Then, when he rolls up his sleeves to perform wudu to pray, Ammi admires his perfect Quran recitation. I admire his well-toned forearms.

Adam, Ammi, and I cook dinner together—after a lot of protesting from Ammi. Adam whittles down her defenses when he puts on some Bollywood music and whips up a perfect cup of tea for her. She smiles as we cook and laugh over spilled flour and messy paratha dough.

Adam and I make Zia's favorite foods for dinner. Stuffed potato parathas, green chutney, biryani, and Egyptian-style baklawa from his grandmother's special recipe.

He stays late, and we talk about his love for old desi movies and mangoes. Zia and Adam bond over Star Wars and games.

After we say good-bye, I turn to Ammi and tell her with a nod, "I agree to baat pakki." A promise to marry him.

Ammi cradles my face and kisses my forehead. "When did you decide that he was good enough?"

"When he made me forget that I had the worst day at work. This is what I want, Ammi, just like what you and Abba had."

Love will follow. If I can just stay the hell away from Daniel.

CHAPTER FOURTEEN

DANIEL

The off-white building with golden lettering announces the Department of Conservation. I feel a glow of pride as I park in the spot that reads *Reserved for the DAG.* Tiny droplets spray my hair as I get out of my car. Rain again. This gloomy weather makes me miss California.

As I click open my umbrella and sprint to the whooshing sliding doors, the scene from the other day flashes before my eyes. Sana and me, on opposite sides of the pane. Her eyes bright and her face flushed, like she was excited about something—or someone. I have no right to be jealous. I'm surprised she's not married or engaged yet. That cannot have been easy for her family.

Kevin, the guard at the door, looks up from his usual chatter with his buddies and yells, "Am I imagining that smile, Mr. Malik? Keep it up."

Grumpy Malik to Smiling Malik. I guess that's a good change. I shake my head as I head to my office.

My computer screen whirs to life. A knock pierces through the quiet of my office, and I swivel in my chair to see who's there.

Eileen, my secretary, is standing at the threshold, holding her coffee tumbler. She's half inside, as if she can't decide whether to come in or have a quick conversation from the hallway. She says in a thick Brooklyn accent, "Mr. Malik, would you like kaw-fee? I'm on my way to the cafeteria."

"I'm okay. Is Ms. Saeed in?" I avoid looking at Eileen, thinking she might read too much into my inquiry about Sana.

Eileen hesitates. "I'm not sure if she'll be in today."

I look up. "That's odd. I was told she doesn't take days off. Is she ill?" Worry laces my words.

"Um . . . Marc knows the situation better than me." Her face is stoic, but she shifts her weight from one leg to the other.

"Eileen, what's going on with Ms. Saeed?"

"All I know, boss"—she steps into my office, closes the door halfway, then lowers her voice a few decibels—"is that someone left her a threatening note. The state police and HR are investigating."

"Someone left her a threatening note?" I repeat stupidly. Fear pulses through me.

She fills me in on the whole incident.

My fist clenches, and I control my anger by digging my heels into the carpet. A scene from when Sana was twelve pops into my head. Some boys at the school had pulled her hijab, which she had recently begun wearing.

"They said I looked like an Al-Qaeda bride," she said as her eyes filled with tears.

"No, you don't," I reassured her. "Don't listen to them; they're idiots."

Her whole body shook as she sobbed. "Why do they hate it so much? I'm still their classmate."

I put a hand to her shoulder, my heartbeat quickening. Things had been changing between us, my body was reacting to even simple, seemingly harmless acts like trying to comfort her. I moved my hand, but she didn't notice. "It'll get better. Maybe give them some time."

I felt helpless not being able to shield her from the cruel place the world had become. I should have said more. Done more.

Eileen clears her throat. "Will that be all, Mr. Malik?"

I nod, and she walks away. I stride outside and circle the building, trying to quell the flames of anger. I'm pissed at a world that cannot seem to stop judging women who wear hijabs—Sana, my mother. People judge you in a single glance, like they somehow know everything about you based on a simple head covering. Or in my case, when I joined school here, my broken English and my very Pakistani accent.

Part of me is hung up on Sana because the school incident occurred at a time when I was a different person. I was vulnerable, innocent, open, and accepting—not this cynical version of myself. I always imagine a parallel reality where our families never fought and we grew up together here. We also shared most of our big moments together. College wouldn't have been so lonely if I'd had friends like her, Ainee, and Ainee's sister Reema by my side. Maybe we would have meant more to each other.

I need to calm the hell down before I see Marc. The sprinkles of rain do little to dampen the fire. I kick a stone from the uneven sidewalk. It doesn't help either. So I let out a "Breathe, dammit" and fill my lungs with air before sprinting up the stairs to Marc's office.

His salmon-pink door has a little sign with MARC BUKOWSKI on it. Despite my two previous attempts to straighten it, it remains crooked. The door is closed, but the sound of raised voices escapes the room.

I knock.

The voices quiet.

Marc croaks, "Come in."

I enter. Around the oval desk, Marc and a pixie brunette with a stern face, talk in a hushed tone. A short younger blond man listens. Marc's office is a haphazard array of papers and files stacked in nooks and crannies.

I meander around one such mountain of files.

"Mr. Malik." He rises. "Glad you paid us a visit."

He claps the back of the younger man's arm. "This is Brian, the other member of our unit. My most trusted employee. He got back from vacation yesterday."

Brian regains his posture after the back clap and flashes a weak grin. His pale complexion is a bit redder after the introduction. He says in a barely audible tone, "Hi."

Then Marc turns to the woman next to him, who scans me head to toe. "This is Debra, our HR rep."

Debra pinches her lips and forces a smile. "He-elloo."

"Is Ms. Saeed in today? I have a conference call scheduled with Nadine's lawyer." I hold my voice steady so that I betray no emotion. I don't want them to see my concern.

Marc sits down, then motions towards a chair across from him. "Have a seat, Mr. Malik. Miss Saeed is not one of our better employees, but Brian is as good as they come. Maybe he can be of some assistance?"

I stay put. "Where is Ms. Saeed?" My voice comes out edgier even though I try to tamp down my bitterness.

My question hangs in the air.

Brian shifts his feet and avoids eye contact.

Debra and Marc glance at each other knowingly.

She clears her throat. "As you know, we have strict privacy policies." She caresses the file sitting on her lap.

I narrow my eyes. "Sana's my staff. Unless it's HIPAA and not work related, I have a right to know why my employee is not at work."

Marc restrains his tone, but it still reeks of a condescending skepticism. "Well, she *says* someone left her a threatening note . . ."

I narrow my gaze but try to keep an even tone. "An employee feels threatened, and all you offer them is a 'she says' like you don't believe them? I must say, even I credited you for running a tighter ship than that. The first step in Supervisor 101 is to take any threat to your employees seriously and do everything in your power to make them feel safe."

"Well, before we could, she requested time off. But who knows? It may be a prank. It's all speculation until the investigation is over. She's requested a temporary move to another work area, and we're thinking of moving her to my office. She put it in writing, so unfortunately, we're required to move her"—the intensity of his voice increases a few decibels—"here."

"Why your office?" I gauge their reaction.

Brian is pale and fidgets with his pen.

Marc is stoic but keeps shaking his leg.

Debra sits still but scans every movement on my face, as if she's trying to read me as I try to read the three of them. I decide to flip the ball into her court. "Debra, what do you think?"

She shakes his head. "Well, Ms. Saeed cannot continue to sit where she is currently situated. She expressed a concern for her safety, and whoever left the note has violated our workplace violence rules. Moving her is the first step; the investigation will follow."

"This office cannot fit another file, let alone a person." I point to the mounds of dusty paper around. "This has to count for some fire code violation. But . . ." I pause, then say, "I may have a solution."

CHAPTER FIFTEEN

SANA

A few days after Adam's visit, I wake to the sound of a bird chirping nearby and a lawn mower growling in the distance. The scent of fresh-cut grass mixed with gas filters through my open window. When Ammi's alarm beeps down the hall, I tiptoe into her room and whisper in her ear, "I'll take care of Zia." I love seeing her this way, curled like a child in the fetal position on her bed. Only in sleep does Ammi seem vulnerable. "Sweet dreams," I say, shutting the door with the utmost care.

I wake Zia, and while he showers, I cook his favorite breakfast—waffles, maple syrup, and a cup of chai. The aromas diffuse through the tiny kitchen.

He enters the room, closes his eyes, inhales deeply, and smiles. He's dressed in his favorite striped shirt and jeans. His hair's still wet.

I point to his uneven shirt. "Z, your buttons are off."

"I want my waffles and tea." He tries to grab the plate I've prepared.

I place the plate on the table before he makes me spill it. "Let me help you."

He ignores me and grunts as he fixes the mismatched buttons himself.

"Perfect." I pull up a chair next to him. "How's school going?"

"It's wookay." He talks with a mouthful of waffles while cutting another piece using his favorite Star Wars cutlery. He's been working on cutting food with his occupational therapist. It's good to see him getting the hang of it after trying for so long.

"How're your teacher and classroom aide?"

He stops midcutting and slumps his shoulders.

"Did something happen? You can tell me. We're best friends, aren't we?" I place my hand over his.

I want to be the best version of myself for my brother. And being around him makes me better.

He continues to eat. "My teacher doesn't like when I hug Grace. And I get punished."

Grace is a girl in his class I suspect he has a crush on. It's difficult for him to articulate his feelings, but he is a teenager with hormones. Unlike most people, he can't read her emotions or drop subtle hints about his feelings. I smile at the thought of my little brother and his first crush. But I have to explain to him about personal space and boundaries and the expectations of living in a society where everyone has to follow certain rules. I wish he were in a better school, somewhere more equipped to facilitate social integration.

"Now that you're seventeen, the social norms are different. You can't touch people without their permission; you've got to respect their personal space." I squeeze his hand and smile.

He puts his fork down. "Why can't I hug?"

"Maybe a high five? Or maybe you can find something she and you can do together that doesn't involve touching? Like draw that character you like from SpongeBob? Or go on the swings? I'll talk to your teacher."

He puts his fork down and looks at the floor. "Okay."

A shuffle and "Salaam alaikum" behind me alert me to Ammi in the kitchen.

"Walaikum salaam, Ammi." I smile and hug her.

She starts opening and closing kitchen cabinets and takes out the pot she cooks biryani in. She glances at me, then mutters, "Your future in-laws are going to be here today. Please change into the coral shalwar kameez in your closet I ironed last night, beti."

"Uff Ammi. I will." I smile. "Let me help you with the biryani." I take the fresh ginger and garlic bulbs from the fridge and begin making the marinade for the chicken.

Zia finishes eating and heads upstairs to his room to complete his tasks for the day. I've gotten him used to a weekend schedule—today, his chores are to organize his dirty clothes and finish his laundry.

The pungent smell of cut onions and fresh coriander and mint leaves fills the air. Ammi sniffles as she chops.

"So many onions? We're just making biryani and samosas, right? Adam said not to cook, Ammi." I point to the tearjerkers. "He's bringing food . . ."

"Ya Allah! You think I won't cook just because he's bringing food? My nose will be cut in front of my damaad and your sasural. I make more for strangers, you know. These are my daughter's in-laws. They deserve much more." She continues to chop the Vidalias like a ninja.

"Ammi, let's just stick to biryani and samosas. I'll bake a dessert if you want. This is too much stress. When is Rana baji coming?"

Ammi starts the dough for the samosas and says, "I told her to bring her hellions and Farooq right before Adam arrives. Her kids will turn the house upside down, and I will have to cook all over again because they will eat everything in sight." Ammi mixes the flour, warm water, and butter, then sprinkles salt and crushed ajwain seeds in the mixture.

I marinate the chicken with the spices and yogurt, then sprinkle some fresh lemon juice and ghee on top before covering the dish and putting it in the fridge. After Ammi lets the dough sit for a bit, she puts the teakettle on the stove.

I squeeze her shoulder. "Don't worry, Ammi. It'll all be fine. Adam doesn't care about these formalities, I'm sure."

At least I hope he doesn't.

I pour Ammi a cup of tea.

She nods. "He is a good man. And from such a good family. When I saw his tattoos, I was determined to say no. But he is such a sweet boy and, mashAllah, recites the Quran beautifully."

There's no turning back now—not that I have anywhere to go.

* * *

Over the next few days, Ammi calls Adam every day. She even gives him all her shorba and secret sauce recipes, which she doesn't do for just anyone.

Sometimes I wonder whose rishta Adam is after—mine or my family's. He talks to Rana and Farooq often and takes Zia out, although Zia is never excited. How has a stranger ingratiated himself into my conservative family like this?

I decide to cut my vacation short—I need an escape from the Adam-fest, and ExGen has been on my mind constantly. If what Daniel suspects is right, that they're doing something illegal and the expansion will only hurt the environmental conditions of the community, then I need to figure out who at ExGen I can talk to. Research more. Every day I spend at home, the communities around

Hempstead, mostly people of color and immigrants like my family, breathe polluted air and drink polluted water.

When Ainee and I get to work, it's clear the whole building knows about the event. Kevin, the security guard, asks, "How are you, Miss Sana?" and his face has that *I feel sorry for you* look.

I smile. "I'm okay, Kev. Hanging in there. How are things with you?"

He smiles with an eye on the large monitor. "Doing well. But you take care, Miss Sana. And let me know if you need anything."

Ainee links her arm with mine as we head to the cafeteria. The last time I was here, I ran into Daniel. I try to convince myself that I don't want to see him, but just the anticipation of seeing him gets my heartbeat thumping.

When I feel a pat on my shoulder, my hand goes to my heart.

It's Melissa. Her pencil-thin eyebrows hitch up, and I'm not sure if it's because she's surprised or scared by my reaction. Her green eyeshadow matches her sea-green poncho. It billows when she moves her arm, like the green-and-yellow parrot wings I saw once on a trip to India. "Sana, how are you, dear? This must be hard."

Around us, ears perk up, and inquiring eyes glance toward us. Gossip travels quickest in the cafeteria.

"I'm good, Melissa. How are you?" I pour tea into a paper cup, pay for it, and wave at Ainee to get going, but she's in a deep discussion with a coworker. We'll be here all morning if we wait for that conversation to end. Ainee ignores me.

"Let me come with you." Melissa puts a lid on her coffee while we walk back to our office. "I was supposed to hear back from HR this morning on your temporary seating. Let me check." At her desk, her keystrokes are violent and rapid. She shakes her head a few times.

I chew my lower lip, trying not to lose it. Will I have to sit in the hall like a misbehaving child at school? Or worse—in Marc's office?

Melissa peers above her screen at me, then clears her throat. "You're in a shared office, next to Eileen." She stands and, with her bracelets jingling in tune with her steps, hurries me toward Eileen's office. "I can help you move."

Wait a second—did she say next to Eileen? My stomach drops. It can't be.

I swallow. "So I'll be with Eileen?"

"No. With Mr. Malik."

I'm not a superstitious person, but there's got to be a reason this cloud in my life shows no signs of lifting. Even sitting next to Marc seems a better alternative. I hope this isn't revenge for Ammi insulting Shahida in front of half of desi Westchester. If Daniel thinks he can rattle me, he doesn't know who he's dealing with.

When we arrive at Daniel's office, he's nowhere to be seen.

Melissa hands me the box with my belongings. "You need to call the help desk and find out when your computer will be set up. Everything else is in the corner."

I turn to see a few white boxes with *SS* written on one side.

The office is as big as I remember, though the addition of my desk makes it less empty. Daniel's space and my corner are clearly defined, with a row of file cabinets between us.

How will I explain this to Ammi? *I work a few feet away from the oldest son of the woman you hate.*

I shudder, then decide no one has to know—not yet.

I dig through my personal items for a picture of Zia and me laughing over a cup of chai. I hold it against the wall, debating placement, then put it down. I don't want Daniel to think I'm a permanent resident here.

I plant my backside into the small chair on my side of the office. It's quiet here, unlike my cubicle, where my thoughts had to compete with watercooler gossip, copier whir, and constant phone buzz because I sat one seat over from our secretary. Here, the hum of the air conditioner and occasional faint footsteps in the hall are the only sounds. No wonder Daniel loves this office; he's separated from other humans as much as possible. But Shahri was always like that—quiet, sitting in the corner with a book or a video game. I'd go bother him, nudge him to join us.

The chair's wheels creak. As much as I appreciate the silence, without a computer, I'm bored. I scan the office while I wait.

Daniel's diplomas and degrees cover the wall. His bookshelf is filled with law books—journals, a collection of essays by Abraham Lincoln, Gandhi's biography. All alphabetized by author, of course. He listens to jazz and reads nonfiction. My childhood friend's interests are yawn inducing.

I venture to Daniel's meticulously organized desk. According to his planner, he and Marc are in a meeting with the mayor of Hempstead till noon. Maybe Daniel has files for me to work on. His chair is twice the size of mine—all leather and oh-so-inviting. I take a seat, the chair reclining as I scoot toward his desk. Whiffs of spearmint and musk emanate from the leather. It's adjusted for a tall person; my feet don't even touch the ground. I swivel to face his computer. The wall behind the computer is checkered with Post-its; one of the Post-its reads *SS moves in*.

SS. My initials in his handwriting. I touch the loops in the letters, reminded of the many cards he wrote to me. My hand goes to the place on my chest where my locket used to be; I stopped wearing it after agreeing to marry Adam. Once, Shahri was my best friend. Now, he's so altered that I didn't even recognize him at first. Shahri hated people and big gatherings; it's surprising he's chosen a profession that involves him constantly interacting with the general public.

We have become reacquainted but must remain perpetually estranged. We may never be friends again, at least not with our families' knowledge. I hope this case ends soon and I never have to see him or hear from him again.

A familiar voice sounds from the doorway. "Comfortable?"

* * *

DANIEL

Sana darts her gaze toward me, her eyes wide. They sparkle with shades of brown before settling into my favorite tint, an earthy shade with a hint of gold. She wears a brown hijab in a similar shade and a long matching cardigan. I like seeing her in my chair.

I'm captivated, and she knows it.

Her face colors. "Sorry." She swings away from me, then jolts upright and darts over to her side of the room.

I resist the urge to say something stupid and make this situation worse. I sit, then swivel my chair to face away from her and start reading emails. When her drawer opens, the rustle of her bracelets fills the room. The wheels of her chair creak as she moves closer to her desk. These little noises distract me. I read an email for the third time, but it still doesn't sink in. I need to move around—or better yet, talk shop with her.

"S—" I almost said her name. I remind myself to be professional. "Ms. Saeed, the advocacy groups for the community in Hempstead want a public hearing after the draft of the ExGen permit is issued. The environmental and community leaders have concerns about air and well water pollution."

She clears her throat. "I completed the permit, and it's up to Marc to sign off. I've put stricter limits on it than Brian did before. Also, I've reviewed the data, and the water quality is showing a weird pattern. I have the data from public records regarding the private wells in front of me." She holds up a file, avoiding my gaze and biting her lower lip.

That draws my attention to her lush lips. I try not to stare, but I'm making it too obvious. I mutter an inward curse, then tell her, "Email it to me, and I'll have a look."

At least from here, I can't smell her perfume.

Sana picks up her phone, and a few moments later my email pings, followed by another email from Nadine's lawyer, Dalia. She and I worked for a private firm together in California before I moved back to the East Coast. She knew someone in the state attorney general's office and recommended me.

Daniel,

Can we have a copy of the permit that the Department of Conservation is issuing? A recent case study has shown an increase in asthma and cancer cases. I have the reports from the labs for the water quality data as well.

Let me know if there are any questions.

Take care,

Dalia Majid

As I read, Sana's scent hits my nostrils, coconut and jasmine. When I turn around, she's standing inches from me. She pinches a folder labeled *ExGen* in bold letters. "There's something you should see . . ."

"What's going on?"

She slides a few forms across to me; most have a red circle around the signatures. She stretches to reach over the expanse of the desk and says, "I looked up the organization charts, and this is not the supervisor who oversees operations. This is an executive."

Maybe because the light hits her pretty face at a certain angle or maybe because I'm too damn distracted, I blurt, "Yaar, Urdu, please." Years ago, I'd say this to her when she spoke English too fast. I was still learning the language; my mind took a bit of time to translate to Urdu. It was my go-to phrase, asking her to slow down. *Yaar* is a moniker for a close friend . . . which we aren't anymore. Old habits die hard.

She stands straight and pushes her cat-eye glasses up. Her hands fidget with the highlighter she grips. Her voice is edgy. "Shahr . . . Mr. Malik, I am not your yaar. My mother, who hasn't stopped grieving for my father, wouldn't appreciate this closeness."

Sana's voice, despite its touchiness, retains her trademark softness. She still doesn't have a mean bone in her body.

My voice matches hers, except mine comes out even edgier. "And you? You didn't mention your own wishes. Do *you* hate me calling you yaar?"

"Mr. Malik." She raises her index finger like a weapon. "If you continue this nonsense, I'll stop caring about procedures. Let's try to maintain professional boundaries; otherwise I'll have to bring this up to HR." She walls me off by crossing her arms over her chest.

After a long glare, like a fire-breathing dragon's before it attacks, she taps on the papers. "Now if you'll excuse me, I'm going on my union-sanctioned break."

When she gets back, she's calmer, and just ending a phone call. From the way she lets out a long, exasperated breath, then irately clicks her pen, I know she's angry. Half of me is exasperated that I care so much, and the other half wonders what the phone call was about. Maybe she's with someone . . .

None of my business, dammit.

I will not meddle. I must not. We're both here to work. She's just a pretty coworker. Nothing else.

"Why did they have to seat me here?" Sana mutters loud enough for me to hear before she lets out a long exhale.

She says it to rile me up. But the need to protect her overtakes the need to lash out.

I walk over to where she sits, reading through the thick file of paperwork. I move my hand to touch her shoulder but then curl my fingers. *Keep it together; she just got done threatening you.*

"Look," I say. "I want you to feel safe here. This shouldn't have happened . . . and it boils my blood that it did. I promise I will make sure it doesn't happen again."

She stays eerily still.

Uff! She hates me.

I've started to walk away when her voice catches me by surprise. "Did you need something? Sorry, I had my earbuds in. I forget people don't know I have them on because my ears are covered."

She's pinched the white AirPod between her thumb and index finger. Her face is somber, and I open my mouth to apologize . . . then I catch that familiar glint in her eye. The same one when she was hidden behind a door ready to scare me with a *boo.* Or when she'd been caught in a lie. She's heard me but wants to pretend she didn't.

I cross my arms and lock my gaze with her; she challenges me but then starts to chew her lip, because this is what Sana does when she's trying to be brave but is doubting herself a little.

I shouldn't notice the way her teeth leave an indent on her lips. But like a creep, I do. She has a hold on me, and I know it. And like an idiot, I moved her here anyway. I should've stayed out of it—being close to her like this will only make it harder to walk away.

Suppressing my grin, I say, "I just wanted to ask if you've emailed Dalia your thoughts on sharing a draft of the permit you've been working on?"

"You're a crappy liar, you know that?" she says with a raised eyebrow.

"Not as bad as you, Saeed."

Before I can say anything else, my phone beeps. It's Saleem. I step outside to take his call. "What's up? Did you see the oncologist?"

"Yeah." His voice is low. "It's not good news."

CHAPTER SIXTEEN

SANA

For the next few days, I work late constantly. Adam and I chat through occasional emails and texts. He's busy getting his business ledgers ready for an audit.

At three o'clock on Friday, the creak of the office door opening announces Daniel's arrival and pulls me out of my trance. He's been distant and curt all week. I want to ask him why. I wonder if he's seeing someone . . .

No, it's none of my business. The distance we've created is perfect—it keeps my stupid heart in check.

"I was wondering if we could set up a meeting with community leaders soon," I say. "The data still looks skewed." I avoid his gaze by fixing mine on the computer.

He mutters without giving me a second glance, "Email me, and I'll have a look."

My hand hovers over the mouse to hit send on the email, but I sense him approaching my desk. My heart's ready to burst out of my chest. *Calm the hell down. We're not in high school anymore.*

He stands behind me, his eyes locked on my screen. "Is this the graph?"

His aftershave is a combination of alpine and musk. I try not to inhale his intoxicating blend. But it's impossible to do without holding my breath. He leans over my right shoulder, and I hold my breath. My gaze wanders to his face. Allah has made him for my eyes to feast on—his perfect cheekbones, this nose, and that neatly trimmed beard. His thick hair is flopping in a way that still reminds me of a younger version of him.

"Ms. Saeed?" His voice is deep, his eyes narrow.

I swallow and murmur, "Yes?"

He glances at the screen. "Is this the graph?"

I tap on the screen. "There are spikes in the metal concentrations, especially during summer. Concentrations can vary due to increased rainfall events. If that were the case here, they should drop, as freshwater would dilute it. There's something here, something they're not telling us."

Speaking of concentration, mine's shot.

He lets out a long breath, and his Adam's apple bobs.

This proximity with him is messing with my head. Ammi's left eye is probably twitching right now.

"The geographic maps of the area show a school not too far away." I try to click Google Maps, but his hand rests on the mouse and accidentally touches mine. Strange tingles shimmy up my spine. *Ignore these stupid sparks and be professional!*

"It's an elementary school. Those goddamn assholes." His eyes darken, and his jaw tightens. Then, just like that, he moves away.

"We need to research the area." He shuffles through the papers on his desk, then begins typing furiously.

My phone rings. Ainee has set Adam's ringtone as a Bollywood song, and Sonu Nigam's voice announces, "Tenu leke main javanga." Which I'm sure Daniel can translate to "I want to take you home" and infer that it's not Ammi calling.

I charge toward my phone before it rings again.

Adam texts when I don't pick up. *When do you get off work?*

I type quickly. *5:30.*

C U then.

Before I can type anything more, Daniel's voice interrupts. "I'm sure the shared office is as hard on you as it is on me. But can we agree on some common courtesies?" He squares his shoulders.

What's gotten him all hot and bothered?

Part of me eggs me on to quit—this office, this job, everything—since things will probably never be the same. Maybe whoever wrote the note will always have an eye on me. And now working with Daniel an arm's length away, and dealing with his hot-and-cold mood swings, I have another headache that I could do without.

I can quit, and start somewhere else.

But what happens to ExGen then? It will go back to Brian and nothing will change. I can't quit. I have to keep going.

Focus on being mad at him, Sana, and not those treacherously gorgeous eyes that leave you tongue-tied. I inhale and count a few seconds before replying. "Sure."

Around four thirty, when I'm about to text Adam and Ainee to meet me in the lobby, I feel a gentle tap on my shoulder. Damn Ainee; I thought she'd wait outside. I pat her hand to let her know I heard her while I save everything. I need to get out of here quickly before Grumpy Malik gets on my case about friends visiting.

But it's not her hand. His thin fingers remain under mine for a brief second, his touch familiar, yet the effect it has on me is nothing close to that of a friendly nudge. Am I so deprived of human touch that I am all flustered with a simple tap? Butterflies stream in my stomach, and a strange, unfamiliar tingling rattles my nerves.

Surprised, I swing back.

Daniel's eyes widen. His hand retreats. He didn't expect me to touch his hand; his eyes mirror my confusion. We've reached an understanding of the whole personal space thing—no touching and no walking into each other's area. But like me, he has a hard time denying this thing between us. But then again, there could've been a fire, and with my noise-canceling headphones on, I wouldn't have known. I certainly feel feverish, as if there's a flame close by.

"San . . . uh . . . Ms. Saeed." He clears his throat. "I wanted to show you something about the data you've been reviewing regarding Nadine Velez. Do you mind?"

My shoulder still burns from his touch. The physical connection was familiar, yet the man remains a mystery. Maybe it's because that touch on the shoulder means so much more. It's a gesture of concern and care. Maybe I'm reading too much into it. I've never been touched like that before.

Ainee said she would come get me around five, so I hesitate. But I don't want him to think I'm not serious about this case, and I'm pretty sure he works until seven every day. "Okay."

He kneels next to me. "Is everything okay?"

"Huh? What do you mean?" My fingers glide over my face to check.

"Wanted to make sure you're not sick." His gaze never leaves me.

"I'm . . . a little surprised." I ignore the heat rushing to my face. I avoid his eyes and stare at his nicely polished brown dress shoes, which match his dark-brown dress pants and crisp white shirt. Even his tie has brown stripes. The man sure knows how to dress.

He walks to his desk and gestures for me to follow.

Daniel offers me his nice leather chair and, while standing, hunches over the desk. He's so tall he has to bend his knees. He taps the monitor, which displays a bar chart showing the actual data versus the data ExGen submitted. There's an obvious anomaly.

I cock my head. "What are the legal implications if they've been reporting false data or tampering with the devices that report the data?" As if his aftershave isn't distracting enough, the leather chair gives off whiffs of spearmint and musk.

He leans closer, then points to another graph that shows the data from the stacks.

"Hefty fines." He gazes at the screen, then my face. He's inches away from me, and I can smell his minty breath. I ignore it and focus on the screen.

I feel his warm gaze as I chew on my lip and wonder how a company can have near-perfect data and no violations, yet the people living nearby have been inflicted with pervasive diseases related to air and groundwater pollution. "How are they getting away with it? Maybe this is bigger than we know."

He nods and moves away. "I know one thing for certain—to get away with something this huge, someone at this plant has an accomplice, either in the city or here."

I nod. "I thought the same thing. I've made an appointment with the Office of Public Records to review the documentation on file." I turn the chair to face him and find he's gone to the file cabinet by my desk.

"That would be the first step." He puts a file back in the cabinet.

I get up, and he and I do the passing dance—we face each other going in opposite directions. I take a step forward, trying to let him by; he takes one back. It's like we're waltzing without holding hands. I hesitate, then stop. We both stand there, looking at each other, unsure what to do next.

I chew my lip, and he stares at me as if he wants to say something.

* * *

DANIEL

Here's my dilemma: when she chews her upper lip, she's still the Sana I knew years ago, not the scornful adult she's grown up to be. The thing about knowing someone when they're younger and less cynical is that you know them on a basic level, before they've been affected by the harsh realities of life. I raise my hand to reach out to the Sana I knew.

"Ahem . . ." Ainee's voice and knock pierce through the quiet office.

I shove my hand in my pocket. I should not get used to her, or this idea of her. My commitment is to the community around ExGen, to give answers to the people who've suffered environmental injustice all these years. I have to keep all attachments at bay.

Ainee's bracelets jangle as she taps Sana's shoulder from the back. "Did you forget, Sana?"

"No. I lost track of time. I was trying to finish up." Sana hugs the file close to her chest and avoids my eyes.

A man stands in the doorway holding a small bouquet of roses. He's a few inches taller than Ainee and wears a black dress shirt, and his hair is pulled back in a ponytail. His jaw tightens as he hands her the flowers. "I didn't realize you worked so late with him." He says *him* with an edge.

My blood courses hotter and faster through my veins. Who is this? Has Sana told him about us?

"I thought we discussed not having social visits during work hours." I address Sana, ignoring him. I can't let this asshole get to me.

Sana blushes a deep red and mutters, "They didn't wait downstairs like I told them." She puts the roses on her desk. "Adam, this is the DAG on the case, Daniel Malik. Mr. Malik, this is my . . . friend Adam."

A friend who brought her roses.

Ainee flicks her gaze between me and Sana and then clamps her mouth shut. A look passes between her and Sana.

I walk to my desk, ignoring my turmoil and the introductions.

Then, as if she senses my mood, Sana asks me, "Will you need anything else tonight? If not, can I leave?"

I heave a sigh and push back the jealous tinges. Without looking back, I say, "By all means, but next time please let me know before you have visitors."

"Mr. Malik . . ." Something in her voice makes me turn. It's the same tone she used when she was trying to get my attention. I swivel my chair and face them. I eye the man smiling at her while she puts on her coat. As much as I disguise my words, they come out as a caustic taunt. "Yes, Ms. Saeed?"

Her face changes color. She doesn't say anything more.

Adam balls his fist, then relaxes it. Then he does the dick move of marking his territory by putting his hand on her back to lead her out, giving me a *She's with me* look.

I want to chop his hand off, but of course that's stupid and juvenile.

Sana stops, a foot in the hall, another in my office, and cranes her neck to look back at me.

I shuffle through the papers and ignore her. Why won't she do what he expects her to and leave me alone?

"Good night, Dan—I mean Mr. Malik. I'll make sure not to have friends here during work hours. I apologize. I hope you'll have a good night."

I pick up the phone to avoid more conversation. Maybe I should be professional and say something like "You too."

Too late.

The click-clacking of her shoes outside the office and her vacant chair inside irritate me. This space suddenly feels empty.

"Concentrate, dammit," I tell myself, and then look through the papers she left me. The pages are laced with her handwriting and smell of that fruity perfume she wears. This must've been the file she was hugging.

I move to the window to check the weather; maybe a quick stroll will clear my head. But outside, the sky is dark, and little drops splatter the window.

Sana, the ponytailed Romeo, and Ainee are huddled near a car. He opens the front passenger door for Sana and the back one for Ainee. Right before getting into his car, Sana looks up and catches me watching her. She holds my gaze and breaks out into a smug smile. Does she know she's succeeded in getting to me? This should never have gotten this far. I need to stop caring.

Adam looks up as well, and when he pats her arm, Sana looks away. He closes Sana's door, circles around to his seat, and waves at me.

Jackass.

CHAPTER SEVENTEEN

DANIEL

I unleash on the punching bag until my knuckles hurt. I wish it were that smug bastard's face. My trainer slaps my back. "Whoa! Someone had a rough day in court."

I punch once more when the image of his hand on her back reemerges in my messed-up brain again. Holy hell. Never have I let myself be affected by a person like this. I hate this feeling of losing control. I hate her for affecting me this way. No, not her. Never her.

"Something like that." I loosen my gloves and reach for a towel to wipe the beads of sweat lining my brow.

"This is a lesson for me to never mess with you, D." He smiles and slaps me with the back of his towel before waving me good-night.

On my drive home, I think about how I would always get mad at Sana when she picked Saleem for a partner for carrom. And how sometimes she would do it just to rattle me.

One Eid, after just such an occurrence, she looked for me all over, only to find me moping in the basement of our house, playing a video game.

"Shahida Auntie is serving dessert." Her bracelets tinkled as she tapped my shoulder.

I shrugged and, despite wanting to look at her, continued playing. Leaning closer, she passed a bowl of pistachio kulfi and falooda over my shoulder. Her henna-painted hands with kundan bracelets surrounded my vision while she tempted me with ice cream.

Tempted as I was, I couldn't let her win. So I tapped my controller and played.

"Sorry," she said, her voice dropping low.

"No you're not."

"Stop being a jerk, Shahri. Sal and I are allowed to be on a team together." She slid the melting ice cream next to me.

"Then go give *him* the ice cream," I scoffed.

"No, I'm here because you barely ate anything and didn't even come upstairs for chai and dessert. C'mon, I saved you a bowl of ice cream, and you're giving me an attitude?"

"Promise to always be on my team."

"Maybe." She chuckled before reaching for the other controller. "Now let me show you how to play this game you keep losing."

We played, and she beat me every single time. But this was how it was: We fought and made up, and I always knew she'd come looking when I was mad. And that I'd do the same for her.

But that was then.

Eighteen years. I've missed out on almost two decades of Sana. Does she still sneeze loudly and then laugh as she did back then? How many Eids together have we missed? Does she even ever wonder what our future would have been like if things had been different?

* * *

At home, Saleem is still in his scrubs, engrossed in a basketball game on the big-screen TV. The house we're leasing is well equipped but too modern. It's almost more fitted for a tech mogul than a desi family of three, with its rigid edges and minimalist furniture. This is why we shipped the comfortable leather couch from our house in California, one of the only remnants from the last house. Saleem stretches his legs on the coffee table and yells at the screen. It's nice to see him relaxed and enjoying a game after the stressful few months we've had, between the move and his divorce.

When I lay my keys on the counter, he looks up at me and says, "What's gotten you so riled up?"

He's the second person to say this; I haven't said a word, and yet, somehow, I'm that see-through. "Looks like your team's losing, little brother." I gesture toward the screen as I gulp down cold water.

His gaze darts back to the screen. "My boys will beat 'em, I'm sure."

After a quick shower, I head back downstairs.

Sal is still perched in front of the TV, though the game appears to be over. Two steaming cups of tea sit on coasters on the rectangular glass table. My mug reads *Bade Bhai*, his endearment for *big brother* engraved on a cup. A birthday gift from him.

"So tea and sympathy? Is that what you need, chote bhai?" I tease him with the special term reserved for a younger brother.

"We won, so no." He raises his right hand for a high five.

I slap his hand and swallow the warm tea. Cinnamon and ginger hit my tongue, and the undertones of honey soothe my throat as I gulp it down. Saleem makes good tea, I'll give him that. It's about the only thing I can trust him not to screw up.

The post-game coverage continues, but he lowers the volume and asks me again, his gaze still on the TV, "What got you so riled up?"

"Nothing much. The usual."

"Stop bullshitting."

"How'd the phone call for a second opinion with the oncologist go?" I switch gears, hoping he'll let this go.

Saleem clicks the TV off. He turns to me and rakes a hand through his hair. "Ammi wants to stop the chemo. I have tried to reason with her, and I'm failing. Can you talk to her? She won't say no to you."

"I'll talk to her, but you've got to understand, she's tired." A glance at his slowly reddening eyes tells me he's holding back tears. "Ever since Uncle's passing, she's been unhappy, and now I think she doesn't have any fight left in her."

It's heart-wrenching to see him come to this realization, the one I'd already reached, that Ammi has given up. Doctors have been telling us for a while that the chemo isn't having much positive effect, but Ammi had some fight in her before we moved here.

She had a tough life. My uncle was passive aggressive, to say the least. He never verbally harassed her but just made things difficult for her. He'd stop talking to her family or attending parties as a family, leaving her to answer all the questions. Ammi was a stickler for tradition, and she died a little each time she had to explain to friends and family why her husband was such a dick.

Saleem runs a jittery hand through his hair. "She should live for us. Aren't we reason enough?"

"Saleem, she loses her appetite for days, and we both work so much. She wanted to move here to be close to her old friends and acquaintances, and you know how that's turned out. Unless we can quit our jobs, take her to Pakistan, and be caregivers full-time, it's not feasible. She is tired." I squeeze his shoulders.

It's a bitter pill to swallow. But I remember the times, back in California, when I ran home because the nurse called to tell me she thought she wasn't breathing. And each time, I held Ammi's hand and prayed until her eyelashes fluttered open.

"Shahri?" she whispered, the last time it happened.

"Ammi. I'm here. Thank Allah you're okay. I was so scared . . ." My voice trailed off, and I held her hand and sobbed.

She swiped my tears and held me close. "Maybe there's a reason why Allah wants me to live . . . I must repent and ask for forgiveness. But soon, you will take me home and bury me next to my mother. Or put me in a river. I can't go on . . ."

"Ammi, please. Don't give up, we will fight it; I talked to the doctor." I pushed down my sobs to take in her soft hands and her smell. The comfort of her soothing voice.

"I don't want to live like this. You have to be strong for Saleem. He's not as strong as you, my son. You will have to pick him up and prepare him." Her eyes shone from the last of the moisture that stuck in the corners of her weary eyes.

"We'll do whatever you want. Just stay, Ammi . . ."

Saleem's voice pulls me out of my head. "I wish I could've given her grandkids. I wish you'd consider marrying a nice desi girl. Whatever it takes to keep her with us."

"I can't just marry someone to make her stay." I give his hand a comforting squeeze. "We will pray for her and keep doing the things that are logical—like we've done in bringing her here, allowing her to say her piece to Soofia Auntie and giving her a chance to say good-bye . . ."

"Why have you sworn off the idea of marriage? Did my marriage screw it up for you? Or are you holding out hope for Sana? If the latter, then at least let her know you care about her. She's not a mind reader, you know."

I ponder the adult Sana I've grown to admire. She isn't vengeful like her mother, but she's not the same girl who trusted me either. But every time I see her, I miss the time we spent together. I see the girl who always saved the bugs and pets and still is loyal to the core.

"She's with someone, I think. He's buying her roses, and they're going out." I draw in a long, cleansing breath.

"Roses? Who is this dude? Is she wearing his ring? Knowing her family, they'd insist on some commitment." The line between his brows deepens.

"She's with someone Soofia Auntie approves of—Ainee was their chaperone, so I assume it's serious. Whatever. Can we not talk about this?" I give him an annoyed look, hoping he'll drop this.

"Look who's talking. You're the golden son, and she's the perfect daughter. You two are similar and so bullheaded, this is just like when we were little—you'd fight, then play together. She's always been a version of you when it comes to family obligations." He nudges my ribs.

"People change; we move on. I have too." I fidget with the fringes of the throw pillow.

"How about this? Ammi called Yasir Uncle yesterday. They talked about the house they grew up in and how she wants to see it . . ."

My heart stops at that name and the implication. Yasir is Ammi and my birth mother's brother.

Saleem shakes his head. "We just lost Abba; the thought of her prepping like it's the end of days scares me."

"She's just talking to Yasir Mamun because she misses him, maybe?" I squeeze his knee to comfort him.

"I wish you could convince Sana somehow, and Ammi could have something to look forward to . . ." Saleem pats my hand.

"That ship has sailed," I say as I scan the TV for a distraction.

CHAPTER EIGHTEEN

SANA

All during the drive into the city, Ainee talks about her wedding preparations and how Haroon is going to pick up food-tasting samples before he meets us at the jewelry store. There, Adam and I are helping Ainee pick up wedding gifts for the family. We drop Ainee at the store and park the car a few blocks away.

The warm spring night is darker than usual because the moon is the shape of half a crescent. We stroll at a casual speed, enjoying the sights of tall, lit-up buildings and taxis honking and stopping at corners to pick up passengers. The air smells of concrete, car exhaust, and food. The wide sidewalk is teeming with people in this city that never sleeps.

A music venue across the street has a line that wraps around the block. The music spills to the street. The hum of the people in line chatting and laughing mixes with sirens blaring in the background. The sidewalk is packed with couples with their arms around each other and the tap of boots and screech of cars braking at the red light.

I point across the street. "That looks like a popular place."

"Very popular. We played here a few times." He looks over and exhales. Adam is such a sweet, charming man, and like a periscope, all parts of him on display.

I tip my head toward the building. "We?"

His shoulders slump, and he gives me a wistful smile. "I used to be in a band. I played the drums. That was a long time ago, though; my band has moved on."

I stop and look up at him for a second. There's so much about him I don't know. But those soft hazel eyes are kind and gentle and filled with respect every time he regards me. And maybe this should be enough. I treasure this trust he places in me. Friendship and trust are the core of all relationships, and we have that. And that should be enough to last a lifetime.

"Do you miss playing live? I bet it was such a rush. My father used to love listening to old Bollywood musical performances in Manhattan. He said live music is just different. The crowd, the energy, it was spectacular."

Adam has a faraway look in his eyes, as if he's scanning his memory to come up with a response that's appropriate and not too heavy for this casual conversation. "My mother is a very successful businesswoman and came from money, not surprisingly. Abba was an accountant before he retired, so neither of them were expecting a boy like me, with all this . . . ?" He points to his wrist tattoo.

I nod. Because I feel the parental pressure to conform as much as he does. Though in my case, some of it comes from that insecurity my parents felt as they tried to rebuild a steady life after leaving everything behind.

"The catalog of disappointments our families have on us," I say. "I get that. But you're obviously not hurting for money, so I thought some of those rules wouldn't apply. You can do what you want as the only son in a desi household." I say it in a teasing tone, so as to get him to acknowledge the little bit of privilege he has over others like me.

"Half desi. My mom is half desi, half Arab. And when my father got sick, everything else took a back seat. My abba needed me. My sisters are gone and my mother is too busy; she hired good help, but what if something happened to him? And I hate taking my mother's money, which comes with so many conditions. So I started my own business."

"That means you couldn't play?"

"Yep." He kicks a small pebble.

"That sucks. I wish they'd see beyond this engineer-and-doctor-are-the-only-good-career-choices bullshit . . ." I realize a little late that I just swore. I put my hands to my lips in an *oops* gesture.

He chuckles. "I knew there was a sassy desi in you somewhere. Let her out more often."

Our elbows touch as he scoots closer to let a runner pass by. That tiny touch should affect me, but all I do is shudder and move away. Opposites are supposed to attract, and Adam with his handsome face and endearing smile should be the perfect yin to my chaotic yang. I need someone like him. Practical, reliable, and he gets along so well with my family.

If only you would move on beyond Daniel.

At the corner, a pushcart vendor sells hot dogs and roasted chestnuts. A wisp of smoke from the aromatic nuts rises, and an earthy waft emanates along with that of burning logs. Another cart sells rice and chicken platters. The sizzle of chicken on the grill and the scent of fresh vegetables on the open flame makes my mouth salivate.

We duck under an awning as a drizzle sets in. "I'll text Ainee that we'll be late." I scan my purse for my phone.

Adam moves in front of me to shield me from the rain, and his sweet gesture melts my heart a little. Maybe he is as good as they come.

"You're quite the knight in shining armor today," I tease.

"Anything for you, milady." He waves his hand in a mock bow.

I prepare to sprint with him, but he lifts up his arms to remove his jacket and covers us both. I can't have Shahri's memories haunting me the rest of my life—but for that to happen, maybe Adam and I need to make some of our own. With our families happy, it should be easy. It has to be easy. I have to live for the present, for Ammi and Zia, and find happiness in these moments.

"Can I ask you something?" I pivot for the pedestrians.

"Sure. I'm an open book." He fixes his gaze on my face.

"Why do you want to be with me? I see you with other girls in the café. They like you. And I mean, this rishta thing and then my crazy family . . . all this doesn't scare you?"

I try to gather all my courage to look him in the eye so I can truly gauge his sincerity.

The pitter-patter of raindrops hitting the roof in a rhythmic tune makes the ambience more intimate than I would have liked. He lets my question sit for a second, then says, "Because you are the kind of girl I can bring home to Abba. A lifer. Someone who knows the value of family and, in the future"—he smiles—"kids."

I break my gaze, purse my lips, then say, "I think we should get an umbrella and brave the rain."

Deflect and distract. Across the street, there's a store open. Adam points and says, "I'm sure they sell umbrellas. Let's get you one."

The store on the corner has a bold neon sign that reads OPEN. It sells everything from clothes to knickknacks and umbrellas. The inside smells of cheap perfume and air freshener. At the back of the store are cute umbrellas in different colors. He pulls out a bright-pink one. "What about this one?"

"So pink." I gag.

He slides the umbrella back in the rack. "I thought all girls like pink."

"This one's a tomboy at heart. All my friends, especially . . ." I chew the inside of my lip to prevent his name from slipping out. "Ainee knows that."

Adam touches his index finger to my nose and grabs a black umbrella next. "How about this?"

I take a step back, and he slackens his arm in disappointment from my reaction to his touch. "Oh, Adam, you go from girly girl to jet black. Is there no in-between?"

"How about gray?"

Gray. It's a bland, boring color. Yet it reminds me of him. Daniel's eyes. I swing back, pick a green umbrella, and step toward the register. "I like this one."

* * *

The swanky jewelry store is just a block away. The megawatts of power illuminating those diamonds could light up an entire Indian village. We even have to be buzzed in. The carpet and chandeliers look like they belong in a castle. A few salespeople stand behind the display counters, and a pretty blonde with shiny red lipstick and long legs waits near the door. As soon as Adam and I enter, she approaches us.

"Are you looking for an engagement ring?" She flicks her gaze between us and widens her maroon-lipstick-covered lips. She's sizing us up to make a sale, but I don't know why it feels intrusive for her to assume we're out searching for a ring. Do we give out couple vibes?

Heat rises up my neck, and Adam senses my discomfort. He shakes his head and addresses her. "Sure, shall I propose to her right here?"

"He's kidding. We're here for our friends." I point to where Ainee and Haroon stand.

The salesperson nods. If she's embarrassed, she doesn't let on. "Follow me, please."

Ainee squeals when she sees us. "Took you guys long enough. I hope you were behaving, Adam." She points her index finger at him. "I'm her chaperone—next time you take a detour, you must ask for permission." She winks at us.

I slap her wrist. "Stop being dramatic."

Haroon and Adam slap each other's back and shake hands as they catch up. Haroon complains in broken Urdu about how long Ainee has been waffling on what she wants to buy.

"Have you chosen anything for Haroon's mother yet?" I nudge her as she rubs her chin.

"I saw two things I liked. I need your opinion." Ainee drags me by the hand to the glass-enclosed trinkets.

Stealing a glance at the guys, I see Haroon smiling and the two of them checking their phone for something.

Ainee, after hemming and hawing, decides on a necklace with sapphires and diamonds and matching chandelier earrings for Haroon's mom. I have to keep reminding her that she can't buy them for herself. Then Adam and I help them with other wedding gifts.

I admire the beautiful rings and bracelets that I will probably never be able to afford in this lifetime. Ammi raised me to be happy with less, not to think of material things as a way to seek happiness.

But there's one ring I can't stop looking at—the setting is similar to that of Shahri's grandmother's ring. Emerald and pearl. That ring sure would make a lot of disappointments better.

"Like something?" Adam whispers close to my ear.

"Nah." I swing around to face him.

"You were looking at this one." He taps on the glass and points with his index finger at a solitaire in an oval setting right next to the emerald.

"Wrong." I cross my arms. "You'll never see me in diamonds. I have issues with the whole diamond industry. The way they function, it's pretty controversial."

I open my mouth to go on about the mining industry and how they exploit the miners and the ecological effects of mining, but then I glance at the sales assistants on the other side of the display and clamp my mouth shut.

"How about fair trade?" He tips his chin toward the sign that says that all their diamonds and gems are fair trade.

"Why are we talking about this?" I feel awkward and move away from him a little. Does he think I expect these things from him?

"Humor me, please." He points at the display case. "Pick your favorite one. You still owe me for the umbrella I bought you." He makes sad puppy eyes, and so, the coward that I am, I oblige.

The display features every setting imaginable. I move on, then linger on a pear-shaped emerald surrounded by a halo of glistening white sapphires. I've always dreamed of a pear-shaped emerald ring. Perhaps because it's Zia's birthstone. Besides, having a ring that looks like Daniel's ring isn't wise. I need to move on, be here, and follow along.

This time he knows which one I'm looking at and points it out to the salesgirl behind the display case. "Can we try that ring?"

My stomach drops. I swallow. "T-try? I don't think he means . . ." I wave off the woman behind the counter, who waits to pull the ring out of the display case.

"Oh, I totally do. Miss, can we try it, please?"

I wipe my sweaty palms on the sides of my trousers.

The woman smiles and hands him the ring. He holds it out and turns to face me. "Try it on for size?"

I'm in unfamiliar territory. I want to swoon and allow myself to be that girl I've always dreamed of being, the version of me leaning my head on someone's shoulder and talking about my day. The one where I live in a decent house and have three kids, two girls and a boy. Except that dream has always included Shahri. Now I want to dream with my eyes open. Of a life with Adam.

Ainee taps on my shoulder. "I leave you two alone for a few hours, and you're buying engagement rings?"

I plaster a smile and say, "I'm just returning a favor. There's no ring buying taking place here."

"We're closing soon." The girl behind the counter points to the big Rolex wall clock in front.

Adam moves the ring back and forth between his thumb and index finger, then extends his hand close to mine and cocks an eyebrow. "May I please have your hand?"

"Why? Adam, let's not make a scene . . ." I swallow and hold my hand back.

"Just to try for size. Please?" He unfolds his hand, the ring in his palm.

Mainly to get him off my back, I let him slip the ring on. It's too small. And I feel as throttled as my poor ring finger. I twist the ring off and give it back to him. Maybe if my family were here, it would seem better. Yes, that's what's missing. It's not him. It's that Ammi, Rana, and Zia aren't here. It'll be different when they're all present.

The saleswoman raises her eyebrows, trying to gauge my reaction. "Don't you love it?"

Love.

The word sends me into an instant panic. If I'm being totally honest with myself, I don't want to be in mere *love* with the one I marry. I want—need—to be his aashiq. The very notion of ishq makes me giddy. The word has no parallel in English. *Love* comes close, but *ishq* is to entwine with your beloved, mind, body, and soul. The ache and passion this word invokes are something I've never felt with anyone in the thirty-three years of my life. I want to be awakened by ishq, intertwined in ishq with all my being.

No. I want to be with Adam and live happily ever after. Love has no place in my life right now. Not now, probably never. An arranged marriage is all I need right now.

"Ainee, I need air." The words barely make it out before I leave the ring in Adam's hand and bolt.

Ainee runs after me. "Are you okay, Sana?" We stop outside the store.

"The whole marriage thing . . . it's so final. Or maybe it's all these changes—you moving in with Haroon after marriage . . . the thought of losing you . . . Plus honestly, I don't even know if I can afford that place by myself and then I'll have to move back home. It's all so overwhelming." I watch the cars zoom past. Ainee's hair flutters in the chilly breeze outside. I put a hand to my heart to calm myself.

"Oh, Sana. I'm sorry, sweetie. You're my friend, and you always will be. We're like sisters. Marrying doesn't mean I'll disappear. And if you give Adam a chance, you'll be married soon too. He is eager to get a ring. I can tell."

Adam and Haroon walk up to us amid our hugging and crying. "Are you okay, Sana?" Adam asks.

"Yeah, we're okay." I give him a faint smile, even though I have a million doubts swirling through my brain.

Adam seems to sense my need for space and stays quiet.

Haroon puts his arms around Ainee. "Let's go get something to eat."

We catch the E train uptown to a sushi place Ainee and I both love.

The restaurant has a couple of stations where they roll fresh sushi. The seating area is all barstools and high-top tables. Long torchiere lamps hang from the ceiling. There's a bar for drinks on the other side of the restaurant, and separating the two is a huge aquarium with colorful tropical fish.

"I understand that soon, all your friends and family are getting together to decide on the date of your new life together. Are you both nervous?" Adam scoots up on the barstool. Somehow he has seamlessly crept into my family and friend circles. That speaks volumes about how committed he is to being with me and for this arrangement to succeed.

"I'm nervous about what comes after," Haroon mutters. "My mom's a great cook. But Ainee can burn an omelet every single time without fail. Plus moving in with her will be interesting . . ." He smiles mischievously.

The floor-to-ceiling windows of the restaurant offer a stunning view of the city block. There is a man in the building across the street, observing the world from his window, and somehow him standing there watching the street below him brings back memories of Daniel from earlier, looking down at me and Adam in the parking lot.

I bet he didn't spare me a second thought after that.

"Earth to Sana." Adam waves his hand. "Try this . . ." He dips a California roll in soy sauce and hovers it close to my mouth.

"I'm all sushied out. But thanks." I cross my arms and lean back.

I don't know how I've become this person. I should've been polite. Why am I so irritable today? "Can we please catch a cab to the car soon?" I look at Ainee to avoid Adam and his sad puppy eyes.

"It's only eight o'clock, Grandma," she scoffs. "But if you're going to be a grump like your old friend, maybe we should put you back on a train by yourself . . ."

Adam scans my face and then asks, "Which old friend?"

I gesture with a zip across my lips for Ainee to shut up, but it's too late. "It was a long time ago. I don't know why Ainee's digging up ancient history."

Ainee crosses her arms. "You work with him every day. How is that ancient?"

That witch. How could Ainee talk about Daniel like somehow she doesn't know the bind I'm in? Or maybe she has picked her corner: Adam over Daniel.

"We were friends when we were little." I avoid his gaze.

"It's one of those old family secrets." Ainee winks.

"I want to know more," Adam says.

I stay silent, because I'm not ready to rehash our families' histories or delve into my childhood trauma. It may be the best thing to let it sit for a bit. Avoid until I can't anymore.

"This is all you'll get today, Adam." Ainee laughs. My death glare warns her not to say anything else.

Adam shrugs. "Hey, my would-be fiancée is a gorgeous, smart woman. If she had suitors in the past, so be it. I'm lucky to lay dibs on her future. And that's all that matters."

There's an awkward silence that descends on our table.

Haroon stretches and rises. "I have early-morning things, jaan. So let's wrap up."

By the time we leave the restaurant and say good-bye to Haroon, it's late. We Uber back to the parking garage, and Adam drives us home.

The drive is long, and Ainee sleeps in the back seat. Adam stares pensively out the dark windshield, and I can tell he's processing our evening together.

"Are you okay?" I ask.

"Yeah, just tired." He gives me a wry smile.

His statement earlier about him being okay with suitors makes me think he's not the jealous kind, unlike Daniel, who was staring at Adam like he wanted to duel with him. I wonder what the difference is. Maybe it's as simple as Adam knowing I will keep my word. Or maybe it's because his attachment is to our agreement and less to me. Either way, I still feel like I owe him an explanation. To clarify things, especially since Daniel and I work together.

"Shahri . . . I mean Daniel and I used to be friends a long time ago. Our families were very close. Then our fathers had a falling-out, and they moved away." I glance outside into the inky sky, which serves as a background for the tall buildings with lights. "But he's back now, and kind of my boss."

"Is it uncomfortable? Working with him?" I feel his gaze warm my face as he tries to gauge my reaction.

"No. We're very different people from who we were back then. I hardly know him." My heart races, and I'm glad for the semi-dark car.

"Well, it's his loss. Because you're amazing. And that brings me to something I've been meaning to ask you . . ." He hesitates. "Can Ammi come see you and put my ring on your finger?" When a Hummer cuts in front of us, he honks and curses under his breath.

I clear my throat. "I would like to meet her, but I have some things coming up with Zia and work."

"You just tell me when, then . . ."

I stay quiet, and the awkward silence continues the rest of the ride.

CHAPTER NINETEEN

DANIEL

As I jog through the early-morning rays, the unease that's gripped me since Friday doesn't settle. Is she serious about him? Goddammit, is it any of my business? I take a longer track and hope to beat this dread and my nonsensical thoughts. It's useless. Exhausted and sweaty, I finally turn around and head home.

As I step inside the kitchen, the sound of the kettle whistling catches me by surprise. Saleem is showered and dressed. He turns around and utters a quick salaam, then asks, "Chai?"

I loosen my shoelaces and shove my shoes in the closet. "Why are you up so early? Do you have a double shift today?" I pour myself a cold glass of water.

"Yeah, since I have no life, like you," he scoffs, "usually they pick me."

"You can have a life, and another wife, if you'd just get your head out of your ass." I gulp down the cool water and smile at him.

"Says the forty-year-old virgin." Saleem guffaws so hard that he chokes on his spit.

"I am not forty. And I'm not saving you when you choke to death." I jab my finger in his ribs.

He straightens and puts his hands up in surrender. "Sorry, I just can't help it. But on a serious note, Ammi is making more calls to her brother to arrange for her to go to Pakistan."

"Did you talk to the doctor about the next steps?" I ask, settling next to him on the barstool. "I mean, Pakistan is not feasible in her condition."

We both know that the journey to Pakistan means she's prepping herself, and us, for the finality of this journey called life. We sit in silence for a few seconds before he leans close and says, "You could make all of this so much easier for her."

The barstool creaks as I swing toward him. "Anything. I'll do anything, if it means giving Ammi even a little comfort."

He stares at the wisp of steam rising from his cup and says, "You see Sana every day. She cares about you, and in my heart I truly believe she loves us more than she hates us. All Sana needs is for someone to talk some sense into her."

Love makes us stupid, incredibly emotional, and a little unstable. Saleem's inconceivable statement just confirms that for me. I run a hand through my hair and retort, "Sana wants nothing to do with our history, Sal. She's moved on. And besides, I like to keep my work and private lives separate."

"I know. But please, can you at least try? For Ammi's sake?" He joins his hand to plead with me.

"She is not the Sana we knew . . . she likes tattooed suitors and roses. She'll reject anything I say." I shake my head and rise, wanting to end this discussion.

"Why? You were inseparable. Do you still feel the same way about her as you did then?"

I shake my head, even though I know my brother knows me too well. "That was a long time ago."

"This fear of rejection is irrational, bhai. Not everyone is like your mother or my father. You can't let the way they treated you constantly determine your life decisions. Isn't this why you've been avoiding all the rishtas and every advance toward you?" His voice is soft, but the weight of his words punches me in the gut.

"That's a low blow." I shuffle up to the stairs to get away from his scrutiny and psychobabble.

After my shower, I stare at myself in the mirror to reflect on my brother's allegations. Is he right? *Am* I scared of rejection? Is this why, despite wanting to, I have yet to have an honest conversation with Sana? Every time I've tried, she's deflected and I haven't pushed. Now, maybe, it's too late.

* * *

A sleepy parking guard smiles as I swipe my card to park, then walk to the building. The early-morning sun filters through the windows in the office. It's quiet and I love it. Because I can get so much work done in this lull without the constant interruption of meetings and phone calls.

Except Sana's empty chair and office space distract me. I have to remind myself that she and I are working together temporarily.

We have an end date.

Better to drown myself in work. I browse through the ExGen file and make a few notes for the meeting tonight.

Around eight, the sounds around me are more pronounced and the hallways busier. Sana's bangles tinkle as she settles into her chair. Her presence both irritates and soothes me.

My fingers glide on the keyboard to keep my heart in check.

"Good morning, Mr. Malik," she says in a singsong voice.

I halt my typing and swing my chair to face her. I will not let her affect my carefully maintained decorum—or my sanity. "We don't have to do this whole 'being civil' thing, Ms. Saeed. It's distracting, to be honest."

I know I'm trying to push her away. I need to recognize that she belongs to another. And what we had has dissipated with the years and distance that separated us. I curse inwardly at myself for becoming someone I loathe in the process.

Gawd. How I wish I could stop myself from falling.

* * *

SANA

He says my name with such venom that I have to do a double take. Part of me wants to ask him to let my friend Shahri out. Another wants to ignore his jabs.

"Who stole your chai this morning?" I mutter under my breath, loud enough for him to hear. But he either didn't hear or he's ignoring me.

Footsteps sound behind me, and I look over my shoulder. He motions to the oval table, where there are a few big maps spread out, some with aerial photos of the ExGen plant. "These are the hot spots for environmental stressors."

I sidle next to him and follow his gaze to various locations on the map. He has at least twenty circled.

Hempstead is a suburb of New York City on Long Island, surrounded by several bodies of water. There's way too much red on this map.

Daniel leans on the table and shakes his head. "I need to make sense of this. They're hiding something in plain sight."

He looks at me intently. I can smell his witch hazel soap and his minty breath. His dark-brown hair is too reachable, his perfect nose too close. Even when he has a scowl on that perfectly angular jaw, it suits him.

A little streak of sunlight seeps from the window and dances on the side of the wall in front of us. “I’m trying to think of who we can talk to there.”

I fix my hijab, and my locket clinks. I don’t know why I put it back on today. I just . . . wanted to wear it.

“Why have you kept it?” he asks gruffly. His icy gaze holds mine.

This break in character surprises me. He’s breaching our professional boundaries by pointing at something personal. How dare he?

“Because, unlike you, I’m sentimental. It’s from a part of my childhood that I choose to I embrace.” My acerbic tone matches his. He’s rubbing off on me and not in a good way. At this rate, we’ll probably never acknowledge to each other that we were once close.

He straightens his back and leans closer, so close that I can hear his uneven breaths and see color reaching the tips of his ears. His breath fans my suddenly flaming hot face. “Sentimentality has no place in the business, is what my uncle always taught me. I was punished for my sentimentality, so you see, I had no choice in the matter. It was either embracing my guardian’s idea or facing consequences. Now, if my mother had kept me like Nadine and fought for me, I’m sure I’d be different.”

Childhood trauma transforms us. Even though he’s not the angsty teenager I knew, the pain is still very real. That hurt that I’ve always known, deep in his heart, is surfacing now. Despite his tough exterior and him pushing me away, I can see it now: he’s still hurting. He’s never *stopped* hurting. Despite that tough DAG persona, he’s still the boy I knew.

Whatever my deficiencies, my parents doted on me. I was loved, wanted, and treasured.

My heart aches for him. My voice doesn't carry even a fraction of the ache that spreads through me like wildfire. "Shahri?"

"My name is Daniel," he says with gritted teeth. He steps to the large window and stares out at the view of the river.

I don't know why I'm not turned off by his anger or his snide comment. Maybe because I've seen it before, the way he hides his hurt by retreating and becoming angry. "I'm sorry for everything, the circumstances. What happened to you wasn't fair." I curl my fingers to curtail my desire to comfort him.

"Don't be. At least as an adult, I've learned not to let my family's meddling dictate my life decisions. I've learned to differentiate between reasonable expectations and thinly veiled guilt trips. And that includes choosing who I marry or don't." He stares into the distance. Glancing at the lapping waves through the window. "So you see, Ms. Saeed, I don't need your pep talk or your sympathy."

How dare he think Ammi is forcing my engagement with Adam?

"I'm not being forced into anything, Mr. Malik. Just because I wear a hijab doesn't mean I'm oppressed." I tuck the locket beneath my hijab and head back to my computer. "I can try to get an organizational chart for ExGen and interview the operators. See if someone is willing to talk."

"I think that might be a good idea." He's become distant once again.

* * *

Daniel goes out for lunch. Ainee knocks on the door soon after.

I step outside and make sure he's left, because God forbid he sees Ainee in the office and starts to lecture me again. "Let's go downstairs to the cafeteria." I open my cabinet to grab my wallet.

"No cafeteria, my stomach is a little upset. Daniel's not coming back, you little scaredy-cat."

I slap her arm and stick my tongue out. "I am not scared. We work together, so I have to respect boundaries."

She cocks an eyebrow. "Is that what we're calling it? 'Work boundaries'? We both know you're both never just going to be casual coworkers. There's too much shit that's passed between our families. And Ammi was telling me that Shahida Auntie is not doing well."

My heart hurts to hear this. "She did look pale and weak at the party. What's going on with her?"

Ainee's face darkens. "Cancer. It's terminal. This is partially why she came back—to reconnect and repent."

I scoff. "It's a few years too late to repent." Even as I say it, I realize how much I sound like my mother.

"Wow. Are you seriously still stuck on that? The men who feuded are long gone, and you wanna continue this . . ." She shakes her head, hoisting herself up on Daniel's desk and moving his papers haphazardly. My stomach drops.

"Stop, Ainee. He'll file a complaint against me. You know how he gets when you move his things."

She smooths the papers and taps her chin. "So you *do* care about him. What's the deal with Adam, then? Is he your sidepiece?"

I slump on my chair. "What the hell are you talking about? Don't you remember that night after the fight at the party? How Ammi threatened to not let me be part of Zia's guardianship unless I found someone?"

The thing about coming clean is once you start, it does become easier. Especially if it's a friend who knows you through and through. At least I hope so.

"Yeah, I remember." She leans in closer.

"Well, Adam and I agreed to give this a try. Marriage, I mean." I speak nervously and study the diamond-shaped patterns on the rug.

"I figured. The poor man is looking at rings! But Sana, you clearly have a thing for Daniel. Do you even *like* Adam?" She crosses her arms now and narrows her eyes at me.

Another thing about good friends is, they know things. I shake my head. "Why do you have to bring Daniel into the mix?"

Ainee presses her palms on Daniel's desk and climbs off. Her voice is a few pitches higher than usual. "Because you need a reality check. Adam is dead serious about you, and you freaked out at the sight of his ring. And you don't even have the decency to tell him that the 'family friend' you work with every day is in fact the boy you've loved forever."

"I don't love him. I'm supposed to hate him." I match her decibel level. "And dammit, Ainee, I had no other option but to accept Adam. And you know it."

The door creaks open, and Marc peeks his bald head inside. He lifts his glasses, scanning us both. "If you ladies are done gossiping, I would like to speak to you, Sana. Fifteen minutes?"

He nods in approval of his own statement and retreats back into the hallway.

Ainee yells, "Please shut the door behind you, thanks!"

He slams the door.

I wave my hand in a keep-your-voice-low gesture. "Marc is still close by."

She shrugs. "Who cares?"

"I do." I huff. "What if he heard you blabbering about Adam?" This whole day has been a dumpster fire.

"What's he going to do? Fire you for being pursued by someone who doesn't even work here? I'd like to see the rules against that in the HR manual." She shrugs. "So, you going to tell either of them? Or your mother? Or is this all going to continue?"

"Either? What do you mean by *either*?" I cross my arms but know very well she means Adam and Daniel.

There's a click on the doorknob again. "Go away, please," Ainee yells.

"I would if it weren't my office," Daniel's voice booms as he enters. "Salaam, Ainee. Good to know you're still a loudmouth."

"Walaikum salaam. Good to know you're still the grump."

Oh, man. I hope he didn't hear any of our conversation. But his face is serene, and no emotion leaks. Ainee mouths, "Good luck with him," and exits.

I wonder what happened to the boy who'd read *Archie* comics with me and laughed when I asked him, "Why can't Archie make up his mind about who he wants to be with? He clearly wants to be with Betty."

He'd smile and say, "Maybe he's still figuring it out. Men are not smart like women."

He liked to read comics because they helped him get better with English when he first moved here. He and I would sit underneath our tree in Ainee's backyard. He would breathe in the smell of fresh-cut grass and say, "I miss summers in Pakistan. My sister, Ayesha, and I played every day until dusk, right until you could hear the call to prayer. She's my only sister. I miss her."

His eyes were red. I could tell he was holding back tears. "Write to her or your mother, then."

He looked at a passing cumulus cloud in the sky and said, "That life's behind me. They didn't want me."

I hesitated a little. "What was your sister like?"

"Kind, sweet, and had a big heart. Always feeding the stray cats and thinking of everyone. Kind of like you." He beamed.

Now it's as if everything we shared was part of another lifetime.

He has his back to me, and his broad shoulders move in a rhythmic tempo as the sounds of keystrokes fill the room. A short rap on the door ceases his movements. He mutters, loud enough for me to hear, "What the hell's the point of a corner office?"

Marc creeps in, as promised. He looks even more disheveled than before. Strands of hair are half in and half out of his comb-over—like he gave up trying to make them settle on top of his shiny bald head. Without so much as a greeting, he says to me, "Are you corresponding with someone at ExGen?" He sniffles, which I recognize as his anger tic.

I stop typing. Marc, as unassuming as he is, can be intimidating when he hovers. "Yes."

Marc sniffles some more and knits his brows. "I need all the emails about the shift supervisor, Nick Abreu."

Daniel has started typing again. His shoulders are tense, but he's still turned away.

"I don't have any emails from Nick yet. I emailed him to get back to me." I drop my voice so Daniel can't hear. It's stupid, but I don't want him to get in the middle of this. I can handle Marc.

Marc cups his ears and says in a loud voice, "What?"

Daniel's chair squeals as he pushes it back to stand. He's full-on McGrump when he approaches us. His dark-gray eyes shoot daggers at Marc. "Can I help you with something?"

Marc steps back. "I was asking Sana to give me the latest on ExGen."

Daniel stands opposite Marc, partially obscuring Marc from my line of vision. Daniel's tall frame and broad shoulders fill out his crisp navy-blue shirt, making Marc appear a foot shorter than him. Daniel's olive skin looks vibrant and healthy in contrast to Marc's sheet-white complexion and stick-man arms peeking out of his 1980s polyester shirt.

Daniel folds his arms, never breaking his death glare on Marc. "Can you please email Eileen to set up an appointment instead of strolling into my office and harassing my staff?" He points to the door as if shooing Marc away.

"Your staff? She works for me." Marc turns his head toward me. "I'm her official supervisor. I sign off on her performance evaluations."

Daniel points his finger at Marc. "Your bosses begged me for help. Do you want me to pull the plug on ExGen? I don't think your boss would appreciate that."

My eyes linger on Daniel. It's becoming a habit. And a dangerous one.

Marc turns toward the door. "I need more details on the public hearing tonight."

"Eileen emailed everyone the agenda last night." Daniel surveys Marc from head to toe. Then, with a final glare, Daniel says, "Anything else?"

I click my mouse to look busy, but I'm dying to see Marc skulk away.

Daniel stands rooted in place until Marc leaves.

Daniel's watch beeps. "Shit. I'm going to be late." He grabs his laptop bag from under his table. "This public hearing is in an old school building in a rough part of town. Can you ride with Brian or Ainee so you don't have to drive there alone?" His eyes soften. Daniel has learned to control his emotions and his words, but his eyes, the way they reflect things he tries so hard to control, tell me the Shahri I knew is still in there, hiding behind this tough DAG. "Parking may be far, and you'll have to walk. I have to swing by the house to check on Ammi; otherwise I'd offer to"—he pauses, as if to weigh the words he's about to say—"carpool."

He wants to check on his sick mother. Uff. Why must he say all the right things while looking at me like he genuinely cares about me? Ammi always says, "Trust the man with the kind eyes, because eyes never lie." It's as if she was talking about this man, and these eyes.

I avert my gaze. "I'm sure I'll be okay."

He hesitates, then scratches his forehead. "Be careful, Sana."

Maybe it's the way he says my name—or maybe because it's been years since I've heard him say my name at all—but my stomach flips. I want this moment to repeat itself on a loop, my name from his beautiful lips. His break in character from my boss, Daniel, to Shahri, my old friend, the one who cared. The one who turns my heart into mush.

"I'll meet you there, and please be on time." He pulls on his jacket, grabs his umbrella, and, when his eyes scan me again, they're icy gray. The sliver of sunlight in his behavior has once again been replaced by aloof detachment.

He leaves the office, and I try to catch Ainee in her cubicle, but she's already left. I text her, but she doesn't respond. She was saying something earlier about her stomach being upset—maybe she left early? I trudge to Brian's, but he's left as well. So now I have two options: take a risk and drive there myself, or miss the meeting. Except I can't miss the meeting. I'm sure it'll be okay to park close by and walk. When the meeting's over, I'll ask someone to walk me back to my car.

I should be okay.

I think.

CHAPTER TWENTY

SANA

I plead with Mirchi to cooperate as I turn the key in the ignition. "Mirchi, please can you be nice and get me there safe and sound?"

She spits, sputters, and mutters. *It's raining and I'm old. Have mercy on me—don't you have Uber?*

I turn on my headlights and windshield wipers. "You're my Uber, woman."

She scoffs. *Hell no. And stop twisting the wiper blades. I reminded you to replace them last time it rained. I'm old, remember? Most of my friends are dead, stored, or recycled.*

"I promise, wallahi, I will take you for a checkup; just please cooperate." I twist the blades to a higher setting.

Maybe it's my promise or maybe she has grown feelings in her metallic heart, but she lets the wipers swipe away the onslaught of moisture. But still, the inky sky is dark, and the drive takes longer than usual.

To top it off, the only parking space available is two long blocks from the school where the public hearing is taking place, and it takes me way too long to parallel park. The drivers behind me honk impatiently and give me nasty stares as they speed by. When I've finally wedged Mirchi into the space, I grab my umbrella, keys, pepper spray, and handbag.

The school building stands out in this dimly lit neighborhood. A big handwritten sign points to the back for the ExGen hearing. An old lady with short, snowy-white hair and cherry-red lipstick points me to the sign-in sheet on the table. Daniel's name is near the top of the list—he signed in a little before five.

The woman smiles and says, "Walk down to the gym, hon. You can't miss it." She points down the hall, and the reindeer antlers on her Christmasy sweater move along with her. Christmas in May? These meetings tend to bring out all kinds. My stomach bubbles with nerves.

In the gym, Daniel, the mayor of Hempstead, and a few other men stand around, talking, on a mini stage with long tables. He's changed into a sky-blue golf shirt that shows off his forearms. He rakes a hand through his thick, wavy hair, then lets it fall in slow motion. I'm suddenly hot. I swipe my warm face and look away.

The gym is filled with chattering people. As the mayor begins to talk, feedback from the microphone fills the room. He adjusts the mic. "Good evening, everyone. I'm glad the rain didn't deter you. As you all know, we're here to discuss the community's concerns and complaints about the expansion permit. Most of you know the rules. If you don't, it's pretty simple. Please be civil and wait for your turn. With that out of the way, let me introduce you to the moderator for the evening, Daniel Malik. He's the deputy attorney general, working with the Department of Conservation on the issuance of the permit for ExGen. He's here to listen to your concerns."

A pretty, red-haired woman I've never seen before sits in the audience next to Nadine Velez. The seat on the other side is empty.

The gym floor projects every sound my squelching rain boots make as I make my way to the vacant seat. I try walking slower, but the sloshing sound only gets worse. I can't run because I might slip and fall. People are starting to stare at me.

Finally I make it to the chair and take my seat. Daniel is talking at the podium, his deep voice filling the room. I remember how he used to sing in the back of our car on long road trips. He always had a deep, soulful voice. I wonder if he still plays his harmonica.

"Thank you, everyone, for being here this evening. I am here for all your concerns about the expansion, not as a regulator but also as someone who cares deeply about the issues. We're here to listen to all your concerns and help assuage any fears." He smiles.

It's the first time I've seen him broadcast a full-blown smile. Infectious, unfettered, and full of sunshine, it's disarming—as if he really wants to be here and listen to them, not just fulfill a work obligation.

I survey the crowd. It's a mixed bag of middle-aged and older folks. Mostly minorities and some white people. An older lady knits and scoffs while a young girl yawns. A sign reading *No Expansion* rests against her legs. These are the citizens of the community whose lives are impacted by our work. Real people, and not only older people but younger one's as well.

I want to listen to every word but am distracted by the red-haired woman whispering to Nadine. "Isn't he amazing? We used to work together."

She's gorgeous, with her perfectly aligned teeth and symmetrical face. I wonder if they were ever closer than being coworkers. He's a handsome, successful man; I'm sure women have been interested.

A loud thunderclap outside breaks my racing thoughts. The hearing continues as the local Sierra chapters comment on how detrimental the expansion would be. They reiterate how Hempstead's air quality hasn't improved over the years and is likely to get worse with the proposed extension.

An older man gets up to speak. "The well water is contaminated. How can we afford to constantly get bottled water? Water is a basic necessity. What should I tell my neighbors?"

Teachers from the nearby school talk about how the kids have been complaining about the water tasting bad, how kids keep getting sick so attendance is down, and how parents decry the air quality, saying it exacerbates their little ones' breathing issues and hives.

As the meeting comes to a close, Daniel says, "If you still have more questions, please either talk to Ms. Saeed, the permit writer for this facility"—he indicates me—"or email us."

The long-legged redhead approaches Daniel, shakes hands with him, and whispers something close to his ear that makes him grin. I guess they have a history.

I stand next to the podium to field questions and pass out flyers. A few people pick up a brochure before leaving. I answer the concerns of the residents who approach, hand them my business card, and ask the community leaders to contact me if they want more information or have any violations to report. Most people care deeply about the issues in this urban city. Most are worried about what will happen to the kids who have gotten sick.

A small population worries we might close the plant. A few of them huddle in the corner with an older man. I recognize him from previous meetings; his name is Phil. A couple of younger men talk animatedly with him. His pale skin is even paler in the bright lights from above.

He wipes the sweat off his brow, then addresses me. "You guys want to clean up the air. But let me tell you something: this plant has been my livelihood since I was sixteen. My family depends on it."

I smile and nod. "I understand."

"I do too." He shakes his head, then points to the younger guys. "But some of the younger men are a little impatient. They think this new permit and the regulations you're about to issue will put us out of work."

I hesitate. When I am about to say something, Daniel joins in. "Phil, as I told you before, we're not shuttering the plant. We'll make it cleaner—better for you and your kids." He extends his hand for a handshake. Then he flicks his gaze over to me. "Ms. Saeed, I would like you to meet someone." Daniel leads me over to the red-haired woman. "This is my friend and former colleague, Dalia. Dalia, this is Sana Saeed, my assistant."

"Nice to meet you." Dalia shakes my hand and smiles. "I've heard a lot about you."

"Good things, hopefully?" I give a humorless, wry smile. As soon as she takes my hand, I sneeze. Then I sneeze again, and shiver. It must be the rain. Though my stomach hurts a little when I sneeze a third time.

Daniel starts up another conversation with some community leaders.

The big clock in the gym reads ten fifteen PM. I don't want to be stuck here with no one to walk out with me. When I wave good-bye, Daniel's eyes meet mine for a second. I see concern and a question in his eyes, but before he says anything, I head out.

I follow an old couple out of the building, hoping for company for my walk back to the car. But they huddle under an umbrella and run to their car, which is parked right by the building in a handicapped spot. The street is desolate and empty.

The wind howls, and a chill whizzes through me. The leaves on the tree sing an eerie tune. My umbrella flips inside out, and some of the spokes break.

As I reach the end of the first block, the unmistakable glare of car headlights comes up from behind me.

Nausea and a sharp stomachache hit me.

The headlights are still there. I glance over my shoulder to try to gauge the distance between me and the car, and crash right into something—or someone.

A solid, warm body catches me.

Then it's dark.

CHAPTER TWENTY-ONE

SANA

I flick my eyes open one at a time; my throat and head hurt. I'm in the back seat of a car, and the front is dark.

A head turns to look at me. The profile is fuzzy, because, I realize, my glasses are gone. Is this real? Why am I in the back of a car? Whose car is it? My skin prickles, and I shiver.

It all comes back to me: a car behind me, headlights, getting feverish and dizzy, passing out.

My heart thumps so hard I can hear the beats like drums.

I should've never come out here alone.

My eyes sting as my whole life circles through my brain: the brush of my graduation tassel as I moved it across my cap, huddling around the table as the news of the lost business sank in, the weight of Zia bundled in my arms the first time I held him, Daniel and I sharing dessert underneath that big tree in Ainee's backyard.

I'll die single and pathetic. Somewhere a little obituary blurb will say: *Sana Saeed, a hijabi dork who leaves behind an empty bank account, a temperamental car, and a judgy family, who will not be attending her funeral because she lied about her double life.*

The car stops.

The front door opens. Then mine.

I close my eyes and scream at the top of my lungs, "Help!"

Someone puts a hand to my mouth. "Shh . . ."

Then his beautiful face appears, the worried look in his dark eyes. My voice breaks when I call out, "Daniel?"

I don't remember how many times in my life I've felt such an utter sense of relief. As if I wanted so badly for it to be him that I wished him here. No one's kidnapping me. Daniel's here.

I hold his arm, and he pulls me in for a hug while I clutch his warm cotton shirt. Something breaks in me. I don't care what he thinks about me, or whether it's appropriate to touch him. My insides are a mess, my aching throat now full of uncried tears of relief. I'm back to being my fifteen-year-old self, and he's the same boy who was my best friend. My comfort from the world when it got ugly.

Daniel sits motionless, as if his whole purpose in life is to hold me. He lets me cling to him like when we were little. He lets me hold him until I finish crying, until every one of my tears has subsided.

He whispers, "It's okay. I'm here."

I swipe my tears and mutter, "How'd you find me?"

"I was following you. But let's get you home." He helps me out of the car. A shiver goes up my spine, so he takes off his coat and wraps it around me. His coat gives off remnants of his cologne—spearmint and cedar, a swoony concoction. He half-carries me to my apartment, with me latched on to his arm for dear life.

* * *

DANIEL

I park and help her up the path toward her second-floor walk-up. The wind howls, and a streak of lightning flares behind the trees that line the back of the complex. Sana bolts to the clearing between the staircase leading downstairs and hurls.

Soon after I ring the bell, Ainee appears at the door in her pajamas. She rubs her eyes, which have dark circles beneath them. Her skin is pale. "Not you too," she groans, taking in Sana's appearance.

Sana drops her hand from my arm quickly, conscious of her friend's eyes on us.

We trudge inside. "Are you all right, Ainee?" I ask.

She shakes her head. "I have food poisoning—I went to the doctor earlier. It was probably the leftover sushi we ate last night." She slumps on the couch.

Sana staggers to the couch too, and I instantly miss her warmth.

"I'm okay, Daniel," she says, craning her neck to look at me. "Thank you so much, but I think I've got it from here."

I scan their faces. Ainee looks like she's ready to retch, and Sana seems like she's going to pass out. I press on. "I can stay for a bit if you need me."

Sana shakes her head. "We'll be fine. I don't want Ammi to have a heart attack." Her face scrunches, and then she lowers her head and upchucks onto the floor.

Ainee jolts upright, pinches her nose, and jogs to the bathroom, yelling over her shoulder, "Cleaning supplies are in the hallway closet."

Sana slumps back on the couch and mutters, "Sorry, I . . ." before passing out.

I have never in my life cleaned vomit. The reason I couldn't be pushed into medical school by my brown mother was because the sight of blood and other bodily fluids turns my stomach. But, doing my best to control my gag reflex, I clean up as quickly as possible before I throw up too and the cycle continues.

When I'm done, I take the lightweight blanket from the back of the couch and drape it over Sana. Her eyes are closed, and I'm sure she's asleep, but when I move my hand, she grabs and holds on to it. "Shahri, please stay."

As much as I hate that name, from her lips it's like a morning birdsong. Like saffron threads melting in milk, coloring it crimson. My heartbeats pummel my ears. She feels something.

"I need my hand to put the cleaning supplies away. I'm right here, though," I whisper close to her ear, but she's out.

In the kitchen, I peek inside the fridge for Gatorade or something similar to help Sana and Ainee replenish their electrolytes.

The fridge is filled with Tupperware upon Tupperware of food in mismatched containers. There's Diet Pepsi cans in every corner, and the freezer is completely empty. I mean, desi moms are obsessed with packing food for an entire village anytime their kids leave, but this fridge is *only* that and nothing else. Nothing to suggest that Sana or Ainee ever cook.

Growing up in Pakistan, we never had Gatorade or anything fancy when we got sick. Amma would boil water and put in equal parts sugar and salt and make us drink it to help keep down the fluids.

After digging through all the bottom cabinets, I finally retrieve a decent pot, then boil the water with salt and sugar and let it cool. Then I go to check on Ainee, because I'm afraid she's passed out.

I knock on the hallway bathroom door. "You okay in there, Ainee?"

The water running inside halts, and she spits out, "Yeah, I'm brushing my teeth. Is the living room, um . . . smelling less pukey?"

Her voice is less shaky, so I tell her, "I made salt and sugar water, if you want."

"Thanks. I'll be right out."

I pace the small living room. This is the first moment I've gotten to take in Sana's home. The living area is a mishmash of styles and a menagerie of colors. Bright-magenta sari curtains and peacock-blue throw pillows are more Ainee, while the tall bookshelves along one wall are more Sana. There's a charcoal drawing of Sana and Ainee, another of Haroon and Zia. Important men in their lives. The deep-purple throw pillows brighten the coffee-colored suede sofas.

I pace some more; Ainee has still not emerged from the bathroom. Sana is listless on the sofa. I ache to comfort her, give her water, and take care of her. But she's made it clear that the idea of me being close to her repulses her. My heart argues, *But she said, "Shahri, stay."*

Shahri. Not Daniel, never Daniel.

After a few long minutes, Ainee appears, freshly showered and with some color back in her face.

I pour the now-warm water into mason jars with lidded covers and bring them out to the living room.

Ainee points to the concoction and then replies, in a slightly disgusted voice. "That looks sad."

Sana stirs again. "Ammi . . ."

She misses her mom. What if her mother finds out that I'm here with her? I need to leave, but before that, I need to make sure she's okay. I reach out to touch her forehead but then halt. I curl my fingers and ask Ainee, "Can you check her temperature?"

Ainee touches her and then nods. "Her forehead's warm. My doctor told me to keep the fluids up. But I am not making her drink that concoction. She needs Gatorade or something."

"Can you try to see if she'll drink while I get her Gatorade from the pharmacy?" I plead with the sensible side of her.

"Ugh. I'll try. Can you pick up the cherry flavor for me? I hate the blue one," Ainee says as she lifts her feet and slips onto the couch next to Sana. "Also, I'm craving nachos."

"Are you serious? You just puked for ten minutes straight. I am not buying you nachos." I shake my head and slip on my shoes.

"I feel better already." She rubs her belly.

"I'll call Haroon and tell him to come over with nachos," I reply.

"And I'll call Adam." She waggles her eyebrows.

"Be my guest," I tell her before I step outside.

On my way to the pharmacy, I make a call.

CHAPTER TWENTY-TWO

SANA

When I regain consciousness, two male voices—one familiar, another not so much—reach my ears through my open bedroom door. The cobwebs around my fuzzy brain clear a bit. The first thought that enters my brain is *Daniel is here*. Or maybe that was all a fever dream.

The voices grow louder. It wasn't a dream. Daniel is still here. I sit upright, and my stomach gurgles.

The other man, not Daniel, says, "I gave her something to stop the nausea. Will you drop the worried-dad routine?"

The voices are coming from the living room. I tiptoe to my doorway to listen.

Daniel's irritation seeps through his words. "Don't be a smartass. I just want her to be okay. I should've never let her drive there alone."

A bout of nausea hits me, and I run to the bathroom. So much for the nausea meds I was apparently given. After I retch, I sit there pulling tightly on the strings of my hoodie. I'm hoping Ainee's snores, coming from where she's asleep on the chair in my room, have masked the sounds of my heaving.

They haven't.

The door opens, and Daniel enters.

If there was ever a romantic notion of him being still attracted to me, it's shattered to bits, right this second. This image of me hunched over vomiting will probably never top any other visuals.

He sits on the bathroom floor next to me and hands me a towel. Using the sink for support, I get up.

"Um . . . I'm fine. I'll be out in a bit."

Thankfully, he realizes I'm asking for privacy. He stands upright and steps outside. "We'll be right outside."

"We?" I wipe my face to avoid looking at him.

"Saleem's here. He's a doctor. You haven't been able to keep much down. I figured I'd ask him to take a look."

"Just give me a few minutes," I tell him as he retreats.

I know Ammi's right eye is twitching. I have not one but two of Shahida's sons here. When we moved in together, Ainee and I promised our mothers we wouldn't have any men in the apartment. We've been living here for six years, and that rule has never been broken.

Until now.

I need to shower.

When we were younger, Shahri and I were in the same Sunday school class at the local mosque. Our teacher was Sister Kahkashan. She had stern glasses and lips thinned in a frown most of the time.

One Sunday, standing next to the chalkboard with Arabic letters, she asked me in her thick accent, "Sister Sana, please recite Surah Kafiruun."

I knew the Surah but was so nervous I got tongue-tied. Shahri raised his hand and asked if he could start to recite it instead.

This brought on whispers from my classmates, and the girls all side-eyed me. Shahri was so popular with them. Before that day, I had always kept our friendship a secret, because I didn't want to have girls asking me details about him. I didn't want to share any part of him with anyone else.

Sister Kahkashan frowned once more and waved her hand at Shahri. "Your name, brother, is not Sana."

The giggles from the girls and meaningful snickers among the boys made me want to die in a pool of shame.

I fought with him after. "You don't have to always come to my rescue; I would have faced her on my own."

We walked in tandem through the long parking lot. Slowing down to match my short steps, he ran a hand through his thick hair and said, "Maybe I was just trying to impress Sister Kahkashan and it had nothing to do with you."

A little scar on the side of his forehead that was usually covered by his floppy hair was exposed. Shahri had told me it was from one of the many times his birth father had beaten him up. There was a broken bottle involved. He'd never shared that with anyone else, not even Saleem.

"Liar." I nudged him.

"You'll never know . . ." He smiled.

* * *

When I get out of the shower, my phone pings with a text from Adam. *How are you feeling?*

Adam? How does he know about last night? Did he call Ainee? Why has my life turned into a Pakistani drama with nonstop plot twists? I already have no idea how I'm going to explain any of this to Ammi. I can't deal with Adam right now.

The house smells of fresh khichdi, basmati, and lentils. My stomach growls.

After a final glance in the mirror, I go out to face the Khalil brothers. Daniel stands an inch taller than Saleem. Where Daniel's hair is wavy, Saleem's is curly. Both are in their sweats, although Saleem looks the more disheveled of the two, as if Daniel dragged him out of bed. They are both ridiculously handsome. Hard to believe we all used to run around in circles in Ainee's backyard all those years ago, Shahri and I always paired together, as did Saleem and Reema.

They both look up as I trudge into the living room.

"Salaam. You look better," Saleem says.

I raise an eyebrow. "Thanks. I feel better. What are you doing here?"

Part of me is irritated they're both here, and another part is so happy to reconnect. This feud was never about them—they were too young to have contributed to it—but their being in the Khalil clan just never worked too well in their favor.

"You break my heart, yaar. Last night you mistook me for Daniel a few times; now I'm a stranger?" Saleem checks my pulse, which has quickened at his comment.

"Did I really?" My hand goes up to my mouth. "What did I say?"

He looks at his watch and says, "Are you sure you want to hear all that?"

I swallow. "I don't remember."

His face contorts from a suppressed smirk. "Don't worry. I won't tell Adam."

My face heats, and I slide farther into the couch. Daniel's laptop sits on the coffee table, and something about the room seems different. It's cleaner, with magazines stacked in the corner, the rug recently vacuumed, and the sofa free of crumbs.

Saleem senses my surprise. "I wish I could take the credit, but it was all Daniel. If you're ever in the market for a house husband, he'd be good. He likes to clean when he's stressed."

"I'm right here, dude." Daniel slaps Saleem's back and then settles a tray on the table.

I look at the meal he's prepared for me, and a lump lodges in my throat. I push the tears down, because how embarrassing would it be for a grown woman to cry at the sight of food? It's not just the nourishment, though; it's the gesture. He knew exactly what to make for me when my belly hurts. Ammi makes this whenever I get sick. This familiarity, this unspoken knowledge we have of each other, catches me by surprise.

Daniel sits next to me and puts his palm against my forehead. "Your fever isn't as bad, but you seem so pale. Everything okay?"

"I remember this." I pat the handle on the tray. "I thought we lost it."

Daniel chuckles, then lifts a mug of tea as he settles into the recliner next to the sofa. "It was all the way in the back of the cabinet, behind the five different types of blenders. Seriously, were they *buy one, get six free* or something?"

"Ainee always just buys new ones if she can't find a part."

He spoons some khichdi into a bowl and hands it to me. "Eat a little."

Even before I taste it, the smell of ghee makes my mouth water. The second the savory rice hits my tongue, flavors explode in my mouth—zeera seeds, sautéed onions, and garlic. I must have groaned, because Daniel's hand touches my back.

I turn to look at him. His eyes are the color of the ocean right before lightning strikes, and I am drowning. I forget to breathe. My skin tingles, and to create space, I lean forward and grab a steamy mug of chai.

Saleem clears his throat. "Easy there, bro. This one might be taken . . ."

Daniel gives his brother a *you're dead* look, then picks up his mug and takes a sip. A lock of his wavy hair falls on his forehead, and I ache to touch it.

I'm losing my grip on myself. I'm falling for him.

No. I cannot. Not him. Anyone but him.

"Thanks so much. Both of you didn't have to stay and take care of me. Give my regards to Shahida Auntie. I'll pray for her recovery." I blow on the steaming cup of ginger tea.

"Maybe you can do a little more than the dua." Saleem's eyes scan Daniel's before they plead with mine. "Because he's better than me, my brother would never ask for anything. But I can."

I twist my fingers and wonder what he's about to ask.

"No, I'm not asking you to marry Daniel." His chestnut eyes gleam with mischief. "But Ammi wants to see you. Can you try and see her, please? I'll be grateful. I'm not beyond begging. Please. It will give her some sense of closure."

Saleem's face is marred with lines of worry as he waits for me to say something. Daniel's more stoic, but I know his feelings mirror his brother's. If I were in their shoes, I'd feel the same way. For the first time in my life, I face an irresolvable predicament. How do I accomplish this without betraying my mother? Shahida may not have directly caused us pain, but by staying quiet, she didn't help matters. The Prophet, may peace be upon him, always forgave the people who had wronged him. Why can't Ammi? I will always be on my mother's side, but this right here has to count for something. Daniel took care of me and Saleem was here to check on me, despite how Ammi has treated them.

I know I may regret this, but I still turn toward Saleem and say, "InshAllah. I will be there this weekend. But please, let's not talk about this to anyone else. I'll talk to Ammi in my own way." I drop my voice to a whisper.

"My lips are sealed." Saleem pinches his fingers and moves them across his face in a zip-up.

"Why does she have this level of hatred?" Daniel asks me. "Even Ainee's mother tried to talk to her when she found out about Ammi's condition and did her best to convince her, but Soofia Auntie completely shut her out."

Maybe it's good that he's asking me this; maybe this can be the closure I've been wanting too. To tell him how we've suffered while they up and left. I cross my arms. "There's so many . . ." I pause. They're both listening to me, intently, really wanting to know. They care. I know they do. And somehow it's disarming. "You know the obvious ones. Your father was a penny-pinching asshole who just had to go after every asset of ours."

Saleem nods, his head lowered. "I agree. That's why I moved out of that house after high school. Bade bhai here had to deal with him after. And this when Father dear paid nothing for college for him."

"I stayed there for Ammi," Daniel replies in a calm voice. "I couldn't leave her to deal with him, especially after Sal left. He blamed her for not loving Sal enough, and shit like that . . . he had issues."

Saleem shakes his head, his face now coloring. "I have no idea why Ammi didn't just walk out on him."

Daniel runs a hand across his face. "Because my mother already did that, and she didn't want to do the same thing. Somehow I felt like I had to see her through this, because my birth mother was partially responsible for this, you know."

I turn to him, wanting so badly to comfort him. I want to hurt anyone who's made him feel this way, like he had to shoulder all the burdens, like somehow he had to repent for his mother's sins.

I swallow the ache and the tears rising to my throat. "My parents were also mad that they failed us. Failed the immigrant dream. That idea of a better life was dying, and the grief from losing friends, their reputation, all at the cost of being away from their families, was too much."

Saleem's voice is rough. "I am so sorry. I wish there was a way . . ."

It makes me wonder if it wouldn't have been so bad if our parents had just sat like this and talked out their issues. But they were different from us; they held on to grudges like traditions. And even as I begin talking, I realize that we are, in that respect, a little better than them. "Ammi was pregnant with Zia when your father sued us. We lost everything. So Abba let the health insurance lapse because he couldn't afford the premiums, and he kept eating biryani and laddus like there was no tomorrow . . ." I trail off, not wanting to go down the *If he'd had insurance, he would have gone to the doctor sooner* road again. "Ammi also blames your father for Zia, because she thinks somehow her stress caused him to be the way he is . . ." I run a hand across my face. Saying it out loud seems so preposterous, yet it's true.

Saleem shakes his head. "Does your mother blame herself for Zia's autism? There's not much evidence in the medical world that supports that."

I don't want to tell him how many discussions Rana and I have had with Ammi about this. My mother, like any other parent, wants her kids to be perfect. She feels the burden of guilt about Zia and transfers it all to Sibte.

"Ammi wants Zia to be like all the other seventeen-year-olds. As much as she wants to control our lives, she also wants us to be independent. I know, the irony of this statement is not lost on me." I give a sad smile. "But the point is, Zia isn't there yet. We can only hope and help him—and pray that he'll be there one day. But she lives with the guilt that, somehow, she's the reason for Zia's Autism . . ." I pause. "I was hoping to get him into a specialized school, but the waiting list for it is too long and tuition too high. So we fight to get him services with the school district. Unlike his current school, they have older kids on the spectrum, on the advisory boards. They help in ways neurotypicals, never can. . ."

Daniel scratches his forehead. "I can help if you want to appeal school districts' placement or to get him more services. . . ."

My shoulders sag, as I think about how many times the teachers at his current school tell me how Zia can't do things instead of appreciating his talents. Understand him, encourage him, and not try to fit him in a box to make sure the funding is secured for him. I want my brother to love being in a school where he's understood and respected for who he is and not how they want him to be.

Silence hangs as we try to process all that's passed between us. Saleem stares at me. His mouth opens and closes on the brink of asking something but doesn't. Finally, he gets the words out. "Which school?"

"Building Bridges."

Daniel massages his forehead and is about to say something when I hear a familiar shuffle of feet as Ainee comes into the room.

She stretches, then looks at our faces and halts. "You're both still here? Skedaddle. Sana's next sympathy suitor and the crazy khandaan are on their way with breakfast. I don't want it to turn into a naan-flying contest. You've got to leave."

CHAPTER TWENTY-THREE

SANA

After Daniel and Saleem leave, my phone pings again.

It's Adam. *Sana? Are you okay? You sent some delirious texts to me yesterday, I'm heading over there with everyone now.*

I hope it's his family he's talking about and not mine. I type, *Is your mom back in town?*

Not mine, ours.:)

What?

Your family is mine, yaar.

Yaar. There's the word I rebuked Daniel in the office for.

I type, then erase, and finally send the least controversial text I can think of. *OK.*

He types back, *See ya soon.*

Ainee sets her teacup down, it clatters, breaking my stream of thoughts. "Daniel filled me in on what happened."

I weigh my words before I speak. "Don't take this the wrong way, but I didn't like the way you rushed them out. They did us a favor. Daniel wasn't expecting anything but some kindness in return."

Ainee chews her lower lip. "If your mother finds out, she's going to be mad. And I'm engaged. You"—she draws a circle around my face—"have to open your eyes, Sana. You're falling for another man while stringing along a sincere man like Adam. We're not living in an Austen novel, you know."

The thing that bothers me is how Ainee, despite not having a mother who hates Daniel, simply feels no attachment to Daniel. Or if she does, it's less than what she feels for Adam. "Why do you talk about Daniel like he's a stranger? We all grew up together, played in your backyard every summer . . ."

"Yeah, you and Shahri were always together. Just like Reema and Saleem. Rana and I hung out with you like extras; it was only after Shahri left that you reluctantly let me into your inner circle."

"What circle? It was just me and you, Ainee."

"Be honest, if Shahri hadn't disappeared, would you still be so close to me?" She asks me with a sincerity in her eyes which surprises me. This isn't the half-here, half-on-her-phone version of Ainee, or the listening-to-me-while-perusing-TV-channels Ainee. This is my friend, who's been hiding this big hurt.

I move next to her and hug her. "I'm so sorry you felt left out, Ainee. I had no idea."

"Meh . . . I guess I should consider myself lucky. The Khalil boys haven't ruined all suitors for me like they did for you and Reema," she scoffs.

My stomach knots. Part of me wants to fight her on this, and another knows that maybe there's some truth there.

Then she smiles and says, "Maybe you two destroyed them also. However accomplished Daniel is, he's still unattached—and Saleem is miserably divorced. I mean, except for your parents, we haven't had any good marriages as examples. My father was hella screwed up, and Sibte uncle was just bitter and mean."

None of this should be news to me, but when we were little, it was all very hush-hush. I knew things were different, but in the desi communities, sometimes symptoms of bad marriages are kept hidden like dirty laundry. Yet, couples stay together, for the kids and for the shame.

"Ammi and Abba had their own challenges, but alhamdulillah, praise be to Allah, there was so much love between them. I think part of Ammi's anger came from losing her husband before your mom and Shahida Auntie. She even said to me once, 'I never wished for him to go, unlike them.'" An ache settles in my belly. I miss my father so much. Maybe, if he were alive, he could have loved Daniel as much as he loved Shahri.

The bell rings then, and Ainee jolts upright. "Let me get it."

I hear a "Please sign here," then a rustle of plastic.

She waves a bouquet of yellow daisies and waggles her eyebrow. "Adam even got the flowers perfect this time—your favorite. Your marriage to him will be so good. This man knows you."

There's something so beautiful about cheerful flowers, like daisies, in that they can lift your mood a few degrees. Even when you've spent the night hunched over a toilet bowl with someone you're hopelessly attracted to.

"This is awfully sweet of Adam." I set the vase on the triangular side table next to me. The typed card says, *Hope you feel better.*

Ainee shuffles through the hallway closet for her rain jacket and slips on her rain boots. "I have some cakes to sample downtown. See you in a bit."

The doorbell rings again, and even before I open it, I can tell from the voices that it's Adam and my family.

A few minutes later, my living room is crowded with people, the sounds of chatter, and the scent of food escaping the pots of food they each carry.

Ammi rushes in, hugs me, then cradles my face. "Beti, you look pale, and these dark circles have aged your face a few years. You should've put some makeup on for Adam."

My mouth opens and shuts when I see Adam. He looks like he made an effort. His long hair is in a ponytail, and he wears a crisp, navy-blue long kameez and matching shalwar pants. He shoots me a dimpled smile. "So sorry. How are you feeling now?" He looks around to make sure no one is looking before he touches my forehead.

Adam's touch is gentle, yet I squirm. I wonder why he didn't bring the daisies instead of having them delivered. Ammi would not approve of such a waste. Mentally I roll my eyes—I hope I'm not turning into Ammi.

He retreats and then surveys my apartment while Ammi and Rana congregate in the kitchen.

Zia settles on the corner reading chair with the TV remote. He fiddles with it and finds his favorite channel.

Adam gestures toward my reading chair and bookshelf before he says, "I can tell which corner belongs to you. And it's certainly not the one with beauty magazines and the shag carpet. It's so clean. I must say, I'm impressed. The way Auntie described your place, I was gearing up for some heavy-duty vacuuming."

I jab my finger at him. "I am sick, so even if it were a pigsty, I should be excused."

He smiles. "Sit down and take it easy. We're here to take care of you, not stress you out."

"I would say, 'Have you met my family?' But of course you have," I scoff. "You drove them here."

"I am marrying them too, remember? Let me see if I can help Auntie," he says, then jaunts toward the kitchen.

Adam joins in Ammi and Rana's talk about recipes. The two of them are so taken by him that they forget to ask about me. Seeing how well they get along, I get jealous. Is this some weird sign he is indeed the one for me? Marriage isn't about two people coming together but about two families joined forever—or until divorce. The Prophet, peace be upon him, puts so much emphasis on community and the family; why shouldn't I?

Rana settles on the love seat with a teacup and saucer in hand. The spicy aroma of cardamom tea fills the space. "I've got to compliment Ainee on her khichdi when she gets back. I'm glad she's not going to burn poor Haroon's food every day. You know, a man's heart is connected to his stomach."

"Are you sure? Then I'm doomed." I nudge her ribs.

"Thankfully for you, he is such a good cook." My sister wags a very judgmental finger at me.

"Yeah, you and Ammi remind me of that often," I mutter, almost under my breath.

Adam helps my mother with the tray of food laden with samosas, mint chutney, and Parle-G cookies. Ammi has brought my favorites.

She sits next to me and side-hugs me.

I lean in. I miss her smell and her soft hands. "Thanks, Ammi. I missed you yesterday."

She pats my cheek and makes a plate for Zia. "Ainee's mother will be so proud of her. MashAllah, she cleans and cooks. I wish some of us were as lucky."

"Ammi, Ainee and I both work, and I have school two nights a week, then assignments. Neither of us has time." I try to hold her hand longer, wondering what'll happen when they learn the truth. Will she still care for me as much? Would she still have cradled my cheek and fussed over me? Would she run over here to check on me if she knew Daniel had been here?

"Haan, haan, I know you're busy, but soon you'll marry this wonderful boy. MashAllah, we're so lucky to have you, Adam. Your mother raised you well." Ammi gives Adam an appreciative glance.

Adam takes a sip of his tea and says, "You can say that my caretakers raised me well. My parents weren't around much. It was me and my sisters. Then they joined the business with my mother, so I'm the black sheep of the family, the only one who's ventured outside the family business."

"Arrey nahin, you're the bright sheep for us." Rana slaps his hand.

When we finish the snacks, Rana gets up, and her feet catch on something.

"Uff, Sana, don't leave stuff lying around like this." She picks up a bag and slams it on the coffee table.

It's the laptop bag. My throat turns dry. Daniel must've forgotten his laptop when Ainee rushed them out of here.

I gulp. "It's not my laptop. Please be careful with it," I warn Ammi as she thumps it on the floor next to Ainee's magazines.

"Okay. I'm putting it with her stuff. Happy?"

"Please be careful with it." I jolt upright and confiscate it from her like smuggled goods.

"Calm down; I'm not throwing it away. I get that these things are expensive, but sheesh . . ." Rana shakes her head as if she's seen my failing report card for the umpteenth time.

Ainee returns home then, and I say a little prayer that she doesn't let anything slip about Daniel having been here.

"Um, can we—"

My words are interrupted by another ring of the doorbell, and I hear Ainee's high-pitched voice. "What the hell are you doing here? Come back another time, please."

"I forgot my laptop." That voice, I'd know it anywhere—except right now, it is the last thing I want to hear. My heart leaps to my throat.

Daniel's heavy footsteps fill the foyer, and a dead silence fills the room. Ammi's face loses color, and Adam crosses his arms.

Ammi puts a hand to her chest. "Shahri?"

Zia throws his arms around Daniel and yells, "Daniel!" Daniel tousles Zia's hair and returns his hug.

Rana approaches him with a furrowed brow. "What are you doing here?"

Adam bores his gaze into my slowly heating face. "Have you still not told Ammi and Rana baji you and Daniel work together? I thought we talked about it the night we were in the city."

Damn him. Now they're all looking at me for an answer.

"I forgot. I've had so much going on, ever since I got back from the city the other night. Then I was sick last night, and . . ." I flick my gaze to Rana, who is chewing the inside of her cheeks to prevent herself from uttering galiyaan at Daniel.

Ammi folds her arms tightly across her chest. "You *work* with Shahri? And you *forgot* to mention it? And what were you and Adam doing in the city? Uff Allah! Unless it was your nikah, I don't want to know."

"Not nikah. We were there helping Ainee and Haroon." I look at their narrowed gazes and keep talking. "Then Adam and I started looking at rings, and—"

Rana squeals. "Rings?" She looks at me and then looks at Adam, who's nervously shifting his weight on the feet. "Where is it? Show me, show me!"

"Oh, um, we didn't actually buy one yet—"

Ammi rushes to my side, her face lit up now, as if she's forgotten she was throwing eye darts at me a moment ago. "But you're planning to, which means a wedding won't be far behind! Both my daughters' responsibilities out of the way—now I can finally sigh in relief."

My sister rushes to my other side, and Ammi brings Adam close to me and hugs us and blesses us both, patting our heads and wiping tears of joy. The commotion causes Zia to look up, but SpongeBob still seems more interesting to him than the family drama, so he stays put.

Daniel's not next to me, not even close. But his intense, unblinking gaze makes my heart ache. Where has he been all my life? Why hasn't anyone else looked at me like this? I've waited and yearned. When I'm old and wrinkled, I will remember this moment. Him, on the verge of walking away. Me, on the precipice of losing him forever. The air between us thrums, and I know he will always be the one who makes my heart sing.

We have an entire conversation with just a look.

He says, *Just once in your life, follow your heart, not what others want.*

I tell him, *But look at them, Shahri; they're so happy. How could I tell them?*

Then why do your eyes search for me and stay on me, even when you stand next to him?

Because, just like my heart, they betray me.

Maybe my body is betraying me as well, because bile rises to my throat, and I run to the bathroom.

Adam knocks. "I didn't realize the talk of the engagement would literally make you throw up."

I lean against the wall and force out a light laugh. "I'll be right out."

Coward. You tell them. Tell them how you feel.

I step outside and immediately regret that decision. Facing conflicts is especially hard when your heart, mind, and duty are so at war.

Adam accepts all the handshakes and hugs as he smiles from ear to ear. He also stares Daniel down.

Daniel is unperturbed. He hands me a bag, then whispers in my ear, his warm breath tickling me and setting a thousand butterflies aflutter. "I hope you liked the daisies. Take your time recovering; no need to rush back to work."

He sent the flowers. Holy smokes.

He spent all night taking care of me, and even when Ainee asked him to leave, despite how my mother treated him, he still sent me flowers. I haven't done anything, not returned a single kind gesture.

In an instant, I make a decision that I'm sure will haunt me for the rest of my life in the Saeed household. "Ammi, I want to visit Shahida Auntie this weekend. She's very sick, and whatever happened, she deserves a chance to say her piece."

I notice Daniel's eyes widen, just slightly, at my words.

Ammi puts a hand on her chest and mutters galiyaan before she points an accusing finger at Daniel. "You. I knew the day I heard you were back that this would happen." Her voice drops when she looks at Adam. "Sana, beti, treasure the good man you have in your life and stop chasing this stupid childhood yaari."

Yaari isn't this strong; this is like a magnetic field. The more I try to resist, the more I get pulled into it.

Rana squeezes Zia's shoulder and gestures that it's time to go. She glares at Daniel before she literally drags Zia out of there. Before I can hug him good-bye.

CHAPTER TWENTY-FOUR

DANIEL

Ammi and Saleem are at the dining table when I enter the room, the tea tray next to them untouched as if they're waiting for me. They give each other knowing glances, and Saleem slaps the chair next to him. "Care to spill . . . ahem . . . some tea?"

I slide onto the chair, but only because Ammi is amused by Saleem's bad jokes. Some color has returned to her face. "Salaam alaikum, Ammi. MashAllah you look better."

Ammi smiles. "Walaikum assalam. I am trying to convince you both I'm fit to travel all alone."

We both say, "No you're not," with such fervor that the nurse looks up from the chart she's working on for Ammi.

I lower my voice and say, "Ammi, please, we're not letting you go anywhere alone."

Ammi heaves a sigh. She extends her frail hand and cradles my cheek. "How much will you both stall the inevitable? I want to be buried next to my father. But I understand that your lives are here; I can't expect you both to drop everything. I talked to my brother, and he will set it all up for me."

I squeeze her hand and hold it close. "We're your sons; you are our responsibility. We will never let you go alone, anywhere, no matter what."

Saleem's eyes have that look, the one I dread. Despair. Loss. Disbelief. The impending death of a parent. It's the same disappointment I saw in his eyes when the doctors in California told us there was no cure left, that everything they did would be palliative and not curative. That it was best to make her remaining days comfortable.

Ammi leans back and says, "I don't want you two to keep moving coasts and countries because of me."

Saleem's voice is determined when he says, "No, Ammi."

After a beat, she replies, "Then you should think about wrapping things up and moving in a week." She heaves a sigh and gestures to the nurse to take her upstairs.

After she's gone to her room, Saleem breaks the silence. "Do you want to talk to Sana?"

I quirk an eyebrow. "About?"

He mimics my brow raise. "I was there last night. You two have a *thing*. If Adam chooses not to care about it, that's his deal. But you cannot leave here without resolving things with her. And before you start your string of denials, I heard you on the phone with a million instructions for the florist."

"What am I supposed to say—'Choose me'? Even if she reciprocates, then what? I stay behind while you and Ammi move to Pakistan? Not going to happen." Thunder claps, and my mood turns dark like the clouds gathering outside. Then I tell him in a low voice, "I was a little surprised when she told Soofia Auntie that she is going to visit Ammi."

Saleem spits out his water. "No way! Wow. Soofia Auntie must've had a heart attack. Were they all there?"

I grab a napkin and clean the water droplets spattered over the kitchen table. "Yeah, her entire khandaan came to see her, and she told her mother and sister. They both, of course, left the house livid."

Saleem lets out a pent-up breath and says, "Well, that's shit I never expected Sana to do. When does she want to visit? Maybe you *are* having an effect on her. Anyway, get your shit together and figure out what you want. We may not have much time left . . ."

Our conversation is interrupted by my watch beeping. It's an email from Sana.

Nick Abreu emailed me. He wants to meet me at Vinnie's Pizza. We're off today, but I figure this is important. I'm sharing the location of the eatery with you, in case you're interested.

Nick Abreu, the elusive shift supervisor at ExGen. The one who hasn't been returning our emails. Nick and I have a history, going back to my stint at another department.

I email her back right away. *Please wait for me.*

CHAPTER TWENTY-FIVE

SANA

I put on a T-shirt and a hoodie and catch the R train to Brooklyn, as Mirchi is still in Hempstead.

The train ride is an hour long, and I try to close my eyes but am constantly being woken up by a woman on her cell phone, gossiping about her boss. Bosses are supposed to be vile, or at least most of mine have been, except for Daniel. But he's not Daniel, he's Shahri.

There's a song Abba used to sing to Ammi: "Mahiya tohe dekhan nu, chuk charkha gali de wich dhawah." The words were from a poem by Bulleh Shah, a Sufi in the seventeenth century. To catch a glimpse of his beloved, he'd put his charkha—spindle—in the street. He thought spinning would distract him, make him forget the ache to see her. But with the spinning came more memories, and it just made him want to see her more.

I now know the meaning so well, because my eyes search for him—just a glance from him and somehow the world is better, the grass greener, air fresher. He changes it all, in an instant, and no matter how much I see him, it's not enough. This isn't ishq—it's worse. It's a disease.

"I wish I could quit," the woman on the phone laments.

I wish I could quit *him*. In this sentiment, we are in agreement.

A long hour later the train halts at the Bay Ridge Avenue station. I follow the printed directions to the meeting spot that Nick emailed me.

His email was cryptic.

Dear Ms. Saeed,

Pls. call me to discuss a time to meet.

Nick Abreu

I called, and he picked up. Over a lot of background noise, he told me he could meet me today at Vinnie's close to the train station. He was visiting family and only had time today.

The umbrella shields me from the rain, and five minutes later I see the pizzeria at the street corner.

Vinnie's Pizza and Subs is a hole-in-the-wall, but clearly popular. As I enter, the bell on the door jingles. There are no empty booths, and there's a line to order. Two big fridges on the right are filled with soda bottles and water. I grab a ginger ale and head to the counter. The thick smell of garlic, tomato sauce, and grease hangs in the air of this small, warm place.

The glass display near the counter has various slices to choose from. My still-weak stomach turns at the sight of mozzarella cheese.

"Will this be all?" the cashier asks when he catches me looking at the pizza pies. He's a short, stout man in his fifties, with curly salt-and-pepper hair and thick sideburns. His eyes are a shade lighter than his hair.

"Yes. Um . . . also, I'm here to meet Nick." My voice comes out as a squeaky whisper. This is part thrilling and part petrifying—as if I'm a spy on the tail of a Mafia boss. The setting fits the role and so does the weather.

The cashier and owner, Vinnie, as advertised on the name tag he wears, looks at me as if I've asked him for the secret ingredient to his sauce. "Which Nick? There's a few 'round here." He waves in a circle around the seated customers.

How many Nicks eat at this restaurant, and do all of them have meetings with brown hijabis like me? Vinnie's absolutely not in the mood to engage with me and clearly wants the line—and his business—to keep moving.

I hesitate before saying, "Abreu."

Vinnie shakes his head again, disappointed in my choice of Nick. "You see that poor sucker in that Yankees hat?" He points to the far side of the refrigerators. "That's your man. Next." He waves to a pimply faced teenager with white headphones bigger than his ears.

I move away and take a few seconds to study the guy sitting next to the big refrigerators. He's younger than I expected, from what I can see. His face is half obscured by his cap and his goatee.

I gather all my confidence and tap on the red laminated table. "Are you Nick Abreu?"

"Depends." He shifts his gaze from the folded slice he's holding. He wears a sports jersey that reads *ExGen*. When he moves, a gold chain with a crucifix moves too. A diamond stud in his left ear winks in the overhead light.

"My name is Sana. I spoke with you earlier." I wave at the empty seat across from him in the booth.

His mouth drops a little as he looks me up and down. He puts his slice down and lets out a breath. "Sure."

My hand trembles, shaking the soda in its can. I guess he wasn't expecting someone like me. I scooch into the booth, holding my can of ginger ale.

"What, no pizza? You one-a those vew-gans?" He takes a bite of his pizza, then dabs his mouth with the napkin.

"Huh? No, I'm staying away from cheese tonight."

He smells of cigarettes and alcohol. Even with my sinuses clogged, the odors are unmistakable.

"What do you want to aks about?" Nick says in a thick Brooklyn accent. He shakes oregano over the second slice of pepperoni. "I don't want no one emailin' me day and night asking about reports."

"ExGen, the data, why aren't you signing off on the reports? Why is the regional director doing the honors?" I steeple my hands under my chin and covertly try to block his boozy cigarette stench. Maybe this wasn't such a good idea. I should have waited until tomorrow.

"So, me, Sam, and Jim are shift supervisors. We never sign papers, 'cause they: meaning the big guys in suits, wanna answer if there are questions—they worry schmucks like us will say somethin'. Ya know? Hell, they payin' me. I don't ask. But I worry about the stuff they be putting out in them pipes."

Stuff? Why am I even here, giving my time to this man who clearly is not in the mood to talk straight? I pop the tab off the ginger ale. "What kind of stuff?"

Nick scratches his chin, then retorts, "Look, you're cute 'n' all. But I'm maaarried." He drags out the word, as if I'm not internally retching at the idea that he'd think I'd be interested.

He points to his ring. "I ain't losing my bread and butter ova this." He finishes his pizza, wipes his face off with the napkin, and throws it on the paper plate.

Why the hell did he drag me out here? To tell me about "stuff"? Man, I suck at tough talk.

Daniel would have glared at him long enough to get something out of him.

The overhead cowbells at the door jingle again, and I turn. Speak of the handsome devil. Daniel stands at the door, scanning the room until he sees me. I guess he read his email. He wears a sweatshirt and sweatpants, as if he came from a run. My pulse quickens as he approaches us. The last time I saw him, so much was left unsaid. I wish we could talk, but this is neither the time nor the place.

I clear my throat. "Nick, my boss wants to join us. Is that okay?"

"Jeez! Didn't realize the whole damn village was invited." He shifts in an effort to bolt.

Despite myself, I stare at him; did he mean that because I'm brown, I must live in a village? Maybe I'm too sensitive because of what happened at work. Is this what happens to people who've been subjected to any level of discrimination, or is this my messed-up brain? I draw in a long breath and let it go. I need him to cooperate.

Daniel's steely gaze locks on Nick. Then he rolls his sleeves up, and I gawk. This man and his forearms will be the death of me. He is so distracting, even in this tense situation.

His deep voice sounds. "Leaving so soon, Nick?"

I slide over so Daniel can sit next to me, but he sits next to Nick, blocking his exit. "Nick and I go way back, right, bud?"

I look at Nick. It's as if he's seen a ghost. All that fake bravado. Seeing him shake in his boots when he was so dismissive of me is making my day.

Daniel glares at me. He would never have advised me to come see him by myself. Nick is a potential witness. I should've waited for him to respond. But then Nick might never have met with me.

"I offered Nick a deal in a case where he would've surely ended up behind bars." Daniel gives me a quick intro before turning to his seatmate. "Nick. Can we talk about what is going on at the plant?" Daniel scans his face.

Why am I even staying? I could be home, binge-watching *Kimmy Schmidt*. Instead, I'm watching a *Jersey Shore/Law and Order* mash-up.

"I'm doing as they tell me." He picks up a napkin to clean the beads of sweat forming on his forehead. "They'll can me. I got a sick kid, ya know."

Daniel softens his tone. "Listen, you'll be protected under the Whistleblower Protection Act. And this is all off the record anyway."

I guess sick kids, or any kids, are Daniel's weakness. He'll be a great dad one day . . .

"I ain't stupid. These are my folks, mi famiglia. I won't rat them out. Maybe I can give you something else—"

"Stop shitting us, will you?" Daniel demands.

"I ain't got nothing on the stacks, Dan. I swear by my wife, Maria."

Of course you would swear by your wife, jerk.

Daniel steeples his hands, his long fingers intertwined. He tells Nick in a calm but stern voice. "Have you forgotten about Victoria, your first wife? She's been asking around."

Nick loses color. "Who the hell is she? I don't know nobody by that name."

Daniel scratches his forehead and shrugs. "Okay, next time my friends in the Family Court office call me, I can point them to Brooklyn. The rest will be easy."

Nick wipes the beads of sweat forming on his forehead. "Please, Dan! I swear, man, that woman is a vengeful bitch."

Daniel slams his fist on the table, which causes the people at the other tables to look in our direction. "Let's make this easy, shall we?

You tell me what's really going on in ExGen. You did not drag us out in the middle of our day off to bullshit with us, did you?"

"There's something going on with the coal ash. They're supposed to collect and haul it away. I'm sayin' maybe they ain't doing that. But Dan, I got kids. I want to do right by them, but if you put me on the stand, I'm denyin' everythin'."

Daniel taps his fingers. "I make no promises. And you, pal, are in no position to negotiate. So, coal ash. If they're not hauling it away safely all the time, what are they doing with it?"

"It's a big hush-hush. They're supposed to haul it to a private pond, because it's toxic when discharged directly into a drinking-water source. These ponds have to be maintained, 'cause leaky liners means heavy metals from coal ash can leak into groundwater. All this is expensive."

Daniel lets out an exasperated breath. "These assholes."

It clicks then. They're not fudging the papers; they're literally dumping the toxic waste *into* the water.

Nick swallows, then continues. "But they ain't doing that all the time. Only when it rains, because rain is a good cover—all the waste just gets hauled away. The heavier the rain, the bigger the dump. But the two of youse didn't hear it from me."

"Nick, you'd better not be lying." Daniel gets up. I guess that's a sign for me to follow him.

Daniel gives Nick one last glare and starts walking. He doesn't wait for me to get up.

I walk, then run to catch up to Daniel. He has his hood on and stops and looks at me with a furrowed brow. "You're out of your mind. Do you ever think?"

"What? I emailed you before I came here, and Nick wasn't going to wait for me. I didn't want to take a chance," I insist.

"What the hell are you talking about? Nick is an asshole. He pled guilty to domestic assault. Twice. After what you've been through, you couldn't wait for me? He could've hurt you. He was drunk in broad daylight. I'd planned to force him to come to the office so he could testify. That's not happening now."

His words bring back memories of the note at the office, and last night after the town hall and how vulnerable I could've been if Daniel hadn't shown up. A shiver runs all the way down my spine.

He crosses his arms and looks at me with a piercing stare. He seems different, distant, right now. It's as if he's trying hard to mark the line in the sand. I almost want to annoy him more just to see if he will spill his guts.

"I emailed you, but I figured you were busy . . . maybe with Dalia? She had eyes for you the other night," I tease him with a straight face.

He shakes his head without sparing me a glance, then says through gritted teeth, "Wow, I didn't take you to be the jealous kind, what with a fiancé and all."

So he *is* jealous. When I look up, he's already a few feet ahead. I yelp, "Slow down, dammit! I can't walk this fast."

Daniel looks over his shoulder. "It's going to rain. Even if Nick's lying, I need to check his story. I'm going over to the ExGen site, but I'll drop you at home first."

The sidewalk is filled with people trying to scamper out of the spitting rain. I try to pivot but am pushed backward by a teenager on a skateboard. I stagger and come within inches of a speeding Vespa. Daniel pulls me away in a swoop as it whooshes by me. My face lands on his chest. He's solid, and all muscle, and his heart thumps are in tandem with mine.

He feels familiar, like home, like Ammi's head massages and chicken biryani. I forget that we're right at a busy intersection with honking cars and shuffling pedestrians.

I'm floating. Is this real?

Daniel's hands brace my elbows, and my hand close to his chest lingers.

Too soon, he separates himself from my grabby hands and avoids my eyes. The rest of the way to his car, he slows and matches my stride. A simple gesture, but it means he cares.

Once we're at his car, he gets the door for me. I try to adjust my seat, but I can't find the damn button to pull the seat forward. What does he do, drive giants around in this car?

"It's on the other side. It's a little button." He points to the edge of the seat.

I touch a button, and with a thump, I lie flat. Daniel rolls his eyes, then leans over and touches a completely different knob. The seat springs upright, and suddenly his face is inches from mine. So close I can count every breath he takes.

"Comfortable?" he asks in a low voice, the one that makes my pulse drum.

I look at his mouth and let my gaze linger.

My phone rings.

CHAPTER TWENTY-SIX

SANA

I love my phone, most of the time. It enables me to watch cat videos and waste a lot of time on Twitter—or "chidiya application," as Ammi likes to say—doom scrolling until I find that one tweet that makes me laugh. But sometimes, like now, I would like for it to be silent.

Daniel slides into the driver's seat, his eyes taking on that distant look.

A missed call from Ainee illuminates my screen, so I text her.

I'm working. Going on site with Daniel. Yes, really. Don't call unless it's urgent.

Daniel says, "I need to get some equipment from the office. I can drop you home first." His face is stoic and his voice even.

"You can just tell me you don't want me to come along." I cross my arms. He goes from protecting me to actively pushing me away. His hot-and-cold attitude is giving me whiplash.

He keeps his eyes fixed ahead and replies, "This is after hours, and Nick could be making this whole thing up. My gut says he isn't, but still . . ."

A boom of thunder startles me as slashes of lightning illuminate the sky ahead. The newly rained-on road is slick and shiny, and splotches of rain splatter the windshield.

"I want to," is all I say.

He tightens his jaw and concentrates on the road. I want to go back to last night, when he cooked and cleaned for me. This curt, professional Daniel makes me want to strangle him.

I glance at the map on the car's screen. We're still forty-five minutes away. I fiddle with the screen, and classical music streams through the speakers.

"What are you, seventy?" I mutter under my breath.

That gains me a lopsided smile before he presses a button. "There's sappy Bollywood here as well, if you want."

"Sappy Bollywood, eh? What happened to Shahri, the boy who danced with me at all the Eid parties to all these sappy songs?" I glimpse his face, his high cheekbones, his neatly trimmed beard, and his wide hands with long fingers steering the car. The light from the outside makes his skin a shade darker. I could sit here and stare at him all night.

"He grew up, and we grew apart, literally and figuratively." His voice is gruff, and then it's quiet.

I scan and tune to the Bollywood channel. The song "Kuch to Hai Tujhse Raabta" comes on. It's a beautiful song about two lovers and how their lives are connected by a thread spanning eternity. I switch it off and draw a sharp breath.

"What's wrong?" he asks.

I stay quiet, mainly because I'm simultaneously mad at him, myself, and the situation we're in. Mostly at myself, for caring so much about this project that has altered my life in so many ways.

He turns the blinker to take the exit for the office. The rain has slowed outside.

"Once we get to the office, I need to get some gear and supplies to collect the samples. What size boots do you wear? Also, can you look through the site maps?" He tips his head toward the back seat. "We can map out the locations."

"I wear a size seven." My reply is curt. Maybe, after this case is over, I can erase him like in a movie, where you get rid of your memories to forget a loved one. Maybe, after this case is over, I can marry Adam, and Daniel can go back to Dalia—who's clearly smitten with him—or some other woman.

"I'll sign out the equipment." He leans over to grab his umbrella from the back seat, and again we're mere inches from each other.

I stare at his lips. He smells great, a little like the rain and mostly a scent that's so intoxicatingly him. I've never kissed anyone before. If I lean forward, I could.

And yet I can't. I won't.

Maybe this wasn't such a good idea.

His face softens; his mouth gapes slightly. He shuts his lips and swallows hard enough to bob his Adam's apple.

I will my eyes to look away, yet I can't.

His eyes hold a question, but then he looks away. He tugs at his hood before he slides out of the car and hides beneath his raised umbrella.

Mostly to distract myself, I grab the big maps. Hempstead has one of the old-fashioned sewer systems. We'll need to sample a nearby body of water where ExGen could dump illegally using their storm or sewer drain. I grab my phone and look up streams and reservoirs close to ExGen that could be locations for possible illegal dumping.

I find several probable locations within a two-mile radius of ExGen: Hempstead Lake, South Pond, Smith Pond, and Mill River, which drains into the surrounding channels and bay. The river is right next to the plant, and certain parts are not accessible by roads. The best samples with higher concentrations would likely be close to the discharge location, which is in the East Rockaway Channel.

The trunk of the car opens, and Daniel puts in a cooler, a long dipper with a cup attached to it, and a couple of rain jackets. He sees me fiddling with the Maps app on his car dashboard and says, "I need your help with the canoe."

Canoe?

"Why do we need a canoe?"

He doesn't answer right away, as if I've asked him an obvious question. "Because the closer we get to the source, the better the samples. The source is buried underwater. Canoeing to the outfall polluting the water is the best way."

I throw my phone inside my purse and leave it in the car. Daniel's pushing the canoe onto the top of the car; his wide hands maneuver it on top of the luggage rack. There's something so appealing about him when he's lost in his thoughts, his hands busy and biceps flexing.

Stop drooling, I remind myself.

But it's as if Allah listened to that checklist I made about my dream man. Daniel is all my duas answered in one forbidden package.

I pull on my hood and finish helping him tie the Department of Conservation canoe on top of his SUV. The gray clouds still hover, and a damp smell hangs in the air. Daniel's hair flops on his forehead a little; tiny droplets bead through the strands when he runs a hand through them. His inky eyelashes fan his face, and a dimple appears, then fades on his cheek.

Maybe it's the way the streetlights hit his face, or the way the wind teases his hair, but my stomach is filled with anticipation. I shouldn't notice his perfectly curled eyelashes or the way his mouth curves when he's thinking, but damn me, I do.

He carefully avoids me as he settles in the car, as if I'm plagued. The back windows have fogged up, and he fidgets with the defogger while I belt in. Once the defrost is going, he asks, "Are you okay with being in a canoe? It might rain, and we'll have to walk through the woods to get to the stream. If you've changed your mind, I can still drop you home. But this is your last chance—I want to get there soon."

I draw in a large breath and retort, "It is my case and I do want to know, so as long as you're not planning to murder me and dump my body in the river, I want to be part of this. And maybe someday tell my kids the story of how I helped catch the bad guys."

He turns the key in the ignition and speaks over the slow hum of the wiper blades. "Marriage, picket fence, two and a half kids, nice colonial in the suburbs. How cliché. Can't say I'm surprised."

My insides burn at his casual condescension. "Bravo, Mr. Malik, you have me all figured out."

He raises his shoulder and casts a quick glance at me. "Isn't it true, though? He was ready to have the nikah last night. And your family was more than willing, as if that is the most important thing and not that you were dehydrated and passing out."

Daniel's words ring true, and they hurt. Ammi and Rana's mission in life *is* to see me married—but it comes from them caring about me. "Don't pass judgment about my family. Your uncle was the scum of the earth. May Allah give his soul peace."

"Ameen. And I don't disagree. But I mean, there is more to life than the ball and the chain, you know? I have had to ward off rishtas for years, for this reason."

Daniel says it with such ease, as if good rishtas are a $9.99 buffet free-for-all.

I glare at him. "Ward them off . . . falling from the sky, were they? Me, I had hmm . . . there was Junaid, who lost his wife days before he decided to find another wife. Rahil, who was looking for a green-card bride, and . . . should I keep going? Or do you get the idea?"

He lets out a whistle. "That bad?"

I shake my head and whisper, "You have no idea."

He shifts and looks at me in disbelief. "Why go through this bullshit? Marriages are a farce anyway."

"Because my mother and sister seem to think of marriage as the only way to a secure future for myself and for taking care of Zia. Can't blame them, can you? Your family did take away any false sense of security we possessed." I dial up my sarcasm a notch, then feel bad because it's not like *he* did all those things.

Daniel's mouth slackens, and the lines on his forehead flatten. He nods and then says, "I heard you telling Ainee about how you agreed to be with Adam for Zia's sake. But you are beautiful and smart. You can tell them how you feel and convince them otherwise, Sana. You don't need Adam or the security that comes with marrying someone whose mother is a famous designer."

The implication is clear—he thinks I'm with Adam for money, when nothing could be further from the truth. Even when he compliments me, telling me he thinks I'm smart and beautiful, he does it with a slight. Just like Darcy did to Elizabeth. "I do, though. Because girls like me never can land boys like you—and by that I mean privileged assholes."

"Hardly," he scoffs. "You forget, even my own mother couldn't keep me, and my aunt, who did, suffered for it. It's not gulab jamun and jalebis over here, either. All I said was you could do better . . ." He says the last part slower, as if he's rethinking every word he's already spoken.

"Adam respects my mother and doesn't cringe at the thought of being Zia's guardian with me. He's a decent man. Everyone in my family is ecstatic about us."

His jaw hardens. "Do you *want* to marry him? Not your mother or your sister—you, Sana, do *you*? Or you have told yourself this lie so many times you're starting to believe it?"

His irritated questions anger me. The other night when he stayed with me, a lot of the lines we'd drawn became murky. The boss-employee line, the we're-going-to-pretend-we're-work-acquaintances line, and the biggest one, the pretend-not-to-care-about-each-other line.

I need to redraw them. Now.

I shake my head, and my voice comes out sharp. "I know my market value, thank you very much. And considering my situation, I think I did well by snagging Adam." My throat squeezes. "And if it's all the same to you, please refrain from commenting on my personal life."

CHAPTER TWENTY-SEVEN

DANIEL

Outside the car, the rain strengthens, and the booms of thunder reverberate. Inside, Sana shoots a fiery glance at me to back off. The sad part is all I want to do is talk to her. I have so many years' worth of things I want to say to her, and yet I keep saying the wrong things, things I shouldn't. Things that end up hurting her.

"I'm sorry," I mutter.

"For?" She crosses her arms and chews her lip.

I weigh my words. "For all the shit my uncle put your family through. I wish I could take it back. I know you blame Ammi, but Ammi stayed quiet because of me. For what it's worth, he regretted his decisions before he died." I hope she believes me. Because it's the truth. My shoulders slacken as the burden I've been carrying for the last eighteen years lifts, even though Sana remains quiet and staring out the window.

After a few minutes of silence, in which I vacillate between doubting that she heard me and being convinced she hates me, she finally speaks. "Shahri, you're too late. Ammi loved Shahida Auntie, but she just disappeared from our lives. She could've called Ammi, apologized, even if she couldn't stop things from happening. Her silence made her complicit, you know."

She called me Shahri. A flicker of hope beams through my heart. I want to tell her I will never disappoint her again, that I've never stopped caring about her and I even rebelled against my uncle. I swallow a knot in my throat and hold my hand back, because in a different world I would offer her comfort. "I wish I could've done something."

My eyes cut to her. Her eyes glisten with tears, and if there was ever a time I felt bitter toward her, it's melted away. There's so much she's saying to me, without saying anything.

What can I say to her to make the hurt disappear? I am never the eloquent one, but today words fail me completely. So I stay quiet. Maybe it's for the best; maybe she's right and this is all too late. The people we love have disappointed us both in ways that will hurt forever.

And she is planning to marry Adam.

The insane part of my brain argues, *But she doesn't love him.*

A streak of lightning illuminates the dark sky and jolts me out of my thoughts.

Sana shivers.

I ask, "Are you cold?"

She shakes her head and leans back, closing her eyes, breathing slowly like she's asleep. Another clap of thunder makes her shudder.

Her mother's words, from when she took me aside at Sana's place, come back to me. "She is with a good man. Adam is kind and respectable. He's the kind who'll stick around and not escape when things get tough. And more importantly, when I look at Adam, I'm not reminded of the life I lost."

I take the exit to the wooded one-lane road, and a few minutes later, we get to the muddy shoulder.

Sana glances outside at the steady droplets streaking the windows. "This is the perfect spot to murder me. Remember, Ainee knows I'm with you."

"By then it'll be too late. I can imagine the headline in the news: *Muslim Girl Runs Away From Crazy Fiancé With her Lover.*"

She scoffs, "You may be a good DAG, but you're a horrible reporter. And we're anything but lovers. You know what would be more sensational? *DAG Drowned by Coworker, Because He Wouldn't Stop Annoying His Wonderful Employee.*"

I can't help my smirk.

We exit the car, and I click the trunk open and take out the box with boots, flashlights, and empty bottles to collect samples. Sana helps me untie the canoe, her oversized boots squeaking as we lower the yellow monstrosity.

I hitch the backpack with supplies onto my shoulder and tie the paddles to the canoe, and we carry it overhead through the woods. Before we left the car, I made sure we had everything, but I have this feeling in the pit of my stomach that I forgot something.

The smell of fresh rain and damp leaves surround us as we stride down the unpaved wooded road. The GPS on my watch shows we're close, and the unmistakable sound of the lapping river, even over the misting rain, seconds the prognosis.

Sana's end of the canoe dips, then drops. I can tell she's straining, but she won't admit it. Finally, when she rests it on top of her head, cushioned only by her hijab, she cries out, "Can we take a quick break? I don't have the upper body strength you do. I need to put my arms down."

We lower the canoe. When she turns to face me, her dark hijab is stuck to her face and hair. A bead of water slithers down her brow.

The sound of crickets, the rain's rhythmic patter, and her breathing are somehow reassuring and intimate. We may never, ever be this close again. I shouldn't think about her in this way—in *any* way. She is with Adam.

But I loved her first.

I never stopped loving her.

I love her.

I've never known anyone like her. Someone who makes me want to trust, despite the way the world has chewed me and spit me out.

The mist turns into a steady rain as we lower the canoe into the water. I offer her my hand to help her climb in, but she ignores it—typical. The boat shakes, and I lose my balance and stagger, but she swoops in and catches my hand before I fall backward.

"Thanks," I say, regaining my equilibrium. I swallow what feels like an avocado pit in my throat. "Sorry about my comment earlier. If you're happy with Adam's rishta, I'm happy for you both."

She helps me pack the sample in the cooler and swipes the tears that I didn't notice until now. Her voice is unsteady when she speaks. "For once in your life, why don't you freaking say what you really want to, Shahri? Or should I call you DAG Daniel Malik?"

Well, if she wants the truth, that's what I'll give her. "Shahri was the name my birth parents gave me, and Khalil was the last name my uncle forced me to take. Those names reminded me of men I never wanted anything to be like or to do with."

I steer the canoe to the next sampling location and try to calm my nerves before speaking again. "I didn't want my family in Pakistan to find me. I thought I could put it all behind me, you know? The scars, everything. So after we left here and moved to California, I urged Ammi and Khalu to allow me to file for a change of name. Uncle was reluctant but eventually gave in."

After a quiet, long minute, Sana says, "And you made it impossible for me to find you too."

I try to take my irritation out on steering the canoe. "I didn't think you were looking."

* * *

SANA

I am so mad at him that if I knew how to swim, I'd jump in the water. "You know what I hate about you the most?"

He gives me a wry smile. "Probably everything?"

The problem with being in a small canoe is that I can't hide anything from him, not that I'm good at hiding my emotions from him anyway. I swallow and stay quiet and meet his gaze.

Another goddamn mistake.

The full moon peeks from the cloudy sky, and Daniel's eyes reveal so much pain that an ache spreads through me. All my life I have looked for validation from my family, and he has done that as well. Somehow we've both taken this burden on ourselves. He has done everything in his power to keep his aunt happy, and I'd do anything if it meant keeping Ammi and Zia happy.

If I could stop myself from falling for Daniel, I would. It's what Ammi would want. But I can't control this. I've become the cautionary tale Ammi always warned Mrs. Sharma about.

"You have this ability to love people, and then just file them away. I don't know how to do that," I say.

"Love?" He huffs and slams the paddle against the water. "You're about to marry Adam."

The sudden motion sways the canoe, and so I grip the paddle with one hand and the boat with the other and snap back, "Dammit, Shahri, why do you care? Can we just finish up here? I think I'm done with the cross-examination for the day." I break the staring contest but not before I quip, "Just because you've cut your family in Pakistan off doesn't make them go away. Face your own demons before you point fingers at me."

I must've touched a nerve ending, because he clamps his mouth shut.

We finish collecting the samples in silence and lug everything back to the car.

I check my phone—there are multiple missed calls and frantic texts from Ainee and Adam wanting to know where I am.

I dial Ainee.

"Leave your sidepiece and come home, please," she hisses into the phone. "Your fiancé and his family are waiting. They're all here."

"I can't hear you well," I lie. "Bad service. I'll see you in a bit." I hang up.

Daniel hitches an eyebrow. "Everything okay?"

"Yeah."

As he drives, I type a long text to Ainee asking her to try to convince Adam to come back another day, as I am too exhausted to entertain. *All I want to do is jump in the shower and not be disturbed until tomorrow.*

Daniel looks at me as if he wants to know what has my fingers flying, but ultimately he decides to leave it alone.

Adam texts again. *I hope you're close.*

I turn off my phone and close my eyes to escape Daniel's questions.

When the car halts, Daniel gets out and opens my door for me.

I slide out, avoiding eye contact. "Thanks for the ride," I mutter.

"Can I see you to your door?"

I tip my head toward the apartment. "We're like ten feet from my door. I'm sure I'll be fine."

The cool air rustles the leaves on the tree behind us, and I hug myself and eye him as he stands firm.

"Maybe the polite thing would be to ask me in for chai?" he says, without batting an eyelash.

"What? No. I'm busy." I step away from him and don't stop until I reach my front door, hoping he'll get the hint.

Of course he doesn't.

The door opens, and Adam flicks his gaze between us.

"I didn't realize you were with him." Adam jabs a finger at Daniel, his jaw pulsing.

"We were working," I tell him as the two men exchange death glares.

Adam turns to me, his face softening. "Sweetheart, I've been calling you for the last half hour. Ammi and Abba have been waiting. Let's go say salaam." He settles his hand in the crook of my elbow to lead me inside. I flinch but go along.

Daniel clenches his fists. "Take it easy, man. We were working. No need to rush her like this; she's had a long day." He steps closer to me.

The last thing I want is for them to get into a fistfight because of me. I'm too tired to deal with their jealousy.

I swallow and begrudgingly bid Daniel a good night. "Shab-b khair."

Adam slams the door before Daniel can reply.

CHAPTER TWENTY-EIGHT

SANA

The voices from the living room hit us as soon as the door closes.

I stop and whisper to Adam, "I'm too tired to entertain. I wish you had warned me."

He takes my hand and gives me a lopsided grin. "Sorry, Ammi came in for like a day. She's flying out tomorrow. I wanted her to meet you." He looks in my eyes now, pleading. I should be happy I get to meet his mother, but my heart's still reeling from everything that just happened with Daniel. I should pull Adam aside and tell him the truth. But right now may not be the best time.

We enter the living room; Ainee sits on the chair, and Adam's mother and father have their backs to me. The coffee table holds a few bottles of sparkling water and a fruit salad. This is a big moment for Adam, and for me, yet all I can think of is Daniel's face when I said good-bye to him. The way his hands felt on mine when he helped me onto the boat, and how even after we fought, he apologized. How I never get tired of being with him.

Adam clears his throat. "Ammi, this is my fiancée, Sana."

The way she runs her gaze up and down and lets out a long exhale tells me that she'd never give me a second glance if it weren't for her son. "Hello." Her voice reeks of such disappointment that I'm tempted to run away, but then I remember him with my family. He always has a smile, through my mother's million probing questions and my sister's subtle hints at doing the proper thing. "And where is the ring?"

Adam swallows. "Working on it, Ammi."

Adam's mother has a striking round face, and her thin nose and her skin tone are just like Adam's. Her chestnut hair with streaks of blond highlights is pulled into a chignon. She looks at me as she adjusts her off-white shawl that complements her cigarette pants and silk tunic. The enormous diamond on her ring finger glitters brightly. Her lips are unnaturally thick, like she got a deal on Botox.

The disappointed mother-in-law is a rite of passage for all desi women. But it's not just her disappointment; it's the sheer chagrin in her eyes that is a gut punch.

"Assalamualaikum," I say, bringing my hand up to my forehead in the traditional desi gesture.

"Walaikum assalam," Adam's parents say in unison.

"Auntie, thank you so much for the generous gifts. Haroon and I couldn't ask for better wedding gifts." Ainee gestures toward a stack of boxes with the logo of Adam's mother's store.

"Oh, it's nothing. This is from my spring collection," she says in a sugary tone. Then she fixes her gaze on Adam's hand resting on my shoulder.

I wiggle away and ask her, "Would you like something other than the fruit? Maybe tea?"

"No thanks. I'm on a fruit-only diet. Adam talks about your family so much; I think he spends more time with your family than his own. I had to come see the girl who has enchanted him." She lifts her eyebrows.

Enchanted. I have heard this word so many times in reference to love marriages; there's a common sentiment that the woman somehow does some magic or jadoo on a poor, hapless man and then he is left with no other way out but to marry her. That one word tells me so much about how she perceives my relationship with Adam.

I dart my gaze to Ainee, who is picture-perfect with her best kundan jewelry and her Instagram-ready hair and makeup, smiling for selfies with her gifts, then stare at my still-damp socks.

Adam's jaw tightens, but he places a hand on my shoulder. "If you had more time here in town, you'd be as taken with Sana and her family as Abba and I are. I kinda sprang this on her, and the fact that she is here shows that she cares, and that's all I need."

"This isn't the place for this bakwas." She gives Adam a stern look.

I feel for him. My mother has control issues, and my sister's issues are too many to count, but they're always a phone call away. For the first time in my life, I recognize the importance of a close-knit, even nosy, family. At least they care to interfere.

I squeeze Adam's hand and straighten my back. "My family loves Adam. If she were here, my mother would say you're both amazing to have raised such a good son."

Adam looks at me, smiles, and mouths a *thank you*, though his forehead's still wrinkled with agitation. "Ammi, Abba, did you want to ask Sana something?"

He tips his head toward the red velvet boxes that sit on the coffee table. His mother reaches for them, her hands hesitant. "These were my mother's; she brought them from India on one of her trips.

They're valued at twenty grand. Please tell me you will keep them in a safe somewhere and not here. Otherwise, I can hold on to them until the nikah."

Adam clears his throat. "I think we discussed Sana keeping them, Ammi."

She clicks the box open. The delicate pearl-and-gold choker gleams in the overhead light. The matching pendant earrings and mother-of-pearl ring sit on burgundy velvet.

Ainee's eyes widen. "They're exquisite. You're so lucky, Sana."

Am I lucky? I paste on a smile and say, "Thank you so much, Auntie."

For the next few seconds, the only sound is the uncomfortable shifting in seats.

Adam's father squeezes his wife's knee. "Sana, these belong to you. We'd love for you to keep them. We're organizing a party in a few weeks where we want to introduce you to everyone, and you should wear them then. And thank you for being in my son's life. He's been so much happier since you've become a part of our lives."

His mother's eyebrows relax when she picks up a single grape from her plate and remarks, "Did Adam speak with you about the legal stuff?"

Phew; it's a relief she knows about the appointment with Zia's attorney tomorrow. I beam at him then and say, "Adam and I are doing that tomorrow, along with the rest of my family."

Her eyes widen. "Oh, I don't think the whole family needs to be involved—I think just the two of you."

Quizzically, I glance at Adam. The tips of his ears are pink.

His father stares at the carpet.

Ainee and I glance at each other.

I explain, "Well, the guardianship is a family affair. So yeah, the lawyer needs to meet with all of us who want to be in the trust for Zia."

His mother leans forward in her chair, then presses her fingertips to her temples as if we're all collectively giving her a massive headache. "Who's Zia?"

Oh. This isn't about my appointment.

Stupid, gullible Sana.

Lena's here to protect her son's assets; she couldn't care less about the wonderful partner he's found. I try to keep my voice steady, but it's still a little shaky. "What other legal things do Adam and I have to talk about?"

Her burgundy lips curve in a smirk. "Adam owns half the shares in my company. He's obviously had a lot of girls—" She stops midsentence when she catches Adam's hand gesture of *cut this out* across his neck. "It's for your own good; a prenup will protect both your assets."

Adam squeezes my hand to calm my rapid, angry breaths.

"I have two hundred dollars in my bank account and a very temperamental 1972 Honda Civic to my name. So you see, assets are the least of my problems. But let me assure you, I want nothing from Adam. Nothing at all. I will gladly sign papers attesting to this at any time. Now, I don't want to take any more of your precious time, Auntie, as you have a flight to catch tomorrow . . ." My tone is acerbic and my arms are folded tightly across my chest.

Lena quips with a sarcastic smile, "Oh, I'm sorry if I offended you. Middle-class pride is such a thing, I know." She joins Adam's father when he rises and starts striding to the door.

Both the men follow her as she stomps out without saying good-bye.

After they leave, Ainee shuts the door. The crease in her forehead deepens as she rests her palms on her hips, her get-ready-for-a-diatribe mode. "Where did that come from? You are never this rude to elders. They were waiting a while for you, so she had a right to be upset, you know? And was that Daniel who came to the door with you? What are you doing, Sana? Adam doesn't deserve this. Hell, even Daniel doesn't deserve this."

I take off my sweatshirt and slump on the couch. I have never, ever talked to any auntie in such a harsh tone, let alone my future mother-in-law. Ainee's right; I should have been more patient, for Adam's sake. "I'm tired . . ."

"Of the lies? The deception? Or the fact that you don't even know the difference between the two?" Ainee sits next to me and levels her eyes with mine.

I scooch away from her. "I promise I'll talk to Adam tomorrow. Am I allowed to shower and sleep?"

She prevents me from getting up and scrunches her nose. "You should shower. But what are you planning to do? And when you find my best friend, can you send her back?"

If Ammi ever needed an ally, she's found one in my best friend. "Maybe Daniel's made me recognize parts of myself that I never knew existed. I can be a little selfish once in a while, you know?"

"Selfish people stay single. And one is a sad, lonely number. And the path you're heading down, you're going to lose it all—for a man who may not even stick around. Khalils have disappeared before; who's going to stop them from packing up and leaving again? Has he committed to anything?"

Is commitment all about saying things out loud? Signing a paper? Abba was committed to being there for us, providing a secure future, and yet that didn't happen. Daniel has not said it in so many words, but in my heart I know he will . . . if only Ammi would agree.

I miss Abba so much. There's a reason why Ammi chose tomorrow for Zia's appointment; it's Abba's death anniversary. She wants to be able to say, when she meets Abba in the hereafter, "Look, I did what I promised you on your deathbed: married my daughters and took care of my son's future."

When night falls, I dream of Daniel and Abba. They sit and chat together like they used to, outside in our small backyard. Daniel asks Abba for my hand and proposes to me in front of my family with his nani's ring.

Too bad dreams always end with a rude awakening.

CHAPTER TWENTY-NINE

SANA

It's a truth universally known that the day you have nowhere to go is the day sleep will elude you. I have the morning off because of Zia's appointment, but I'm awake at six.

Faint daylight filters through my curtains, and the chatter of the birds lets me know I'm not the only one awake. Last night's dream plays in my brain like those reels on projectors we used to watch old Bollywood movies on in our backyard every summer.

In my dream, Abba smiled and held Shahri's hand. He called him beta again, all the bitterness and animosity gone.

I shower and put on my favorite full-sleeved, beige cotton shirt and a long, flowy, dark-brown skirt and matching hijab. Cherry lip balm with mascara and eyeliner.

The velvet box with the jewelry that Lena so reluctantly gave me sits on the vanity.

My phone buzzes. It's Ammi.

"Salaam," she says. "I talked to the lawyer already and told him you and Rana will be there, along with your . . ." She hesitates. "Significant others."

"Ammi, about Adam . . ." I swallow.

"What?" she asks, her breathing heavy.

Am I making her panic? "Ammi, everything okay? Why are you wheezing? Did you take your medicine?" My voice is laced with worry.

"Just speed walking with Mrs. Sharma and another neighbor." In the background, I hear women gossiping. "Did you hear Mrs. Ahmed's daughter eloped with a gora?"

"Okay, Ammi, take it easy. I'll meet you there." I get ready to hang up.

"What were you saying earlier about Adam?" she whispers into the phone as the background chatter lessens.

I should've kept my mouth shut. I tell her, "Lena Auntie came last night with Adam and his dad."

"Sacchi. MashAllah! I heard Adam say she was giving you the khandani choker. He was saying she was saving it for Adam's would-be wife, even though his sister wanted it," Ammi gushes, her voice now elated and the chatter from behind her more pronounced.

She puts a hand to the mouthpiece and repeats it to her friends, embellishing the value of the jewelry a little.

We say good-bye, and I look at my watch. It's nearly eleven. I grab my bag and drive to the lawyer's office an hour away. At a stoplight, I text Adam a reminder: *Salaam. See you there around noon.*

He doesn't respond.

Maybe he's driving? I arrive to find that Ammi, my sister Rana, and Farooq are already there. But no sign of Adam. The agita in the pit of my stomach turns to dread as the big wall clock in the waiting room ticks away.

Still no Adam. Is he mad about what happened with Lena yesterday? Adam has always shown up when he's said he would, so my stomach clenches at the thought of all the things that could've gone wrong.

The pretty paralegal walks in, click-clacking her heels. "Mr. Watson can see you now."

"Um . . . I'm still waiting for my . . . fiancé. Can you give us a couple of minutes?"

Even she notices that my use of the word *fiancé* took some effort. She does that thing with her lips like she's going to frown but draws them into a straight line instead. "Sure, but Mr. Watson has another appointment in an hour. The wait will cut into your time." She pinches the files that read *Zia Saeed*.

Rana turns to me. "Ammi, Farooq, and I will get started. We have a lot to discuss." She gets up, and they follow the paralegal inside.

Stuck outside, pacing, my stomach in knots, I call Adam. It rings, but he doesn't pick up. I leave him an urgent voice mail. Maybe he's in the parking lot? I walk to the other side but don't see his car. I pace some more. It's almost a quarter after.

I call Tease.

The woman who works the register picks up. "May I take your order?"

"It's Sana. Is Adam there?"

"No. Sorry, but we're busy. Call his cell." She hangs up.

Witch.

I have to face the facts: he's not coming.

As I step into Mr. Watson's office, all eyes are on me. Papers and files are stacked on a big desk.

"So, as I was telling your family, Ms. Saeed, we have to file the paperwork in court a few months before Zia turns eighteen." He stacks some papers and then lines them up. "Your family wants to set up a trust fund for him. As I understand it, your mother wants to have power of attorney, but also to set up a trust for his medical, as well as financial, needs from here on out."

He explains the different options. Then he gives my mother forms to fill out for Zia. With a few minutes to spare before our time is up, he gathers the papers in a stack.

As we step out of the office, Ammi asks, "What happened to Adam?"

"I wasn't able to reach him. Maybe something came up?" I keep walking, hoping to get away from their gazes. I cringe at the pity in their eyes. I can take their silent treatment, their angry glances, even their I-told-you-so looks. It's the *poor Sana* I can't stand.

"Ammi, I have to get to work. I'll talk to you later, inshAllah." I hug her and wave good-bye.

Ammi squeezes my shoulder and says, "Maybe something happened at the restaurant. Did you call him there?"

I nod.

She defends him some more, and I realize: she genuinely likes Adam. Not just because he's not Shahri, but because she sees something more in him than just a spouse for me. She sees someone who takes a genuine interest in cooking, and when he talks to her in broken Urdu, they connect. It breaks my heart that I let it get this far.

* * *

DANIEL

Kevin waves as I rush in. On the wall above him, the picture of the governor gleams in a streak of sunlight filtering through the big windows. As much as I've gotten used to this environment, it's all temporary. Once I finish this case, I'll be assigned elsewhere.

I review my mental list of things to work on today. I hope I'll be less distracted without Sana in the office today.

The ding of the elevator catches me by surprise. I lodge a hand inside to stop the closing doors.

I apologize to the sole rider in the elevator. "Sorry."

Her soft voice echoes as the doors close. "Daniel?"

I lift my gaze to her beautiful face. Her brown eyes have strands of red as she sniffles.

I fold my arms across my chest to physically prevent myself from touching her.

She adjusts the strap of the bag on her shoulder and avoids me.

Dammit, Sana, don't make this hard! I want to yell into the silence that surrounds us. *Your tears still break me.*

Without preface, I say, "I thought you were going to be out all day. The secretary told me this morning."

She looks up and swallows with an inaudible gulp. "I finished earlier than I thought."

I rake a hand through my hair, deciding which Sana I'd rather talk to—the angry one who shares or this version who holds things close to her chest. But the need to make sure she's okay overpowers my need to keep my sanity and ego. "Sana, please. You know we can still talk."

Screech.

The light flickers above, followed by a jolt.

Then a complete standstill.

What the actual hell? I can't be stuck here. Not alone with her.

Sana's eyes widen. "What's happening?" Her voice quivers.

"I'm not sure." I press the emergency button and then dig out my phone.

She grabs my arm, holding on tight. Her touch is harmless, yet electricity jolts through me. She's a live wire to my messed-up system, igniting all kinds of emotions with minimal contact.

"Kevin, the elevator's stuck." I speak quickly into the receiver.

"They're on it. But it could be an hour or so. They were doing some electrical work earlier that caused power failures. Sorry."

Sana starts to shake. Her face has gone pale, and her breathing is rapid and shallow. "An hour? No way. I can't breathe."

I break the no-touch rule and frame her shoulders with both hands. "Sana. Look at me, please." Beneath my fingers, her shallow breaths rack her. She latches on to my arm to steady herself, then slides down the elevator wall, freaking out.

From my messenger bag, I dig out the law journals I was reading earlier and spread them on the floor. "Sit on these; this floor is disgusting."

"Dammit, you're not helping," she hisses, but slides onto the spread-out papers.

She pulls up her knees and swallows, shaking her hands as if she can't feel them.

"Breathe," I tell her. *Yet I forget to breathe when she's around . . .* I put my index finger near my pulse. "Put your finger here and breathe in through your nose."

She draws a quick breath in and glances at my hand, then replicates my action. I knew she had claustrophobia when we were little, but I didn't realize she still has it. Going through the midtown tunnel with her in the car when we were young meant I had to distract her with my singing or games.

I squeeze her free hand. "You got this."

We breathe in sync for a minute or so before she's inhaling normally again. She lets go of my hand and leans back. "Thanks." She pulls her knees close and rests her chin on them.

I decide to prod. "So, you want to tell me what's got you all upset? Apart from the whole elevator thing, I mean."

"Nothing." She avoids my gaze.

"The thing is, Soni-yo, you're a bad liar. What did he do?" Soni-yo is the name I had for her when we were little. She doesn't flinch or raise her eyes when I say that, so I assume she's okay with it. It's progress.

The stainless steel of the elevator feels cold against my back as I give myself permission to slide next to her.

She avoids me by staring ahead. "Keep the questions for your billable hours."

"I'm a lawyer because I want to help people. If I cared about the money, I'd work in private practice somewhere and not be a bureaucrat."

She fidgets with the fringe of her hijab for a bit before she answers. "People always break my trust, but that's nothing new."

"Maybe you're trusting the wrong type of people. What did he do now, ask for nikah within a week? But be honest, that's not it. What's really bothering you?" Sana is not just upset; there's a sadness in her eyes that makes my heart twist.

She stops fidgeting and says in a low voice, "It's Abba's barsi today, seventeen years since he passed. And I don't know, I thought I'd be someone he'd be proud of, you know, a perfect daughter. But I don't know what I'm becoming. I'm lying to Ammi, and myself, and I don't know . . ." She swipes her face. "It's your fault."

"Me? What did I do?"

She jabs her index finger at me. "It'd be easier, you know."

Now her eyes flick to mine, brimming with tears, and I do know: this agony is not mine alone. We're in this together. Suffering, yet hoping.

"Let's go see him," I say. "When we get out of here, let's go visit his grave."

She widens her eyes. "I've never been to his grave. I just couldn't bring myself to go."

"Why not? Didn't you ever feel like reading the Quran for him? I still go to my dear old uncle's grave, even though he treated me like shit. There's something so freeing about letting go of pent-up anger." It feels like something is changing between us, like we're going back to where we were, when it was me as Shahri and her, my Soni.

"I don't know if it was just anger. I felt *betrayed* by Abba. He hid how the business was doing. Every time he'd come back late from work, he had this look on his face. Ammi would ask him if everything was okay, and he would lie and say things were fine and that it would all work out. He was the king of *everything's under control.* Fast-forward a few years, and he dies from a heart attack and we learn we are thousands of dollars in debt. So, you see, everything was not okay. I wish he had told us the truth and prepared us instead of hiding behind the lies." She twists the corner of the long lace at the end of her hijab. "I hated the not knowing."

"I'm sorry," I say. "I know this whole *I'm the man of the house* complex was because that's how desi men were raised back then. Men don't cry. Men are the providers. But it doesn't make it right. I agree that truth is always the answer."

The lights flicker on again.

The elevator jerks to a start.

The movement shoves her against me. Her hand lodges against my heart. This is the closest we've ever been as grown-ups, apart from when she was sick and I had to carry her. I feel exposed. She smells of coconut and jasmine and feels so good. Better than all my dreams and expectation. I'm sure she sees my desires dancing in my eyes.

Right here, right now, we only have eyes for each other. Our wild hearts beat in sync, like they've always known this rhythm.

My addiction to her is subtle. When her eyes shine bright, a small surge of dopamine hits my mind, and when her lips part, it's overwhelming. I have been around an alcoholic, so I know this; some addictions are harder, but the addiction that seeps through without any volition are tougher. Like her. And her gorgeous lips. If I were a poet, I'd write a couplet about her Cupid's bow and the way I forget to breathe when she smiles.

I lean close, just to breathe her in, just a tiny bit closer. To ease this madness that is her, that she only can cure.

She parts her lips and runs her hand on her face.

The door dings open, and she moves away. I miss her. She's my oasis and my shelter. And I crave her, which is frustrating to someone like me, who's tried so hard to control everything in life. She consumes me, and I have no idea why I can't control it.

As she steps outside, her phone pings. She moves away from me, and her voice is a little upbeat. Maybe it's him. All I can hear is, "I couldn't face Ammi. We have to talk."

Reluctantly, I stride to my office.

A few minutes later her footfalls alert me to her presence. I swing my chair around, and she's right behind me.

Her face is a little brighter than before, and with a tiny, tentative smile, she asks, "Were you serious about accompanying me to Abba's grave?"

At this moment, if she were to ask me to accompany her to Jahannam, I would say yes. I flick my wrist to check on the time, then glance at my calendar on the desk. No appointments. Thank Allah!

"Absolutely." I reach for my coat and ask her, "You're okay to drive with me?"

"No, I'll take Mirchi." She slings her bag on her shoulder and shuffles her feet to bolt upright.

"What's Mirchi?" I ask.

"My car; actually, it was Abba's car. I call it Mirchi 'cause she has such an attitude." She beams.

Of course I know Mirchi. It was the car I was driven away from her in, that day. The old lady was in her prime then. And so many of my nightmares still feature her.

"I want you to make it there alive. Can we please carpool? It's good for the environment. Plus my car is fully electric." I have no idea why I'm pleading with her.

She scrunches her forehead and relents. "Fine. But fair warning, I haven't been to his grave, so we may have to look for his qabr."

I shrug and say, "Well, he's not going anywhere. So I'm sure we will find him."

A faint smile dances on her lips as she slaps my shoulder. "Respect, please."

It's incredible how even a tiny smile from her changes my day.

* * *

SANA

Daniel focuses on the road, and after an hour of quiet we reach our destination. We look for Abba's grave for a while, and Daniel is ultimately the one who spots it. Not me, the child, but him, the hated one.

Abba's grave is marked with our names and the date of his death. Grief is a place that when you revisit, it's as if you never left. I had thought by not being here, not seeing him buried, I could lock the pain away. And yes, with the passing years I have learned to live with this bullet lodged in my heart, but seeing his grave loosens something in me, an ache that's like a poker lodged in my heart, sharp and running through me quickly. I bend down to touch the headstone, but my legs become jelly and I sit next to the grave.

Daniel follows suit, dress pants and all. I haven't cried much since the day Abba was pronounced dead at the hospital. The memory of that fateful day is fresh in my mind: sirens, hospital, machines, and how I felt when they told me. Like I was falling into an abyss.

But now, tears, warm and plenty, rush through me. When my glasses fog, Daniel takes out a handkerchief and cleans them for me before placing them back on my nose.

He squeezes my shoulder and nods, and I know my sadness is shared. He lifts his hand in a prayer and makes a long recitation of all the duas he remembers. His incantation is like a soothing hymn and I follow, and we both stay there quiet for a while.

My heart is full, when I see Daniel like this, praying intently, with his eyes clothes. Like a son would for their father. How did I ever think he didn't care.

I lean my head on his shoulder. "You know, I saw him in a dream yesterday, talking to you."

"That's something . . . because I saw him in a dream not too long ago too. He was dressed in his white shalwar kameez. And you were in my dream too, but we were both younger." His voice doesn't break, but I know he's fighting tears. "He told me to go home—and he told you to make sure I did." His voice breaks a little, and he swallows. "Sana, I . . ."

His words are interrupted by the sound of footsteps.

I move away from him and jolt upright.

But it's too late. Ammi and Adam are standing just feet away. And if Ammi's eyes could kill, Daniel and I would be dead.

CHAPTER THIRTY

SANA

Ammi's chest rises and falls vigorously as she raises a finger in Daniel's direction and talks with gritted teeth. "I know the reason why you all came back. But don't you dare think I will let you destroy my family again. I won't let you sully his grave and his name any more. Sana, we're leaving."

Daniel folds his hands and pleads. "Soofia Auntie, please, I was just praying for him. I didn't mean to upset you in any way. Despite everything, I loved Zayn Uncle. He was like a father to me."

Ammi shakes her head and doubles down. "Either you leave, or I call the police."

"But Ammi!" I say, my voice unsteady. "I asked him to bring me here. I saw Abba in a dream yesterday . . . he and Shahri were together, just like the old days."

There is always this romantic notion in all the movies where the heroine eats, prays, and gives her heart to be with the one she loves.

But what happens to someone like me, with a divided heart? Daniel holds a piece, so does Ammi, and the largest part and the center of my heart is Zia. I wish there were a piece with Adam's name. But as much as I search, I come up empty.

I glance at Adam and can tell from his face that he knows.

Do I let my mother suffer on the anniversary of the day she was widowed? Do I stay and defend Daniel, who is here because of me? Or do I tell Adam that I love Daniel and have never stopped? So many people Daniel has cared about have given up on him . . . and the longer I stay quiet, the more I am becoming one of them.

Ammi is quiet, silently glaring. I glance at Daniel, and the piece that he holds of my heart shatters into a million more. His eyes have threads of red, like he's about to unravel. Right now he isn't the tough DAG who makes asshats like Nick crap their pants, but my Shahri, who's always been abandoned by those who should've stood by him.

Ammi finally whispers close to my ear, "Go with Adam and wait in the car. I will join you shortly."

Daniel nods when I glance up at him. The disappointed, shoulders-slumped nod of a defeated man.

Adam puts a hand on my shoulder. I swipe my tears and sidle next to him as he takes hurried steps toward his car. I look over my shoulder as Ammi tells Daniel, loud enough for us to hear, "You have no right to do this. This is not appropriate. If Adam walks away, she's ruined. Who will marry her then?"

Ammi is asking the wrong question. I wish she'd ask him if he's ready to marry me, despite everything. I know the answer as much as I know my heartbeats.

* * *

DANIEL

At home, Saleem's completely engrossed in a basketball game. He's wearing his Lakers jersey and rooting them on, shouting at the TV. A mug of chai sits on the coffee table.

When he hears my footsteps, he says over his shoulder, eyes still on the game, "Don't do it, bro. I've been there and don't recommend it."

I eye his worn-out T-shirt and sweats and tease him. "Are none of the nurses hitting on you, bro? Is that why you're constantly in your sweats?"

He waves his hands up and down his sweats and says, "Maybe this is to ward off the nurses. So how did Soofia Auntie not have a heart attack, her engaged daughter out with the enemy?" Word travels fast in this town.

I scan the score on screen. His team's winning. "Oh, she was mad, and I tell you her intuition or auntie network is strong, because she somehow knew we were there and showed up with Adam and laid the guilt thick on Sana. She accused me of ruining Sana's marriage prospects and gave me the 'she's ruined if Adam breaks up with her' line. It made me think."

Saleem peels his eyes from the screen and narrows them. "Thinking too much is your favorite pastime. Gimme a quick summary of the part after the thought process." He takes a sip from his mug.

I lean back and stare at the ceiling. "Soofia Auntie is right, in a way. I have no right over Sana. Adam and Sana are engaged, and he is a part of their family. But it's *because* I respect Sana and her family that I want to prove to Soofia Auntie that I intend to commit to Sana."

"I like that you're doing the honorable thing. But I'm going to be real with you, bade bhai. It's going to be a cold day in Jahannam before Soofia Auntie accepts your rishta."

I glare at him. "Maybe she won't, but I have to try. I can't let this what-if control my life. Maybe if I tell her how Sana and I feel about each other, it'll convince her—surely she can see how Sana feels about me. Sana went to her father's grave, today, for the first time, with me. She picked *me*. It has to mean something."

A loud roar announces his team's win. I give him a high five. He slaps my hand and then says, "I can usually tell in the last few minutes of the game if my team's going to win or lose. Does it mean I stop watching? No. Because despite it all, I hope and pray. I'll do the same for you, bade bhai. But do get a haircut and put on a nice shalwar kameez. No flowers, but a jasmine plant will suffice. You know desi moms and their aversion to money spent buying flowers."

"It's like Ammi says: 'Ummeed pai duniya qayam hai.' Hope is what keeps the world spinning."

"This is not hope. It's delusion," Saleem quips before he says good-night.

* * *

My morning run isn't calming my belly butterflies. I try to push the pace but still can't get into my zone. I give up and turn back before I finish my favorite 5K loop.

What if Sal is right? What if she throws me out? Soofia Auntie is never one to mince words. But . . . what if Sana and I can convince her? I wouldn't bet on myself if I were the gambling type, but maybe sometimes all you can do is put yourself out there and pray.

After a shower, I dress in a navy-blue shalwar kameez. As I run a comb through my hair, I see why Saleem suggested a haircut.

Mental checklist of things to do:

Pick up the jasmine plant and the fruit basket.

Ring.

I pull out the cardboard box with all my childhood things. My nani's ring. The only thing of value my birth mother sent with me. Ammi kept it with her until I was old enough to take care of it responsibly. As I click the latch open, the light catches the emerald, and it twinkles. It would look beautiful on Sana's slender fingers. I wonder if it'll fit her? Maybe I'll need to get it fitted. The box feels smooth under my fingertips as I slide it into the pocket of my kameez.

I wish an elder could come with me and follow the tradition and say the right things. But Ammi is too sick. I didn't expect to have to arrange my own rishta, but here we are.

I hop downstairs to the kitchen, where Saleem, freshly showered and holding a mug of chai, is fixing breakfast.

"Whoa. Going somewhere?" I raise an eyebrow at his fancy black shalwar kameez.

"Yeah, with you as an elder." My younger brother actually says it with a straight face.

"Seriously?" I scoff. "Thanks, but I'm already on a slippery slope with Soofia Auntie."

He folds his arms and speaks in a haughty, pinched-up voice. "I can play the part of your elderly aunt perfectly. Shahri, what's with this hair? It's so long and in your eyes. Get a haircut, son."

"But your daughter loves my hair." I reach up and wiggle the lock that always falls into my face. "She stares at this particular strand longingly—if you know what I mean." I smooth my hair, then wink at him.

He puts a hand to his chest and widens his eyes in mock surprise. "Hai Allah. Nalaiq. I'm your mother's age. Please don't make these obscene eye gestures. Surely your ammi didn't teach you that."

I laugh. "Can we go, please? I want this to be over with." I nudge him. "I still have to pick up a jasmine plant and fruit basket."

"I've got it all taken care of." He grabs a fruit basket out of the fridge. "The jasmine plant is behind you."

I smile, surprised. "Thank you."

After I park the car in front of Soofia Auntie's house, I start doubting my decision and drum the steering wheel. My fingers shake a little as I check my breath, wipe my face, and run a quick comb through my hair. I peek outside. A curtain in the window flutters, then is drawn back before I glimpse who's checking on us.

A slap on my back takes me out of my reverie. Saleem tips his head toward the house. "Someone saw us. Unless you want them to call the cops, let's go in."

I scratch my chin. "Maybe we should've called instead . . ."

Saleem shakes his head. "I was starting to like this adventurous side of you, showing up here after the last time you saw her and the conversation ended with *Stay away from Sana*. Come on, don't chicken out now."

"Are you done?" I take a deep breath and step out of the car.

In this neighborhood, attached townhomes run down both sides of the block. A Bollywood song filters out of a neighboring home along with the familiar smell of sautéed onions. It's the stark opposite of where we live, with its big lots and fenced secured entry.

At the front steps, I grab the railing to reassure myself this is really happening. The rickety railing quivers as badly as my nerves.

The door opens without so much as a shuffle of feet, which tells me they were literally waiting for us to knock. "Salaam, Auntie and Zia." I raise my hand in the traditional greeting.

Soofia Auntie doesn't smile. Her face is that of a poker player unwilling to reveal their hand. Zia's behind her. His hands flail, but his face lights up like a rising sun.

Zia whispers something in his mother's ear. When she nods, he asks, "Can I have a hug, Daniel?" He talks in a monotone, but his face is so expressive. He's genuinely happy to see me, unlike Soofia Auntie.

"Sure." I extend my arms toward him, and he settles into a hug. It's amazing the therapeutic effect of human touch. His bear hug calms me.

"Walaikum assalam. Come inside." She waves to her living room. "Zia, finish your homework, please." She points upstairs.

Zia stomps his feet but agrees to walk away. Before he goes, he says, "I like you, Daniel. More than Adam."

His affirmation means so much to me, knowing how much Sana loves her little brother. His words make this easier, although I know Soofia Auntie is nothing like Zia.

Saleem holds out the gift basket for her. "Auntie, a little something for you."

She smiles and hesitates, as if she's trying to decipher the meaning behind this gesture. I'm certain that the cogs of her brain are quickly piecing together why I'm here. If she knows, she's not letting on. "You shouldn't have. I'm diabetic, and Zia's not a big fruit person. But it's good to see you both under . . . better circumstances. MashAllah, such handsome young men you've grown up to be. Your mother must be proud. I've heard a lot about your accomplishments through Sana and Ainee."

The living room has almond-brown sofas with plastic covers pushed against the walls. A picture of Kabbah and the holy city hangs on the wall. A framed calligraphy with Arabic verses is right next to it.

Soofia Auntie gestures toward the kitchen. "Come in here; I put a fresh kettle on for chai. Sana and Adam are going to set a date for their shaadi soon. I have, in exchange, agreed to let her visit your mother tonight. I hope this is a visit to thank me for that . . . if not, there's really nothing else to talk about."

I swallow, and Saleem and I follow her to the kitchen. The dread settles in the air, and we sit awkwardly for a long, excruciating minute. Soofia Auntie intimidates me because I respect her so much; despite her misgivings, she and her husband treated me like their own, when my own uncle didn't.

But I have to say my piece. Our truth. There's just no other way.

I smile and finally tell her. "Soofia Auntie, Saleem and I are here for Sana's rishta."

Maybe I should've built up to it or eased into this conversation, but without a current relationship with her beyond bad memories, it's best to lay this out in the open.

She stays quiet and stares at her hand for a long time.

Saleem and I look at each other for clues.

She shakes her head, then lifts an accusing finger. "I am stunned. After I explicitly told you to get this straight, how dare you come here? Sana is going to marry Adam—I have given Abdullah and Adam's mother Lena my word. If she doesn't keep my word, I will wish her dead. You see, I'm not like your uncle, who never kept his word to us."

"Adam is not right for her, Auntie," I say softly. "Don't you want Sana to be happy? You must know she has doubts."

Soofia Auntie leans back in her chair. "You young people think love is sweeping gestures and declarations. Love is commitment, like Adam is willing to do, despite the fact that I have nothing to give except my good wishes—no dowry, nothing but my daughter. He and his father have given us such respect, and they are a well-to-do Syed family. He's the only son, and will inherit most of his mother's fortune, and still is a hardworking business owner. I don't see anything wrong with him. I'm convinced when they marry, love will follow."

Saleem pulls his chair close to her. "It's not just gestures. I guarantee that Daniel means this. We're committed, and he is the deputy attorney general. He is so layaq. Worthy. He and Sana have had this undeniable bond ever since they were little—I know I see it, and I am sure Adam does too. Think about Sana and her happiness. If Adam doesn't see this, he's blind, or something is up with him."

Soofia Auntie jabs her finger at me. "Adam is a practical man. No one is perfect. You're not—that's why your divorce happened. But Shahri's issues are much bigger. Do you think anyone with a respectable family will give their daughter to someone who's najayaz?"

Najayaz. *Illegitimate.*

"I can never ever agree to this union," she continues. "I have to show Sana's father my face in Jannah, inshAllah."

Saleem's voice booms. "That is nothing but stupid gossip, Auntie! You and I both know that. Please, don't do this."

My stomach drops. "What the hell are you both talking about?"

"Let's go, Daniel." He bolts up and nudges me.

I glance at him. His face, which is almost always calm, is anything but. He doesn't even look back at me before storming out. I follow him outside. "You want to tell me what's going on? Why is my entire legitimacy being questioned?"

CHAPTER THIRTY-ONE

SANA

The nights that I spend restless are not my favorite, but I feel nervous and a little giddy from the excitement of seeing Shahida Auntie. I texted Daniel earlier, but he said he was tired and would talk more later. He was curt and distant. Is what Ammi said to him at the graveyard still bothering him?

I wanted to talk to Adam on the drive home, but Ammi sat next to him, and they happily chatted about setting a date for our baat pakki and engagement party. When Adam walked me to my apartment door, I stopped before stepping inside and asked, "Hey, can we talk about what happened for a minute? Ammi wants to forget what happened, but I can't. I need to sort this mess out."

Adam jammed his hands in his pockets and shrugged. "What's the rush? We have our whole lives to sort out things. I'm committed to making it work, and my abba has been so happy lately. You know he asked Ammi to design a few dresses for you. Abba never asks Ammi for anything."

"Adam, we cannot live for other people. Are *you* happy? Is this what you want as well?"

He looked away. "I am happy. My father's happiness makes me happy, and you are so wonderful, and I know we will have a wonderful future. Our families mesh so well together."

"Yeah, but what about us?" I asked again, trying to read his eyes, to gauge his feelings.

I finally told him the truth that I had been avoiding. "I want to be honest with you. Daniel and I have a history, and it . . ."

Adam gave me a wry smile, devoid of mirth. His eyes were laced with an emotion I had seen when we first met: sadness. Whatever he was grappling with wasn't something he wanted to think about. "I have felt that rush of being in love, except it wasn't love. It was a fleeting attraction, and it ran its course. Afterward, I realized it wasn't love; it was my hormones or whatever."

I wanted to say that maybe what he felt for that person and what I felt for Daniel were different. This flame had eighteen years to burn out, yet it still threatens to consume me.

Ainee's knock on my door interrupts my thoughts. "Are you decent?"

I slap my laptop shut. It's the week before finals, and my life is total and utter chaos.

I yell back at her. "When has that ever stopped you from barging in? Come in. I'm preparing for finals next week."

Ainee walks in. Her slick hair is loose, and her peach lip gloss shimmers. She's dressed in a long pastel dress.

She plays with a loose strand of hair and asks, "So, you're planning to be indoors studying all week, sans your suitors?"

Ainee is fishing; she knows I'm supposed to go see Shahida Auntie today. I can feel a quip coming, but I play along.

I shrug and tell her what she knows. "Daniel is picking me up in a bit to see Shahida Auntie."

"Must be nice, having two suitors in tow; if one fails, you have a backup. And what a backup—Daniel Malik, who half our office thirsts for . . ." She doesn't mask the sarcasm in her voice.

I'm tired of people throwing dirt on Daniel's name. I retort back, "Adam knows I'm going to visit Shahida Auntie. And I hinted to him about my feelings for Daniel."

Ainee puts a hand to her chest. "Whoa! Bravo. So, what, you'll dump him and go to Shahida Auntie's house, where dear old Shahri will propose with his nani's ring in front of his dying mother? That's a Bollywood twist I didn't see coming. Since today is going to be a big day, you'll need to dress the part."

She winks, then opens my messy closet. After shuffling hangers back and forth, she finds the dress and lays it on my bed.

What if this is the dress I get engaged in? Daniel has never mentioned a proposal, but I believe I know him enough to know that he will, eventually. And if he does, will I say yes? What will I tell Ammi? Because she will never agree.

But what I do know, with absolute certainty, is that I cannot marry Adam. It's too big a lie. And he doesn't deserve it. He deserves someone who is not completely in love with another.

When Ainee speaks again, her voice is softer. More genuine. "I'll be there to catch you after the blowup. Although I will remind you that you are making a mistake. Adam will be heartbroken." Ainee's face softens. "Both of your families are involved."

"I know. But if I continue, it'll break both of our hearts eventually. That's not how I want my marriage to be, full of regrets and bitterness."

I take a quick shower, then get dressed in the dress, hijab, and jewelry Ainee left out for me.

The bell rings.

My heart drums in my ears, and my pulse quickens when I open the door.

A gamut of emotions pass across Daniel's face when he glances at me, from hints of surprise to love and, finally, indifference. Like the Daniel I first met, not my friend Shahri. He's handsome in his crisp shalwar kameez and floppy hair but seems to be having an internal battle. When he speaks, he's curt. "Walaikum assalam. Ready?"

I cross my arms. He annoys me with his hot and cold. I wish he'd just tell me what the hell has gotten him so distant again. "You know you don't have to chauffeur me around. I can get a ride with someone."

"I promised to take you, and Ammi wants me to do this." He avoids my stern glance and makes his way out without waiting for my answer.

I step into my heels and mutter, "Which side of you is this now? Decide who the hell you want to be."

While I lock up, his phone rings. "I have to take this. Meet you by the car."

I want to demand to know what's bothering him, why he's pushing me away. Tell him we have come too far and I'm willing to really fight for him, give up my secure life with Adam. Part of me wants him to get his head examined. But I also know him enough to know that something triggered his need to put his walls up again.

I follow him to the car. He leans on the passenger side door, his eyes obscured by sunglasses. Dammit. More ways he's shutting me out. He mutters into the phone, "See you in a bit."

Daniel swings the door open for me, and I lose my battle of wills. "Is Shahida Auntie okay?" It's not a loaded question, but I figure maybe this is something he's willing to offer. Maybe.

He closes the door but hovers close. “Well. Depends.”

“On what?”

“On what you mean by that. Is she physically okay? Yes.”

“Dear Allah! What’s with you, Shahri?”

“Daniel. My name is Daniel.”

At this, I want to shake his broad shoulders that fit that off-white kameez so perfectly and muss his floppy hair until he tells me what’s going on, or turn around and go home. But that would mean giving up; besides, I want to see his mother.

The passenger seat is reclined all the way back. I grunt to adjust it. “Who do you transport in this car? Jinns?”

He scratches his forehead. “It’s Saleem. He likes to stretch out. But this morning we had a fruit basket and a . . . never mind.”

We drive in utter silence until we reach their development. In this part of Westchester County, buildings are surrounded by green open spaces. We’re so far out in the burbs, I’m quite sure we’re in a different zip code. Well-paved roads lined with streetlights. Hardly any traffic. I’m fairly sure I see white horses running wild in front of one house we drive by. What the hell? Am I going to see unicorns next? Maybe the rich do have things we peons only dream about.

On the horizon, the sun sets in an orange glow, and the sky is starting to darken. Daniel pulls up next to a beautiful modern house spread across a wide yard. The tires crunch as he shifts into park. Manicured hedges line the circular driveway, and the scent of jasmine and marigold tinges the air.

I look around before I start climbing the front steps. The sheer number of floor-to-ceiling windows in this mini-mansion surprises me. It must be true: the rich live in glass houses.

I stand there so long, Shahri—no, *Daniel* when he’s in this mood—takes my arm and urges me along. “Chickening out?”

“Of course not.”

An older white woman with short hair and glasses around her neck opens the door for us. "Good evening, Mr. M."

"Good evening, Mary-Ann. This is a family friend, Sana Saeed. She's here to see Ammi. Sana, this is our nurse, Mary-Ann."

"You know how I feel about visitors. No more than twenty minutes." She taps her wristwatch for emphasis. The tiered, cut-crystal chandelier reflects on the face of her Apple watch.

I follow him up the circular staircase. What strikes me is how quiet the house is. Maybe it's because I've always lived in apartment buildings and busy neighborhoods with women like Mrs. Sharma for nosy neighbors, but it's almost never this quiet. He skips up a few steps at a time, while I struggle to keep up.

"Twenty minutes, and use the hand sanitizer outside the rooms, please." Mary-Ann's voice carries up the stairs.

I catch my breath and glance up to where Daniel waits for me.

His eyebrow quirks up. "You okay?"

I nod.

He leads me down a long corridor to a master suite. We sanitize our hands before entering. Inside the room, almost all the light comes from the sunset. Now I see the logic behind these windows, especially for someone like Shahida Auntie. She can feel close to the outdoors without actually being there and exposed to all the germs. Her private bubble with a view.

"Salaam, Auntie." I move next to her. Her face is pale, her hair thin and white as snow. Last time we met, at Ainee's engagement party, things were so chaotic. It seems like that was ages ago. The big armchair completely dwarfs her. The sun setting casts a glow on her face.

She tilts my chin up. "Sit closer, beti. It's been a while since I saw you."

Her voice is the one thing about her that hasn't altered. It brings flashbacks of her always telling Ammi how much she loved seeing me and Shahri play together, and how grateful she was that I had gotten him out of his shell. Things were good then, or maybe that's how it always seemed, seen through the haze of childhood memories.

"How are you, Auntie? It's so good to see you." I press her hand to my cheek.

"I'm so glad to see you too. So much time has gone by. Daniel tells me you are about to be engaged. If I had a daughter, I'd wish she were like you. I see so much of myself in you. This is why I always wanted you for my Daniel." She holds my hand and kisses it with such tenderness that my heart aches.

"Auntie, I've always loved you, despite all the things that went on. I know Ammi blames you for not stopping Sibte Uncle, but I know that even if you tried, he wouldn't have listened. The way he treated Shahri all his life, he wouldn't have cared about anyone, let alone us."

Daniel sits next to her on the other side. "Ammi, please, I don't want you to stress over this; it's in the past. And inshAllah, things will get better."

Footsteps sound, softened by the wall-to-wall carpet. I glance at the door. It's Saleem.

He seems surprised. "Sana? After what happened earlier, I didn't think you would be here." He glances at Daniel, then clamps his mouth shut.

I'm definitely missing something, but it would be rude to interrupt Shahida, so I stay quiet. I'll have a sidebar with Saleem later.

Shahida beams at her sons. "There are things in my life I am proud of and other things I regret. Mere bacchey are my pride and joy. Sue didn't deserve Saleem. And no one has ever been good enough for my Daniel . . . because I always thought of you. The two of you have something special; I've always known that. But then I find out you are about to be engaged. I did what you are doing years ago . . . and let me tell you, it never worked for anyone involved—not for me, or my late husband, or my sons."

She shifts in her seat, and I steal a glance at Daniel and Saleem. They both are such good sons; I see why she is proud. I also hear the pain in her voice from a toxic relationship. My heart aches when I tell her, "I plan to tell Ammi tomorrow that I'm not marrying Adam."

Daniel's mouth opens wide in shock, and his eyebrows hitch up. "Really?"

Shahida lets out a sharp exhale. "I know Soofia—she holds grudges as close to her heart as the ones she loves. I grieve the loss of our friendship to this day; I'm sure she does too, which is why she's bitter. I should've said more, done more. She was my closest friend, my confidante. But what she hasn't yet learned is that sometimes we have to trust our kids."

Shahida points to her side table, and Saleem retrieves a manila envelope. "This is for you and Daniel. Now, I know you two haven't had all the conversations that need to be had, or made any decisions, but I hope you'll indulge me for a moment."

I glance at Daniel, who looks just as confused as I feel.

"I know how happy you make Daniel," Shahida continues. "So I will say this: choose wisely, even if it's your own family. And ultimately, whoever you choose, I will always love you, beti." She hands me the envelope. "Here's a little something for the two of you, whether you choose to be with him or not. I'm leaving you both Ainee's mother's house. She was selling, and I had always intended to give you some of your childhood back. You two both had so many memories in that house, and it's the only house remaining of our good times together. I'd hoped you'd both build your lives there."

I can't believe my ears. A *house*? But it's the finality in Shahida's voice that makes my heart sink. I swallow. "Are you . . . going somewhere?" I knew something seemed off, but I don't want her to say they're going back to California.

"We're moving to Pakistan at the end of this week." Daniel's voice is flat.

"P-Pakistan?" I'm having difficulty swallowing the lump lodged in my throat.

He can't leave. Not now.

"Sorry, beti. I'm making them take me to Pakistan, to be buried next to my family. I've nothing left here. I want to spend my last few months surrounded by my family. I had hoped to see Daniel married, but my body's giving up on me, and the prospects of Soofia forgiving me seem slim." She wheezes, then takes a gulp of water.

"I am going to talk to Ammi, Shahida Auntie. But—" My thoughts and words halt when Mary-Ann's shrill voice interrupts us.

"Let's wrap this up, everyone." She taps on her wristwatch.

"Let me say good-bye to her. Please." My voice breaks, and I kneel next to her and lower my head in her lap as I did when I was little. "Auntie, I'm so sorry I didn't come here sooner." I release all the tears I've kept in check. "May Allah give you shifa and health. I wish you could stay . . ."

She wipes her tears and whispers close to my ear, "Take care of him for me."

After a final good-bye, I drag myself away from Shahida and climb downstairs with Daniel and Saleem. I stop next to the door. "When were you planning to tell me?"

Daniel breaks his gaze. "Things happen. Ammi's doctors want us to think about the next steps."

"So what? You're just going to leave? Just like that?"

"We have a lot to deal with here," Saleem interjects. "We tried, Sana. Be sure to ask Soofia Auntie why she would do such a thing—"

Daniel raises his hand. "Let's not do this right now, Sal." Then he walks to the door hurriedly. "Let me drop you home."

I know there is a piece missing in this whole conversation, something that happened between Ammi and Daniel, something that's made him cynical about us.

But he has made a decision about us without feeling the need to talk to me. Daniel and Shahri are so not alike. Shahri would never do what Daniel just did.

"No need." I shake my head. "I can find my way home."

* * *

It hurts that he didn't protest when I asked to be left alone. I wanted him to come after me.

I wipe my tears as my Uber approaches me.

The driver, Rahman, is a friendly guy from Bangladesh who tells me about his family back home and blasts Bangla songs from the car stereo. But I can't stop thinking about how Daniel is leaving me again—and this time, he has a choice.

My phone rings. It's Zia. My heart rate picks up; he never calls this late.

Zia sobs. "Ammi's not waking up."

CHAPTER THIRTY-TWO

SANA

As I process Zia's words, part of me is terrified and another can't believe it. How bad can things get before they get better?

I hear Zia pacing with some noise in the background, then his panicked voice comes on the phone again. "Why's she not waking up?"

"Zia, call 911!" My heartbeat drums in my ears.

"I called already. They're coming. Rana's coming too." He hangs up abruptly.

My heart lurches. My hands shake as I call my sister, but her phone's busy. Ainee's phone is switched off.

"Can you drive faster?" I ask Rahman. "I need to get home immediately."

"I'll take a shortcut. But I won't drive over the speed limit. I don't want a ticket."

Flashbacks from visiting my father in the hospital storm my brain anew. I can't lose Ammi and I don't want to lose Daniel, yet both are slipping away.

I check my phone so many times that Rahman consoles me. "InshAllah, it will all be okay, sister."

His kind words calm my anxiety a little.

Finally, at home, I thank Rahman and step out of the Uber. As I unlock the front door, Adam texts me: *On my way to get you.*

Then my sister: *Ammi is at University Hospital ED. Meet us there. I sent Adam to get you.*

I pace, waiting for Adam. When he arrives, I run to his car. He squeezes my hand.

"Soofia Auntie is critical but stable. It was a diabetic attack. I spoke to Rana; she's there with her. Zia is home with her mother-in-law."

I want to cry so badly but swallow my tears. Maybe it's because Daniel has completely shut me out, but having a shoulder to lean on is comforting. Daniel has taken all the sparks and magic, but this friendship Adam and I share is still special. He's here for me. I look out at the dark sky and say a silent prayer for Ammi.

Rana and Ammi's reliance on Adam more than me is irksome, and their excluding me even more so. But I shouldn't blame my sister too much. Adam has, in such a short period of time, slid into our tight family unit. How will I detach him without wrenching my family to the core?

"I'm so worried about her."

"Don't worry; they're all there with her. I'll get you there as soon as possible and will stay as long as you want me to," he says in a soothing, calm voice.

Daniel isn't here. Adam is here, and committed to staying. Why am I so blinded by stupid emotions?

The whole time he's driving, I recite the Quran, assuring myself Ammi's outcome is not going to be the same as Abba's. I can't lose my only parent. Just the thought gives me shivers.

When we get to the hospital, Adam puts his hand around my shoulders and whispers, "She'll be okay."

When we walk into the intensive care unit, memories of my father being here come back. The tile floors gleaming in the white overhead lights, the smell of Lysol, the squeak of wheels and the hurried footsteps—all of it comes back afresh. I remember, even after seventeen years, every single detail about that day. Trauma, in a way, is like déjà vu—it all inevitably comes back, and you relive all the emotions, this time even stronger.

On the way to the nurses' station to check on my mother, I run into my brother-in-law. "Where's Ammi?"

"She's in with the doctor. She's stable, but her sugar was high." He exhales. "Rana is in the waiting room. I'm heading home. My mother is with the kids alone."

"Is Zia okay?" My poor brother must be a wreck. Has someone explained to him what's going on? As much as I want to call him, Ammi takes priority now.

In the waiting area, Rana sits with her shoulders hunched and her lips moving along with the prayer beads in her hands. My eyes sting with tears. Her reddened eyes tell me she's been crying. My sister never cries, but clearly this broke her too.

She pulls me into a hug and sobs, her tears wetting my hijab. I rub her back in circles and console her. "She'll be okay. I promise."

"How is she? Any updates?" Adam asks.

The waiting room seems quiet, except for the TV playing HGTV shows.

Rana swipes her face and replies, "Not yet. If everything goes well, she might be able to breathe on her own by tomorrow."

"I'll stay here if you need to leave, Rana baji," I say. "Did you talk to Zia? Adam, you can leave too—it's late. Thanks for everything."

"Zia's better now. I gave him something for anxiety before I left, so he was sleeping last time I checked," Rana tells me. "Adam, stay with Sana if you can, please. I don't want you to be all alone, Sana."

Adam graciously smiles. "You don't have to ask. I'll be here with Sana as long as she'll tolerate me."

My sister hugs me and thanks Adam. Farooq and Rana walk hand in hand toward the hospital exit; my sister leans on his shoulder, and he squeezes her hand reassuringly. A look passes between them, and the lines on my sister's face soften. After all these years, they still love each other.

Adam's voice breaks my thoughts. "The nurse says we can visit for fifteen minutes. I'll find the attending physician to give you an update on her situation."

He runs a hand through his hair as we trudge to the nurses' station. It's quiet except for beeping monitors and chatter there. A nurse looks at me with tired eyes. She points to the logbook. "Please fill out the forms so I can give you a badge."

Once inside the semi-dark, depressing ICU room, we see Ammi. She's still unconscious, her body hooked to the machines.

"Is it okay to sit next to her?" I ask the nurse checking her IV.

"Yeah, she's out of danger, but we have to keep her another night. Hopefully, tomorrow she can be transferred to a general room."

I lean on Adam's shoulder. "All my life, my mother has been my rock. She's my only parent—" My voice cracks.

"I brought some Zamzam for her. Maybe the holy water will help her heal." He gives me a little bottle.

I take a bit of the water and touch her forehead. Her warm body and rhythmic heartbeats are a comfort. I pull a chair next to her and fall asleep watching her breathe.

* * *

DANIEL

The movers have taken out some boxes, but the ones Ammi wants us to look through, sort, and donate are stacked in a corner.

The cool breeze ruffles the curtain, and the bright sunlight brings my attention to the immense task at hand—the sorting through twenty plus years of my life. My Pakistani passport, letters from my birth parents. My birth certificate and passport both have the names of my dead father. My high school diploma bears my old name, Shahri Khalil.

Soofia has made my existence into a question mark. Who am I? Was I born out of a wedlock? Was I a secret my mother didn't want; is this why I was shipped away? My adult mind needs answers to all these questions. The scar has been cut open again before it has healed.

Maybe going back will give me a better sense of belonging. I have never belonged anywhere but with Sana, so maybe going back will be good, to heal and find my footing again.

Footfalls echo behind me.

Saleem clears his throat. "Will you be able to sort through these? Or should we ship it all back to Pakistan? Since my wonderful divorce, I have had meager belongings. I never thought I'd be grateful for the split," he scoffs.

After moving as much as I have, moving should be easy; at least that's what I've told myself. I'll cut off all ties and start anew. "I'm not one for baggage—literal or figurative. I think most of my clothes and things are sorted, and I'll take these few boxes."

"Yeah. Did you go through everything? What's in there?" He reaches for the box I'm holding.

Before he can grab it, I close it up and shove it inside my bare closet.

"What are you hiding, big brother?"

"None of your business." I glare. "So, did you tell Reema you're moving?"

"Yup, but she's pretty busy with work. I gave her my number in case she decides to connect in the future." He shrugs casually, but I know there's something between these two, more than he lets on.

I smile and slap the back of his shoulder.

"Bade bhai, you know that Soofia Auntie is not right about you," he says. "This is all a rumor. Nothing to it. Ammi would never keep such a big thing from you." He shakes his head. "Sana seemed sincere when she said she was going to talk to her mother. Did you try calling her?"

"I did, and when she didn't pick up, I gave it a rest. Maybe she needs to figure this out. I don't know. Even if her mother had accepted me, it wouldn't be fair to ask Sana to give up everything and move. It's a lot to think about."

He looks outside the window where the big truck is being loaded with boxes. "Ammi doesn't have much time left . . . why can't Sana come for a few weeks, if you have a nikah? And then you can move back? Ask her. Communicate."

"I don't want her to look forward to my mother dying so we can be together. If she isn't with Adam, maybe we can make things work long-distance and see how it goes. But I need to do some things for my own sanity before I drag her along. Maybe I need to get some answers before I can go back to Soofia. If Sana fights with her entire family for me, then I owe it to her to be back to help her convince them."

Saleem slaps my back. "And if Sana doesn't fight for you, maybe she isn't the one for you."

"If she isn't, then I'm not sure about anyone or anything else. She's the only one I've ever loved."

"Love. It too shall pass," Saleem tells me before walking away.

* * *

When I peek inside Ammi's room, the nurse is helping her up. She shuffles to the recliner near the open window. The breeze carries the scent of sweet honeysuckle from the garden outside.

Her face is pale and thin, but her eyes gleam. "How are you holding up?" she asks, extending her hand.

I take it and crouch on the floor next to her. "For the first time in a very long time, I feel defeated. I tried to do the right thing, and not only did Soofia shoot me down, she . . . questioned the circumstances of my birth."

Ammi strokes my hair. "These are just vile rumors, son. Soofia is punishing you for my mistakes."

"But even if it's a rumor, it makes me think—is this why she gave me up? Because I was that tarnish on her reputation? Maybe I reminded her of all things shameful in her life . . ."

She cradles my face. "Forgive your mother. Your mother, my sister, wanted a better life for you, one she could never give you. It was a sacrifice for her. She loves you. Maybe going back will be good. Maybe it's time you get your answers from her."

Ammi's words give me some comfort, but she lets her sister off the hook too easily.

"Ammi, love isn't just words. I could've had a life in Pakistan and been happy. I would've worked hard. Why did she have to rip me from everyone I knew and loved?"

"She did what she felt she had to." She picks up a photo of me graduating from UC Berkeley and smiles. "I won't be here long, but

I'm happy you will have another mother to see you succeed, and hopefully marry and have grandkids."

I swallow and pat her hand. "I only have one mother. You."

"No, you don't. Also, you must know that all I want is for you to be happy." She gestures toward the closet. "Can you get me a box from the safe? It's red velvet. I kept my heirloom bracelets for Sana. I'm not even sure if they'll fit her, but before I go, they should go to her. Maybe something to remember me by."

After I retrieve the box for her, she opens it and holds out the bracelets for me. The gold bracelets have patterns of flowers, and the inlaid emeralds match my grandmother's ring.

"I love Sana," says Ammi. "She balances you." She looks up at me, wiping the corner of her eye with her long dupatta. "Give her the bracelets and tell her I wouldn't have parted with them for anyone but her. I wanted to give them to her but I didn't want her to think I was trying to bribe her into marrying you. If I had hopes of living to see you get married, I would keep them."

"InshAllah, you will have a long life." I pat her warm hand.

"I have no illusions about my health." Ammi leans back and hands me the manila envelope Sana left behind when she left in a huff, then points to the box with bracelets. "Give these to her, son. Please. And don't give up her."

* * *

I call Sana's phone, and it goes to voice mail again.

I'm forced to call Ainee. Her phone rings a few times before she picks up. "Daniel?"

"Salaam, Ainee, sorry to bother you. I have a few things that my mother wanted to give to Sana. Is it possible for me to drop them off?"

"Just let her be. Her mother's in the hospital. The last person she needs to see is you."

Soofia Auntie is in the hospital? "What happened?"

"None of your business," Ainee snaps.

Whatever it is, Sana must be devastated. I need to see her, be there for her.

I let out a long breath and say, "Look, I promise it'll be quick. Can you text me the address?"

She hesitates. "Okay, but I'll hunt you down if you hurt her more."

* * *

I pick up a plant and stop by the front desk. The older white lady asks me for my ID and the room number I'm visiting. Her badge reads *Helen*.

"It's Mrs. Soofia Saeed. I don't know her room number," I say.

Helen glances at me from over the top of her glasses while picking up the phone receiver. "Let me check if they're okay to receive visitors."

She calls, and the conversation lasts for more than a minute. From behind the glass, I catch snippets of conversation, and I can gather that I am not welcome.

But then Helen hangs up and says, "Ms. Saeed will accompany you upstairs. Please wait in the lobby."

I pace with the plant under the white overhead tube lights until I hear familiar footsteps. It's Sana.

Her face is pale; she looks beautiful but tired, with red-rimmed eyes and dry lips. Before I can get a word out, tears flood her eyes and she runs and hugs me. I swallow and hold her. We envelop each other like a soft cardigan on a cold winter day. And I know: I will fight anyone and everyone for her.

When people start to stare, I create a few inches of distance between us. "How is Soofia Auntie?"

She wipes her tears. "Ammi's better. We have a surprise planned for Ammi when she opens her eyes later."

I'm confused by her statement. "I thought she's okay?"

She nods and signals toward a chair to sit. "They're reducing her dosage, so she should be more conscious. She is supposed to open her eyes in a bit, so they're setting the room up for her—they'll text me when they're ready. So you can be part of the surprise."

I'm astonished that Sana's family is not objecting to me being here. Granted, her mother can't protest, but Rana cannot be happy about my presence.. "Is Rana upstairs?"

Sana stares absently at the circular moving door and shrugs. "Yeah, they're all up there. So is Adam."

Adam is here and Rana and her family as well, yet no one objects?

"What's that?" She points to the bag.

I smile. "You left in a huff, but these are the property papers. And Ammi wanted you to have something else . . ." I shift in the seat and swing toward her. "I'm leaving for Pakistan soon. There's . . . a lot we need to talk about."

She swallows audibly and locks gazes with me. In the reflection of her eyes I see a version of myself I like, maybe even love.

Her phone beeps.

She jolts upright. "They're ready."

I follow her to the elevator, and we walk in step to Soofia's room. The smell of roses fills the hallway even before we enter.

When Soofia sees us, the disgust in her weak voice is pronounced. "What is he doing here?"

Adam straightens from the decorations he's setting up, which read: *Mujhsey shadi karogi?* Will you marry me?

Adam is dressed in a black sherwani and kneels on one knee, holding a small box. Rana, Farooq, and Zia are right behind him.

Sana has a hand to her lips in surprise and steps forward in a daze. "What's all this, Adam?"

"A ring and a question. I want you to have my ring, so that everyone knows." He flicks a gaze in my direction before focusing back on Sana.

"Adam . . . can we—"

Even before she finishes, Soofia interjects. "Answer him, Sana."

Sana extends her hand to his arm to ask him to stand up; he does, but slips the ring on her right hand as he does so.

I've had enough. I leave the plant next to Sana and her excited family and get the hell out of there. When I hear footsteps behind me, I speed up my strides. I am so done.

"Shahri!" Sana calls out and catches up to me.

I stop and face her. "Why are you following me, Sana? You've made your choice. I trusted you, despite myself, but I should've known better. My instincts have kept me safe up until now . . ." My voice breaks.

The toll of the move, this whole situation, is just too much.

"I am going to talk to them," she says, twisting her fingers. The glint from the ring catching the overhead light serves as a good eye-opener. What am I doing here? Her mother will never agree, and Sana will never hurt her ailing mother.

"I can't, Sana. Not after what I saw in there. You won't choose me over them, and they don't want any piece of me. So this is good-bye."

She catches my shirt in her fists. We stay still for a moment; I revel in her warmth. My heart, my soul, and every pore of my body recognizes the high of being with her. This madness is a marż, only calmed by her; too bad I'm addicted to the one thing I'll never have. It's a bad wager and yet my heart still wants to bet on her.

Despite myself, I finally tell her: "I love you."

CHAPTER THIRTY-THREE

SANA

Daniel's words make my heart feel like it's going to burst into the tiny boondis of a motichoor laddu. I hold his hands, and the pent-up tears spill over and run down my face. My throat hurts from holding back the sobs. Clinging to him for my sanity, I lose myself in his scent. His arms feel like my permanent home. My tears darken his gray T-shirt. He's still, like that night when I fell apart in his arms, but I know today he won't stay. All I may ever have are these last few moments with him.

"Shahri. Please stay."

He lets go of me and says in a bitter tone, "To see you get married to him? You wear his ring as a punishment. I can't stay to see you suffer like this. Maybe, after I go away, you will like him more?"

"I—" Before I finish, he leaves. No good-bye. No promise of tomorrow. No looking back even once.

It's a merry-go-round, our qismet. He's left me crying again.

Footsteps approach. "Sana," Adam calls out. "Come on, your mom is asking about you." He grabs my hand, and I wonder why he's ignoring what just happened.

"Adam, can we talk for a minute?" I tug at his hand.

"Sure." He tips his head in the direction of the sign that says *Cafeteria*.

He doesn't let go of my hand with his ring until we enter a big hall with circular tables set up throughout. The skylights make the area bright. I wonder if they do that because hospitals are depressing in general. They're certainly trying, with the natural light and cheery yellow paint on the walls.

The hum of chatter and registers dinging fills the air. I pay for our tea and sit with Adam at a corner table. I pry his ring from my finger and set it between us on the table. "Adam, I can't marry you."

His eyes widen. "But why? I thought we had an agreement. Ammi is so happy seeing us together."

I look him in the eye. "Adam, I'm so sorry for doing this to you, but I had convinced myself all this time that being like my mother and sister and following their path would be the way to a perfect marriage. What I didn't factor in was that I will never be over Shahri. He will have a part of me, always. It would not be fair to you to come into this agreement with half of my heart."

He clears his throat. "But he's left. And maybe you just need some time to get over this. No great love lasts—eventually, like grief, you get over it."

I shake my head; he clearly hasn't felt the sharp pang of grief. Every time I pass by a store Abba used to love, or when Ammi cooks one of his favorite foods, the symptoms of grief and loss are back with a vengeance. And it's as if they never left. It's not that you get over your loss, it's more that you learn to live with it. Like a knife lodged in your chest, it only hurts when someone pokes at the wound. Love is the same—maybe you learn to live with it and deal with the pain anytime something reminds you of the one your heart truly belongs to.

"I hope you will get over this disappointment, Adam, and find someone who can love you like you deserve to be loved."

He stares at my bare hand, with his ring resting on the laminate cafeteria table. "So you've given up on us. What will you tell your mother?"

The doctors next to us pick up their trays and move. I wonder if they've overheard our conversation. "Once Ammi is out of here, I'll tell her the truth. And you don't have to come here anymore. The only thing binding you to my family is me, and now that it's over between us, everyone needs time to recover and settle down. I know this cannot be easy for you either."

He slaps his hands on the table. "You're cutting me off completely?" Adam is clearly more wounded over being cut off from my family than not being engaged to me. It surprises me a little.

"I'm not right for you . . . ," I say weakly.

"Will you think about us?" His hand hovers near my shoulder.

"No," I tell him with a certainty I've known for a long time.

* * *

The next morning as I enter the office building, a small podium with the agency logo and a few mics on it is set up, as if a press conference is about to happen.

"We're here from the *Sun*," one reporter says, approaching me and flashing his press tag. "We've heard there's going to be an announcement about alleged toxic waste dumping by ExGen. We know you're the agency representative on this case, Ms. Saeed."

"Don't you mean Mr. Malik?" Then again, he's left, so maybe I am it? "Um . . . please direct all questions to the press office." I sprint to the building.

Inside, I lean against Kevin's desk to catch my breath. "What's going on, Kev? Why are these reporters parked outside?"

Kevin is unperturbed by the commotion. "Oh, Miss Sana, don't worry. The commissioner is making an announcement later."

The elevator ride to my floor reminds me of the day Daniel and I got stuck. It sucks to be here in our empty office where Daniel is imprinted on everything. Daniel's side of the office is bare. I sit on his chair, which still holds the aroma of his citrus-and-musk aftershave. I breathe it in.

I can't be like this. I'll talk to Debra and ask to be moved back to my old desk. Even though they never found the culprit who wrote that note.

A big thick yellow file sits on my desk. The yellow sticky note on the front reads, *Open the encrypted files I sent you. All the instructions are in there.*

Damn. Daniel was here. I log on from my desk and click to read the email: *Sana, read this. The encryption password is Ainee's parents' home address with no caps or spaces.*

I type in Ainee's address, and voilà, the message opens on my computer.

Sana:

I left you all the lab results from the samples we collected (environmental enforcement has a copy). The results confirm what I suspected. ExGen is dumping a lot of these chemicals in the water in levels way above the regulated limit. With the implementation of the Clean Water Act, these coal plants are supposed to collect and haul the chemicals to a lined pool, but the expense of it outweighed any concerns they may have had.

If you look at the history of compliance, they've had issues with maintaining these pools, with their neglect leading to spills. Every time they have a massive rain event, they dump for two reasons:

1. They don't have to worry about liners malfunctioning.
2. They don't have to worry about detection limits due to the dilution.

I've talked to the AG's office. Also, there is an internal investigation being conducted on Marc and a few others involved, so please do not give them anything regarding the case.

I sit back, digesting this, and something behind my computer monitor catches my eye. A bouquet of yellow daisies. I hold one close to my nose.

Underneath the vase is a handwritten letter.

Salaam, Soni,

I know you love Persuasion so I will quote Austen. I must leave, uncertain of my fate, and if you had given me a look, or even affirmed that you do love me, it would have been easier to find a way to stay. But you chose to wear his ring. I can't fight a losing battle. I know exactly when to walk away. Even Austen couldn't have written a more tragic ending.

Who would have thought I'd ever trust someone enough to fall in love? Just admitting this as I write these words feels surreal. But I feel it with every cell of my being. How else could I memorize your face like I have—that mole on your left cheek, that line in the middle of your forehead that deepens when you're angry?

This is what they never tell you about love. It is the most exhilarating feeling in the world. Like a flame that starts in the pit of your stomach, and spreads, consuming you.

I can't stay. The only other person I've ever loved, besides you, is dying, and she wants me to go home with her.

I hope you'll be happy with Adam always.

I hear footsteps and feel someone's gaze. I turn to see who it is.

Brian, Marc's right-hand man, stands at the door. He taps on the table where my files are. "Hey, Sana, did you get the email?"

It's seven thirty AM on a Monday. Why is he here?

"Not yet. What email? Is Marc here?"

"Marc is busy. Um . . . I need you to hand over ExGen. It's been decided that I'm taking it back." He holds his hand out.

I stare at him. Does this rat think I'll give him the files without a fight? "The DAG and I are working on the discovery and the permit stay."

"Well, read the email and respond. Pronto." He huffs.

I swivel my chair to face him and give him the Bollywood mother-in-law glance-over. "I will. And if there'll be nothing else, please close the door on your way out."

He mutters something about insubordination and slams the door loud enough for all the mice in the building to run for cover.

* * *

DANIEL

Islamabad, Pakistan

Rebirth. That's how I pictured this trip—not just cathartic, not just a trip down memory lane, but a return to my roots. Unlike Ammi, I'm not dying, but the part of me born here has been dead for too long.

Since I've been back here, I've been cut off from my life back in the States. Part of it is deliberate, although I didn't plan on losing my phone at the airport. I miss Sana, though. Her smile, her eyes, and her coconut perfume. Every time I'm near any woman who smells like her, the scent triggers memories of that gentle upturn of her lips when she's about to break into a smile. And the way she plays with her locket. How she's kept it close to her heart, even after so many years.

Ammi's prognosis is dire, but at least she has an appetite. I'll take that. Better than in the U.S., where she stopped eating, making it harder to continue the chemo.

With Saleem around to watch over her, I have lots of spare time. I'm not used to sitting around, so I sign on with a refugee program. And begin my investigation into Soofia Auntie's denunciation.

You're najayaz.

It's not so much about being illegitimate—that stings, but I can handle it. I've risen above my past. It's the not-knowing that mauls my heart. And so, after confirming my birth family is still in the same neighborhood where I left them, I try to retrace my address from my memory.

Every city in Pakistan has its own rhythm, its own unique voice. Lahore with its history, food, culture, and tight corners. Karachi with its metropolitan vibe, a melting pot of new and old cities. And Islamabad has the beauty and the mountain backdrop and the new-city vibe, with its modern buildings, green parks, and hip cafés and eateries. It's not bustling like Karachi or historic like Lahore, but it has its own charm. Being here makes me realize that I have missed its sounds, its humanity, and its will to survive.

Maybe this is why Soofia and I never got along—we're too much alike. Too stubborn and angry to make peace. Even if it means depriving ourselves of the happiness that would have helped us get closure.

As soon as I leave the main city and enter the poorer neighborhood, the traffic piles on, and the cacophony of noise is jarring. The unpaved roads, a swarm of flies, and a strong stench of open sewer canal welcome me.

Dust from the unpaved road covers the Jeep I'm driving. This little town is busier than I remembered, but in twenty-six years, things have changed. Cell phone chimes and the sound of Bollywood songs from the nearby tea stalls and shops mix with the sounds of chatter from the bazaar.

I've dreamt of this place so many times. Now that I'm here, though, it's unreal. Faint memories of running around, playing in these dusty roads, fill my mind. Poverty is bitingly real when you've experienced the comforts of a developed country.

I drag the gear and shift the car into park. The little street that leads up to my house is too tight to fit a car. A moped that passes too close to me takes me by surprise.

The driver halts the moped and yells, "Shahri bhai?"

"Yes. And you are?" I say in Urdu.

"You don't recognize me?" he replies, also in Urdu, as he loosens the strap on his helmet.

When he cradles his helmet and runs a hand through his light-brown hair, I see the resemblance. Same square face and green eyes. This is my brother. My youngest sibling. He was just a baby when I left.

It's amazing how I don't feel the emotions I was expecting to feel. I don't feel that sense of hatred, only grief. Of not knowing him, of having let my anger get in the way of connecting with my other siblings.

I swallow and extend my hand, racking my brain to come up with his name.

"It's Faisal." He squeezes my hand and pats the back of his seat. "Come home with me."

Home. Is this home? When was the last time anything felt like home? It's people, not places, that make a home. This is an epiphany that comes too late, as I hold on to my life while my younger brother drives over another bump on the brick road.

He stops in front of a house I thought only existed in my memories. It's bigger than the homes around it. The tamarind-brown exterior with beige walls gave it the name Kathai haveli. He parks in front of the iron gate. It's still white, with rust seeping through the chipping paint.

I stand at the threshold of the house. Green patches of mold discolor the bottoms of the walls.

My nomad heart is anchored to this house, this place. And the vault of memories that I've tightly locked reappear. Of me running through these streets, having so little, yet being content.

Faisal shouts, "He's here!" then takes me inside to a modest living area and seats me on an old, patched sofa.

The dingy walls and chipped floor tiles tell me this living room has seen better days. The furniture is dusty. Despite my grudges, it hits me: I could have helped them, could have sent them money.

Then I see her.

Amma. My mother, the woman I spent all my life hating. She opens the front door and rushes in my direction. She's wearing a shalwar kameez. With the corner of her dupatta, which is wrapped around her head like a scarf, she wipes her tears. She sits next to me and cradles my face in her hands. I want to retreat, yet I don't. Her hands feel rough. Hours of kitchen work and cleaning have taken a toll on her. Without recent pictures to compare her to, she seems like a shadow from the early days.

And then she holds me close to her. She smells of my childhood—of warm spices, as if she's just finished cooking. I have so many questions, but right now none of them matter.

Faisal brings me chai and introduces me to my three younger brothers and my only sister, Ayesha. The whole family gathers around and is so impressed with my life and all I have achieved.

When they are all busy making arrangements for dinner, Amma and I get a moment of quiet. She asks me with a slight crease to her forehead, "Why are you really here, puttar?"

Of course she knows—she held me before anyone else, and she knows things I may hide from the world. I steeple my hands together and avoid her eyes. "I had to confirm something I heard about . . . the way I was born."

"Not this bakwas again." She leans back and breaks into a humorless laugh. "That you were born out of wedlock is a nasty rumor spread by my own brother-in-law. His poor ego was hurt by how I could love another man over him."

My mind reels from this news. My uncle was a vengeful man, but spreading malicious rumors was beneath even him.

"I had to elope with your father, but we had our nikah even before I ran away. I had gone to your grandfather with my husband, and he had refused to acknowledge our marriage. I had no choice. Then you were born a few weeks early, premature. That just made things worse. I have a certificate from the doctor of your premature birth and that you stayed in the hospital a few weeks after you were born." She lets out a long exhale and searches my face.

There are two sides of me warring: one that wants to believe her because she is my mother, and another, the inner skeptic, the one who's taught me to be wary and helped me survive.

She senses my struggle as I run my hand over my face.

At this, she squeezes my shoulder. "I can give you the papers, but that seed of doubt has been planted in your brain, and maybe nothing I say will matter, but my Allah and I know you were born of a nikah. This vicious rumor was spread in America, where I couldn't defend myself from your scornful uncle."

I squeeze my temples and then tell her, "Uncle was bitter. I just never thought he'd stoop to this level."

"Oh, he absolutely could. My poor sister suffered because of him. I know she spared me that fate, but at a very high price. You see, your grandfather would have killed me and your father if Shahida didn't marry Sibte." Ammi wipes her eyes. "This is why when she couldn't have more kids, I gave you to her. She promised a better life for you, son. I know you don't trust me. But I wish you would."

I nod and give her a wry smile. "Give me some time." It's the best answer I can come up with in these circumstances. This wound I've carried has festered for years and won't heal overnight.

She smiles and squeezes my hand. "Okay, puttar. How is Shahida doing now? Any better?"

"Not too good. This is also why I am here. She wants you to come back to the house and be with her. That house is as much yours as hers, she said."

I watch her wipe off her tears and rush to pack.

Later Faisal shows me all the newspaper clippings and old photos of me before I became Daniel. They've kept all these parts of me close to their hearts, while I've tried to push them away.

Love is holding on, and sometimes when you are in something more than love, in Ishq, it's also about letting go.

My mother letting me go was love. And now, surrounded by my siblings I feel adored.

I am home.

CHAPTER THIRTY-FOUR

SANA

The headline from a week ago still haunts me: *EXGEN HALTS PLANS TO EXPAND*. It should feel like a triumph, but somehow, it doesn't.

It's not because my entire office thinks I'm a rat, but because even people like Kevin, alongside whom I've worked with for most of my career here, look at me differently. For an agency whose motto is to put people and the environment first, its members don't seem to agree. But I suppose it's a violation of the trust they've put in me somehow.

Ainee texts me. *Are you playing hooky again?*

I tap my thumb on my phone before texting her back. I've been on unpaid leave after Daniel left and the ExGen case wrapped up. Marc and Brian both took plea deals and named their coconspirators at ExGen. ExGen agreed to hefty fines, to halt expansion, and to remediate the damage over the next few years.

Today is supposed to be my first day back at work. I should have been there an hour ago. But I can't seem to bring myself to go.

My phone's ring startles me.

Ainee starts talking as soon as I pick up. "Where are you?" she asks.

"I'm getting ready to go to work," I tell her, and reluctantly start to pick out my most confident outfit for facing all the speculation.

"Good, I'm glad! How's your mother?"

"Ammi is home. She's doing well."

"Alhamdulillah! It's good to hear that Soofia Auntie is home."

"Ainee, tell me I'm not stupid to quit. I just can't continue working there, with them looking at me like I'm going to put a knife in their back the second they turn. I can't, not without Daniel," I blurt out, and realize I shouldn't have said that. I seem so weak.

Ainee huffs. "Nah, I gave my two weeks' notice at work today too, earlier than I wanted to, and I'm not even in your department. I can't face the weird side-eyes either. They think since I'm best friends with you, I'm the coconspirator. Talk about paranoia."

"Yeah, I don't know what I'm going to do after this; looking for a job in this market is going to suck. But I'm going to graduate soon, and hopefully something better will come along. I may have to move out earlier from the apartment than I wanted to, but maybe it's for the best. Ammi and Zia need me to be close to them now."

After we hang up, I put on an off-white silk blouse, black pleated long skirt, and matching chiffon scarf. Once I'm dressed and outside, I start Mirchi with a prayer and then mutter, "I hope I'm not making a mistake."

Mirchi groans in a familiar way and lets out a sputtering exhale. *The mistake was to let that sweet-ass man go and be stuck here with me. This job and you are going nowhere.*

At work, most people ignore me. And then there are the awkward smiles and wordless nods. The only person who is even close to friendly is Melissa.

I turn on my computer and type and delete the email a few times before I hit send.

To Whom It May Concern:

Please consider this my resignation, as per the procedure set forth in the Human Resources policy.

Thank you for your consideration,

Sana Saeed

Dread fills my stomach. What have I done? How will I help my family? Should I retract it? I swipe the nervous sweat from my forehead and pace the office. There's no sign Daniel was ever here.

An ache spreads through me, and I grab an empty box and start filling it with my things. Once I've emptied my office, I stop by Melissa's desk to say good-bye.

Melissa is busy looking at kaftan websites when I tap on her shoulder. She swings her chair and puts a hand to her chest. "Oh, thank God! You scared me."

She clicks the website closed, then points to the cart with my boxes. "Moving again?"

I give her a humorless smile and shrug. "Yes, for good."

"Those sons of bit—" She stops herself when someone walks by, then lowers her voice. "Did they fire you? Even after that leech Brian confessed?"

I sit down on the chair next to her. "Confessed to what?"

Her face changes color. "You didn't know? To writing the note to scare you off."

My heartbeats drum in my ear. I always had a feeling that Marc and Brian wanted me to hand over the case, after I started digging more than they'd liked. But that hateful, putrid note was too much—because Brian actually felt that way toward me.

"That's vile. But no, I'm quitting," I tell her. I feel the need to get out for air, to escape this place filled with bad memories.

"Oh, hon. I'm so sorry. Good luck with everything. And call me if you need anything."

She swings her chair back to her screen and waves good-bye as if she's just read the weather report to me. I push the cart with my belongings out of the building and wonder how the hell I'm going to break the news to Ammi.

* * *

The weeks pass in a haze. I thought being away from my workplace memories of Daniel would diminish. I also thought having Ammi healthier and at home would make me happy.

I was wrong.

Even if I ignore the emptiness in the pit of my stomach, my sleepless nights have taken their toll. I stare at the dark circles underneath my eyes and wonder if I should finally start watching TikTok makeup tutorials.

All my emails and texts to Daniel have gone unanswered. I've thought about calling Saleem, but I don't know what to say. Maybe it's better this way. If Daniel and I were meant to be together, it would've happened. I think.

Now I'm losing Ainee to Haroon. Back at our apartment, boxes surround her. All her belongings are scattered around, clothes dangling everywhere.

"It's a mess in here." I pick up some socks and T-shirts that have been tossed into a corner.

She glances up and swipes the hair covering her face. "I can't find the lease we signed for the Williamsburg apartment." She pats the floor next to her. "Sit here. I need to ask you for a huge favor."

My eyes widen. "O . . . kay, you're scaring me a little."

"It's about the move." Her gaze fixates on my face, as if she's trying to gauge my reaction.

Ainee never hesitates to speak her mind. Her attitude now makes me think she's about to ask me for something big.

"So, you know how my mother sold you our Scarsdale house? I kind of need to buy it back—or lease it or something."

"I haven't even opened that damn envelope; I've been too busy with all the other crap. Why do you want the house?"

"Haroon's job is giving him a huge promotion, and we have to move up to Westchester. We're excited but stressed. My mother-in-law will want us to move in with her if she finds out we don't have a place. So I want to get a place, sign the lease, *then* tell them, so she can't pressure us to move in with them. I have to cancel the Williamsburg lease regardless."

I want to help, but the house is in both our names, and I can't lease it to her without Daniel's signature on the lease paperwork. Even if I let them live there without a lease, I'd want to ask him first. I don't want him or Shahida Auntie to ever think I took advantage. But being that he's completely shut me out, I have no idea how to have this conversation with him.

"I emailed Saleem and Daniel last night and haven't heard," Ainee says. "I need to know soon." She dusts her hands and gets up. "I don't know what to do."

"Maybe Shahida Auntie's health is keeping them busy? What would you like me to do?" I raise my eyebrows.

"Call him again, please?"

"I've been trying." I swing away, because I don't want her to see the tears collecting in the corners of my eyes. It's amazing how Ainee *now* wants me to talk to Daniel—when she needs something.

Ainee shakes her head and then says, "You look like you're in mourning. All you need is a white sari, and you will be the perfect Bollywood grieving widow."

CHAPTER THIRTY-FIVE

SANA

Moving back home is bittersweet. Being desi, I don't take moving home with Zia and Ammi as a defeat, but it sucks that at this phase of my life, my mother has to take me in instead of me trying to help her out.

Ammi, though, is elated. When she found out that I'm moving home, she started cooking and gossiping, prepping for my return. It's good to see that life is somewhat normal in terms of her health. She's asked me a few times why Adam hasn't called on her, and I've told her he's away. But today I have to tell her the truth.

Mirchi doesn't betray me and gets me to Ammi's in one piece. As I park and walk up the front path, the smell of biryani and curry hits me.

Zia opens the door and yells, "Baji! Ammi, look, baji is here."

"Ammi, salaam. Are you okay?" I close the door with my hip, my hands full of boxes and a bag of McDonald's for Zia, adding whiffs of french fries and a fish sandwich to the other spicy aromas in the house. "Teddy bear, I got you McDonald's."

Zia grabs the brown bag out of my hands.

I ruffle his hair. "Hey, you okay? Have you been behaving with Ammi?"

"I missed you," Zia says, before he shoves a few fries into his mouth. "Guess what? I got into that school."

"Building Bridges?" Finally, some good news! "That's awesome! Where's Ammi?"

"I'm here." Ammi climbs down the stairs, carrying a package in her hands. "Yeah, they called me. Fees all paid. A scholarship or something, they said. We have to go in next week." Her face isn't beaming with pride, though. Strange. This is where she'd usually say she's thankful.

"Everything okay, Ammi? You're feeling all right?" I squeeze her hand.

The crease on her forehead deepens. "Yeah, I need to talk to you about something." She turns to my brother. "Zia, Sana and I have to talk for a few minutes. Can you go to your room?"

Ammi holds my hand, and we move to the round kitchen table. She is never this intense unless something serious is bothering her. I worry about her health, but I cannot keep lying.

Sitting across from her, I let the words tumble out before I lose my nerve. "Ammi, Adam and I—we're not together. I've been meaning to tell you." I hold her hand and avoid her probing gaze.

"I know. Adam had been calling and checking up on me, and then he stopped, did not return my calls. Rana tried calling him, but he didn't pick up. I don't know what is up with you two, but I had Zia's trust redrafted to just include you and Rana. I just think it's better if things stay within the family . . ." She sighs. "Relationships aren't what they used to be."

"Please, Ammi, try to understand . . ." I plead with folded hands.

She pulls her chair close. "This came in the mail today. I don't know why Shahida sent it here instead of your apartment, but here." She hands me a package.

I look at the return address. Islamabad, Pakistan.

"What is it?" I raise my eyebrows, questioningly.

"Letters, written by Shahri to you. Not that it matters now. They're gone but still won't leave you alone. I've been meaning to talk to you about something, though . . ." She avoids my gaze.

The silence hangs between us. "Ammi?"

"Do you remember the night I got sick?" She leans forward in her chair, the lines on her forehead deepening.

"How can I forget?"

Her voice is stoic. "I was upset because Shahri and Saleem came over to ask for your hand in marriage."

They *what*?

Pausing, she heaves a long sigh. "I refused, and told him to never bring this up again. Then Shahida called me and told me I was the reason for your unhappiness. She said, 'Sana will betray you, because she loves Shahri too much.'"

My back straightens. "Shahida Auntie said those exact words, Ammi?" I gaze into her eyes intently.

She scratches her nose. This is Ammi's tell for when she's nervous. "Well, it was implied. So I showed her. I *knew* I could make you choose me over him."

Is she saying what I think she's saying?

I swallow and try to keep my voice even. "Did . . . you do this to yourself, Ammi? Please tell me that what I'm thinking is not what you *actually* did?"

Heat rushes to her face, and her breathing is quick. "Yes, I injected myself with double insulin. But it was a timed dose. I had told Rana earlier I wasn't feeling well, so she was on alert as well."

I cradle my head in my hands. My mother is blind in her prejudices, but this stupidity could have actually gotten her killed.

My hands quiver from anger, and my face heats. "You could have *died*, Ammi. Then what good would this stupid feud be? Do you hate him so much? What did Daniel ever do to you, Ammi? All that man has seen is abandonment and hatred—from his uncle, his parents, and now me. He left without a single word of complaint against you, Ammi. For the hate you spew against him, he hasn't reciprocated even a tiny ounce. Uff, my Allah, what have I done . . ."

Ammi shakes her head. "I hate Shahri because *he* is the reason the argument started between your father and his uncle. Your father would always tell Sibte to be nice to the poor orphan boy. And his uncle, the arrogant, egotistical ass, didn't like it. Were you not there when we were evicted? And yet you were choosing them over us. Visiting Shahida when I told you not to . . . the next step would've been an elopement between you two. And then, Allah kasam, how would I face my friends in the community and their gossip?"

My mother is obviously too far gone in her rage. "Ammi, you've been blinded in anger. Shahri is not like his uncle—you want to blame him for his uncle's actions, when he was a victim of that wretched man's actions as well."

I hold my head in hands and say in a defeated tone, "I love him. I have forgiven Shahri. I've also forgiven his uncle, because he's gone. Carrying this burden of hatred is too much, Ammi. The Prophet forgave his beloved uncle's murderer; you can't even forgive an innocent man. Think about this, Ammi—don't let this hatred blind you to reason."

Ammi slaps the table. "If I'm blind in rage, you're blind too—in Shahri's ishq. You cannot see that a good man like Adam doesn't come along every day. You are engaged to him. Go back to him—"

"I *was* engaged to him. I couldn't do this to Adam."

"You're acting like a petulant child. Ishq vishq is temporary. I'll talk to Adam's father." She puts out a hand to squeeze my shoulder.

I take a long intake of breath, hoping to calm the anger rushing through my veins. My mother is capable of rational thought. Why can't she see this? See that the man who is the cause of our misery is dead and his reticent wife on the verge of death?

She twists the ring that she still wears on her right ring finger, a reminder of my father's that she carries with her every single day. Being a widow at forty must've been rough. And she never felt the need to remarry. That's love. But with this love comes grief. The grief that's thriving, and manifests in so many ways.

I hold her hand on my shoulder and say, "There's not a day when I don't miss Abba. And yes, it's unfair we lost him early. But we can't look to blame just them for his death. I know you still grieve him, and keep that hatred alive like his memory. But forgiving Shahida and her family will not diminish your love. In fact, Abba would've forgiven Shahri too, if he were alive."

"You are out of your mind, Sana." Ammi retreats her hand and looks away. Before she breaks her gaze, I see the drops of tears in the corners of her eyes.

"Ammi, please, try to understand."

"The day I forget about Sibte and what he did to us will be the day I stop living . . ."

I jolt upright; my vision is blurry because the warm tears fog my glasses. I fumble with my keys and tell her before darting away, "I can't with you right now, Ammi. I chose you. Daniel told me he loved me, and I stared blankly at him when every single pore in my body was screaming to say the words back to him. You know why I didn't? Because I chose you. I always choose you."

Before I leave, I hug Zia and kiss his forehead. "Hey, you take good care of Ammi until I see you again. I need to go back to Ainee's to clear my head, but please call me if anything happens."

He wipes my kiss off. "Okay, but Ammi is fine now, right, baji? I don't want her in the hospital."

"I don't either. And tell her I love her, despite everything. I just need to be away from here for a bit." I bite back a choking sob and swing away.

Daniel fought for us. He swallowed his pride and went to my mother's door, knowing full well how that conversation would go. Yet he never complained or said a bad word about Ammi to me.

How could I let such a person walk away?

* * *

Back at the apartment, Ainee's still packing. "Salaam, habibi. I didn't think I'd see you back so soon. And with no food in tow—have a fight with mama bear?" She sneezes as she pulls out another box from underneath the sofa. It's books. She scrunches her face and dumps them in the trash can.

My insides protest. "Ainee, that's a crime; please don't throw away books! And yeah, Ammi and I argued. But in my defense, she did something incredibly dangerous."

"What, did she fake her death or something? Desi moms are drama queens, you know that. Haven't you seen that movie where Mahira's mother puts a knife against her neck to prevent her from marrying Fawad? She will come around eventually. Haroon's mom once threatened to never eat again unless he stopped seeing me. She came around." She shrugs and slides the box of books in my direction. "Sometimes it's good to purge. Start new." She pauses, then comes to sit next to me. "And if you can't, go to him. Collect the pieces of your ego and your lost backbone and tell him how you feel. Otherwise, as they say, you're just spitting in the wind."

"What? Did you just read *Idioms for Idiots* recently? But I have no money, Ainee. I have to think twice about going to Long Island, let alone Islamabad."

"Nothing good in life is easy. Let's have some tea and brainstorm." She goes to the kitchen and starts the kettle.

I can't ask my mother or sister for money. They will completely disown me if I even attempt it. Ainee is stretched thin, between the move and her wedding. I log on to my bank account. My balance is $200.25.

Then I check my emails, and one from HR catches my eye. A 401(k) transfer.

"I think I have an idea."

"Oh, Sana, no. I ain't setting up a GoFundMe. Or robbing a bank, just so you know."

I squeeze her shoulder. "I'll take money out of my retirement account. Since I'm moving jobs, I have to transfer my 401(k) anyway. I'll have to pay penalties, but what the heck—"

"You do love him." She smiles as she sips her tea.

I jab her in the ribs, paying her back for the million times she's done it to me. "I do—and always have. Now, help me find some cheap tickets, woman."

* * *

DANIEL

It's been a couple of weeks since I brought my birth mother to Ammi. Now the sisters can be together. It's nice to have both my families close, but it's getting harder to find excuses to avoid the relentless, twice-multiplied matchmaking that's the center of their world. The emotional blackmail alone is torture.

Instead of getting ready for another wedding/rishta setup, I'm out running.

I wonder about my birth mother's motivations for all these setups. Is it to brag about her American passport-holder son? Or is she hoping to climb the social ladder by marrying me off to a rich girl? Or is it something about having a son who's single at thirty-four, the talk of the town? Maybe it's some type of guilt to marry me off as a social obligation. In my heart, I know this has got to be more than her wanting me to be happily settled. Or maybe I'm just a cynic.

The girls she picks are all pretty, well educated, and from good families, but no matter how much I say, "I'm not looking," or, "I don't want to get married at all," Amma doesn't get the message.

I sneak into the house through the back door.

My mother is outside my door waiting.

"Puttar, you're not ready? Remember, we're all invited tonight." She fixes her sari and points to my sweaty state.

"Amma, you should go. I don't want to delay you." I pivot past her to my room and grab a towel. "Have a good time. I'm going to shower."

She scrunches her face disapprovingly. "I told everyone you're accompanying us; we will wait. No one is expecting us to be on time anyway."

I let out an exasperated breath. "I don't feel like socializing. Can I skip this time?"

She shakes her head. "Whatever you want. After all, I have no rights over you . . . who am I, anyway?" Her eyes fill with tears.

Dammit. "Let me shower and get ready—but please, I'll drive myself. You should go with the driver and the rest of the family."

* * *

Of course, they wait for me, and I get dragged to the wedding in the car along with the rest of my family. The driver drops us in front of the banquet hall, and Amma holds my hand and leads me inside.

A huge chandelier illuminates the hall. The chairs have golden bows tied in the back, and the off-white tablecloths are decorated with a round motif in gold beadwork topped with rose-and-jasmine centerpieces.

A server in a white shalwar kameez meanders through the crowd with kebabs. The air smells of barbecue, fresh roses, and expensive perfume.

My birth mother mingles while I distract myself with my phone. A tap on my shoulder pulls me to attention. I raise my head. My mother is in front of me with her arm around a petite girl.

Amma says, "Son, this is Zaynab. Why don't you two sit and chat?" Amma raises her eyebrows and gestures toward an empty table.

Zaynab and I endure the most awkward silence ever. She and I have nothing in common, and it reminds me that my mother really knows very little about me. Zaynab barely looks eighteen. The part of my brain where I kept my hopes and dreams—and Sana—is now corrupt. Perhaps forever.

"So . . ." Zaynab flicks her hair and asks, "What is it you do?"

I stifle a yawn. "I work for the NGO Lawyers for Peace. They help refugees through a shelter set up close to the border. I spend most weekdays there helping out, whether it's talking to the checkpoint officers or being a driver or teacher. Someti—"

She's lost interest and examines her manicure.

I switch gears. "Also, I have no interest in getting married right now. It's nothing against you, but I don't want to lead you on. Now I'll smile because my mother's looking at us"—I wave at Amma—"but this is only to make her happy in hopes she'll leave me alone."

The girl is horrified. Her dark eyes widen, and her cheeks turn red. She curses me in Punjabi. "Just because you're rich and handsome, you think you can humiliate me like this—*sala*."

She picks up her clutch and mobile and marches away.

My mother looks at me with questioning eyes.

I shrug.

I was an ass to Zaynab. But I've thwarted any further attempts at a second meeting and dissolved any hopes of romantic entanglements. I don't care if she hates me for the rest of my life. In fact, I hope she gossips and tells all of Islamabad society what a jerk I am. Hopefully, that will end Amma's endless matchmaking.

I loosen the collar of my sherwani, straighten my back, and smile at my approaching mother.

She shakes her head and mutters under her breath, "Who is the chudail who did this to you? I'd like to meet her and ask her to give me my son back."

I run a hand through my hair and deflect. "There is no witch, Amma."

"I have a few years on you son, and I have been there and made the same mistakes as you." She lifts her glass of mango lassi in an I-challenge-you-to-lie-to-my-face gesture.

Zaynab is back, and approaching us with her family. I try to read the vibes, because I'm afraid her brothers might be upset by how I ignored her. Except they're all smiling as they walk in our direction.

Zaynab's father slaps my shoulder and speaks in Urdu. "Salaam. You should visit us, son. Zaynab has told us a lot of great things about you."

My mouth is agape. I glance at Zaynab, who hides behind her father.

"InshAllah, soon." My mother jumps in and gives them the fakest smile ever. They talk about getting together, and I try to make eye contact with Zaynab to say, *What the hell?* She avoids me just as much as her family hounds us.

Amma finally bids them good-night and asks the driver to bring the car up front. Once we're away from Zaynab's family, she says, "That was a close call. I'm so happy things went well. Keep next Friday available."

I make a mental note to not be available.

* * *

Working at the refugee center is hard work. Not the reviewing-documents kind of work but labor intensive, helping to build shelter homes in abandoned buildings and being anything they need me to be during the day.

On any given day I could be a laborer, teacher, cleaner, or a handyman. It's tiring but fulfilling. I'm truly needed here, and it keeps my mind busy. I'm so tired at night that I barely have time to return calls. But Saleem has called a few times, so I make it a point to call him when I sit down to eat at night.

"Salaam. Everything okay?" I ask as soon as he picks up.

"Yeah. I was wondering if you're going to be home Thursday night as usual?" His voice is casual, which eases the tension.

I dip the hard loaf into the watery lentil soup and reply while chewing. "No. I'm not planning on being there before Saturday."

The mosquitoes buzz near my ear and distract me while Saleem speaks. "Ammi needs to go to the hospital, and I was hoping you could be there to help."

I squash a mosquito with my right hand and answer. "I'll move things around but will leave before the evening, is that okay? I'm trying to avoid Zaynab's family." I give up on the bread and decide to just down the lentil soup.

"Are you going to live like a darvesh? Honestly, are you punishing yourself for what happened with Sana? Because I will tell you, it's not your fault. Talk to her. Or forgive her and move on."

"No. She is engaged to Adam. I've made my case to her, and to her family. I have to respect their decision. Can we not talk about this—"

Saleem cuts me off. "What if she realized her mistake? Would you forgive her? What if she came to you right now and apologized?"

I spit out the watery soup and chuckle. "She couldn't say the three words back to me. I hardly think her to be the type to jump on a plane to apologize."

"For someone who's given up on her, you're really bitter. Okay, Mr. Darvesh. See you Thursday." He hangs up abruptly.

Strange man.

* * *

SANA

What the hell did I get myself into? I've pulled thousands of dollars from my retirement account and bought a nonrefundable ticket to Islamabad, a place I've never been.

The airline agent places my passport and boarding pass in my hand. "Boarding starts in an hour at gate ten."

I told Rana about the trip last night. She clutched her dupatta and paced for a while. It was late at night, Farooq was away on a business trip, her kids and Zia were already asleep. Zia and I were spending a night at her house because I wanted to be away from my mother.

"I love him. I thought I could be like you and Farooq. Learn to love Adam. But I had not foreseen Daniel coming into my life.

Can you believe he went to Ammi to beg for me? And even after she humiliated him, he still came to see her in the hospital." I swallowed a lump, and my voice broke. "He told me he loved me . . . and I let him walk out that hospital door."

Rana wiped my tears and sat on the chair next to me. A breeze that carried the smell of gardenias floated through the open cracks of her large kitchen window, along with the sounds of summer—cicadas and that faint sound of someone riding a motorbike.

She held me and let me cry, then she cradled my face. "If it weren't for the fact that he got Zia into that school, I'd still hate him. I will talk to Ammi, tell him how he's saved your life, and now helped Zia. Maybe she'll see that even though he didn't do all those evil things to us years ago, he's trying to repent for his evil uncle."

"Daniel did what?" I held her elbow to contain my surprise.

"Yeah. Farooq got a call from Zia's school before he left. They wanted to confirm Zia's attendance in the fall. The principal didn't mean to spill that Daniel had paid for Zia and that he had worked pro bono for some of the volunteers who work there. It made me think, then. He knew you were with Adam, yet he still did that." She patted my hand. "He *must* love you. And what Farooq and I have is wonderful, but what you two have—who am I kidding, have *always* had—is something written in your qismet. *He* is your qismet."

The weight of what she'd said hit my heart—and hard. Daniel cared enough that he'd gotten Zia into the school.

Rana slipped a weighty envelope, filled with cash, into my hand then.

"I don't need this. I took out—" I paused. Maybe not best to tell her I'd taken out the money from my 401(k) to fund this trip; I wasn't in the mood for a lecture.

Before heading to security, I stop and give Ainee a hug and whisper, "Tell me I'm not stupid to do this."

"Yes, you are. But if he's not answering your calls, this is the only way. Otherwise, you'll always wonder what could've been. Plus I'm sick of you being Ms. Mopey." She dries her tears with the back of her hand. "Now, go get the grump. And if he's already snagged, at least get him to sign the lease papers for me." Ainee smiles through her tears and waves me away.

* * *

Islamabad, Pakistan

Islamabad International Airport is full of people waving at their loved ones. I look around but see no familiar faces. I don't know if anyone's here to receive me. Saleem knows I'm arriving today, but maybe he's busy with his mom. Maybe I'm not a priority to anyone because I decided on a whim to come. I sit on a bench and move the luggage cart to my side while I dig out their address.

"You know, someone could just take this luggage cart and walk away. You'd never know," a familiar voice booms.

Saleem! Alhamdulillah. What a relief.

He smiles at me and grabs the luggage cart.

I burst into tears.

Saleem looks at me, probably wondering why I'm reduced to tears at the mere sight of him saying hello.

"I'm sorry to put you through this," I tell Saleem. "I hope you didn't go to much trouble."

Saleem slides next to me and gives me a charming smile. "You are no trouble. You know that, Sana." He runs a hand through his hair and glances at me. "How does Adam feel about you coming here? I know Ainee said you needed some papers signed, quickly?"

"Adam and I are not together," I say. But how do I tell him that I've left everything I hold dear to be here, and I can't go back without seeing Daniel and telling him how I feel?

But maybe I'm too late? After all, every relationship has a threshold, an expiration date when we give up, stop hoping, and move on.

Saleem signals someone in the small cluster of people outside the airport. Two men dash toward him to assist with the luggage cart.

A large black Mercedes pulls up, and a uniformed man with a thick mustache opens the front door for Saleem and then the back door for me.

"I haven't told him," Saleem tells me succinctly. "He's away until Thursday." He avoids my gaze and tells the driver to take it slow on the bumpy road in heavily accented Urdu.

My heart twists. It's like the hide-and-seek game Shahri and I used to play: He comes after me, then I chase him halfway around the world. Then I get here, and he's gone somewhere else. I change the subject. "How is Shahida Auntie?"

"She's the same. Happier, though. She's eating, which is a good thing."

The thought of seeing Shahida Auntie excites me. Maybe, even if Daniel wants nothing to do with me, I can still see her.

We pull up at Saleem's office. As he opens the door, he tells the driver in Urdu, "Please drop her off at home."

He's leaving me alone? I panic a bit. "Where are you off to?"

"I have to finish something at work. I'll see you later tonight."

He gets out, then turns around and leans into the vehicle, his forehead pinched.

My heart jumps to my throat. What's next?

"You remember my mother's sister is Shahri's birth mom. She's old-fashioned and a little blunt, but she has a good heart." He smiles awkwardly and walks off.

My shoulders drop.

Saleem just told me—and not so subtly—that Daniel's mom is a typical Bollywood mother-in-law. I have the urge to turn back around but I don't have an alternative plan. In fact, I'm here without a plan at all, other than to find Daniel. What kind of a grown-ass woman comes to a foreign country without a backup plan?

The driver snakes the car through miles of heavy traffic before arriving at a huge house that could be straight out of *Architectural Digest*. It's a British-era off-white home with tall columns and a wrap-around balcony that spans most of the second floor of the house. The thing that's the most striking and totally smells and looks like big money is the expansive manicured gardens. The tall pine trees around the grounds are green and well maintained. Vibrant flowers lining the fence are in bloom. Sweet jasmine blossoms, hibiscus, and frangipani tickle my nose with their fresh scents. Lush tropical flowers and tall trees provide the perfect setting for an outdoor party—or a wedding.

When we were young, Shahri talked about this home and about how most of the family weddings were held outdoors to accommodate the hundreds that were usually part of such gatherings. It feels special to see this house, and to see parts of his life I didn't know as well in America.

Sentries stand on either side of a gate that opens as the car approaches. A long, semicircular driveway leads to the main house.

At the entrance, the driver opens my door and then gets my luggage.

I fix my hijab in the rearview mirror and put on a fresh coat of lip gloss.

The doorman opens the front door, and the driver carries my luggage upstairs while the doorman ushers me into an ornate room the size of a ballroom. Every wall is adorned with landscapes. The sofa has detailed mahogany trimmings. Freshly cut roses in a cut-crystal vase embellish the scallop-top coffee table.

A middle-aged woman pushes a tea cart, and the smell of freshly fried samosas wafts through the room. She sits by the table and gestures to the silver teapot. "Can I pour you some tea?" She doesn't say another word. Instead, she sits and quietly makes tea. Her clothes are mismatched. She's wearing flip-flops, and a long dupatta obscures half her uncombed hair while strands stick out from the sides. She smells of fried onions and curry.

A stern voice thunders through the room. "Bua. I asked you to give tea and leave. You may go now."

I turn to see who it is. The impressive voice doesn't match the woman's skinny frame. She wears a beautifully embroidered shalwar kameez, a matching shawl that wraps around her arms, and a chiffon hijab.

"Salaam. You must be Sana." She sits across from me and looks me up and down a few times. "You look exhausted." She calls the woman again. "Bua, after she's done eating, please show her to her room so she can freshen up."

"Thank you for your kindness, but can you show me to Shahida Auntie?" I better not ask her about Daniel.

"She's sleeping. She's not taking visitors. We have to be very careful with her and keep her room sanitized." She picks up a cup and pours some tea. Her eyes fix on me, and she heaves a sigh, as if she's disappointed in my appearance.

My nails dig into my palms. "Is it possible to see her at some point today?"

"Beti," she enunciates in Urdu. "Why don't you freshen up and shower, and we will take it from there." She cocks an eyebrow and takes a sip of her tea, then picks up a plate of cookies to offer me. "Have some. These are sugar-free."

"Thanks so much, but I'm not that hungry. I'm sorry, I must have missed the introductions. Are you her cousin?"

"No. I'm her sister, Zahida."

My heart drops into my stomach. Shit.

Daniel's birth mother is direct, all right, and she clearly hates me. Maybe hate is a strong word. But she knows about me. Does she know that Daniel loves me and my mother rejected him? Zahida regards me head to toe again.

I decide I will be like Daniel; I will just lay it out and be honest with her. But before I form the words, she lets out a long, exasperated breath, then says, "My son that I have just reunited with has turned into a dervish, given up on his family, and treats rishtas like plague. Because of you. Have you come here to gloat? Why can't you let him be?"

So this is the consensus. That somehow I'm here to rob Daniel of his sanity, when it's the opposite. But I can't let my vanity cloud my judgment. I lock my gaze with her and say, "Auntie, Daniel has talked about you most of his life and not in a pleasant way, and even though he never said it explicitly, I know he loved you so much. He was constantly at war with himself to write to you. In his heart he believed that despite you giving him up, you loved him. Sometimes, as we both know, things aren't always how they seem." I take a breath. "I had thought it was wise to choose the path of least resistance. Get engaged to another, make Ammi and my family happy. That was until I saw Daniel. I love Daniel—so much so that I'm here, leaving everything I hold dear behind. Before today, I'd barely traveled to another state without my family, let alone across continents."

Zahida stays quiet for a minute, as if she's weighing her words, her eyes never leaving my face. When she finally speaks, her voice is stern. "Your mother accused me and my innocent son. Do you know Islamabad society? If there was any truth to that rumor, my son wouldn't be getting rishtas from the most prestigious families. It was a rumor started by my scorned brother-in-law, who couldn't take it that I left him. So I faced the same dilemmas as you, and I made the decision that haunted me and my kids for the rest of my life. My life is a cautionary tale, but I love my son too much. Even though I have no faith in impulse-driven things like love."

"Sibte Uncle was capable of that and much worse. But please believe me when I say that I love your son, and there has never been a time I haven't. Impulsive as it may have been to come here, it wasn't easy. I'm not even sure if my mother will ever want to see me again."

"She will. Ammis are all dramatic, but eventually, if she's anything like me, she will see that her happiness is linked to yours." Zahida shrugs. "And I know my son, and know his happiness is linked to yours. Even if I am not convinced that you deserve him."

My heart lifts with hope. "I will do anything."

She raises an eyebrow. "I wouldn't be so hasty to commit to what I'm about to suggest."

CHAPTER THIRTY-SIX

DANIEL

The plan was for me to meet Ammi and Saleem at the hospital, where we would discuss palliative care with her oncologist, and then drop them home and return to work. Saleem called me at the last minute to meet him at home.

The sun is setting in golden hues as I approach the house. The tall trees have twinkling lights wrapped around them. As the house appears from behind the lights, it becomes evident the balconies have lights wrapped around their angular edges as well. Then I see my uncle's Bentley, and it becomes certain that something is going on.

I park the Jeep and rush inside. The whole house is decorated as if there's a wedding party in progress. I hear my uncle and his wife yelling instructions to the staff about food. What did I miss?

Faisal, my younger brother, catches me by the wrist and gestures toward my room upstairs. "I'm so glad you're here. Amma told me to make sure you change and come to the main dining area as soon as possible."

I snap my hand away. "What the hell is going on here?"

His phone beeps. He puts a hand to the mic and tells me to hurry up. Then he says a loud salaam and swings in the direction of the chatter in the main living room.

Whatever this is, I do need to shower after the long drive in the ninety-degree heat. I lock my bedroom door. There's a note pinned on the mirror. It says *Open me* in Saleem's chicken-scratch handwriting. How the hell do doctors prescribe anything with this shitty lettering?

Pls wear the clothes we've left for you on the bed.

Your mother wants her mother's ring back, since you've obviously given up on marrying, so make sure to bring that with you.

Groom a little, too—pictures last a lifetime. And also Ammi will be watching on FaceTime, as her appointment got switched. So hurry up, and remember she's wanted this for us for a long time.

I call Saleem a few times, then Amma, then all the other members of my family, but no one picks up. I throw the phone on my bed and follow the stupid note because I want whatever this nonsense is to end.

Maybe Saleem came to his senses and eloped.

Nah, not him. Who else, then? Faisal?

I shower and change into the navy-blue shalwar kameez and trim my beard and comb my hair. Then I look through my side-table drawer for Nani's ring. Maybe it's better if Amma gives it to Faisal or Saleem. I always imagined Sana with it, but now that will never happen. I exhale, slip the ring into my pocket, and head to the party downstairs.

The dining room is filled with my family. Saleem approaches me with a phone in hand, and on the screen I see the nurse holding the phone close to Ammi.

Saleem points at me. "Dulha didn't run away, Ammi."

Dulha? What on earth? I'm not the groom he's referring to, I hope.

Then I see that the white ornate sofas have been rearranged, and there's a swing in the middle of the room decorated with strings of roses twisted on each of the beams that hold the long swing together. On it is seated a woman wearing a veil that covers her face entirely. She's dressed in colors that match with mine.

Is this a big setup? Holy shit. It is.

The whole room is quiet.

My birth mother approaches me, her heels reverberating in the quiet room. "Do you have the ring, puttar?"

I'm livid. But Ammi is watching, so I lower my voice. "What's all this?"

Saleem puts the phone close to my face and yells, "Surprise engagement party!"

"Who is getting engaged?"

"You are. Now let's not keep the lovely lady waiting. She's traveled quite a distance." He tips his head in the direction of the girl on the swing.

The whole room is now looking at me, including my mothers, uncles, and their families. A no would disappoint them all. I could give a middle finger to everyone and walk out of here. But I can't. This is how Sana's changed me. She's shown me that sometimes you have to sacrifice your own desires to please those you love. Love is not just about things we want; it's also about trusting the decisions of those around me. She is somewhat happy with Adam, and maybe I will be too. Maybe I'll learn to like Zaynab.

Maybe it's enough.

"You are so full of shit," I whisper in Saleem's ear and approach her.

Amma leads me to the seat next to her on the traditional swing. The jhula sways a little when I slide onto it.

Everyone applauds. And I see my mother, Saleem, and Uncle all exhale in relief. Even they're surprised by my willingness to go along with this crazy plan.

Saleem gives the phone to Faisal and announces to the room, "Salaam, everyone. And apologies, bade bhai, for throwing this curve ball at you. Marriage, as they say, is a life sentence that has some benefits."

Whistles and hoots from my uncles follow that line, while the women titter and smile. Saleem continues. "But I'm so glad he has found someone who will chase him, even when he's given up on her. This must be love. With this, I ask you all to pray for them and shower them with your blessings."

Everyone applauds, and an uncle older than Yasir recites the Surah Fatiha. After he finishes, the ladies all gather around us and ask Zaynab to lift her hand.

Amma nudges me. "Ring?"

This is when I start to deflate. This was Sana's ring. Am I ready for this?

Saleem whispers close to my ear, "I have a backup ring if you lost Nani's."

I dig in my pocket and retrieve the ring. The woman lifts her hand.

The hand is . . . familiar.

I blink. This cannot be. Maybe my mind is playing tricks on me. I have conjured up memories of Sana, when she cannot be here.

I blink twice. It's still the same hand.

I swallow. "Zaynab?"

She squirms and lifts her veil. "Who's Zaynab?"

Saleem moves next to her quickly and yelps, "Sana, goddammit! Why couldn't you follow the script?"

My heart leaps. Sana is really here. We're getting engaged.

Then Zia, Soofia Auntie, and Rana make their way through the crowd.

I can't believe this.

When Sana's eyes meet mine, I forget that we're surrounded by our families in Pakistan—I lift her hand and kiss the back of her wrist.

A few more whistles, and someone calls out, "You need to pay maher!"

Sana snatches her hand back and blushes. My beautiful bride. More beautiful than any dream.

She smiles and says, "This isn't halal. Pay maher and have nikah."

I chuckle. "Where's the qazi? I'm ready for the nikah."

Soofia Auntie chides, "Let's get through the engagement. We landed this morning; don't make us go looking for a wedding venue tonight."

Sana wiggles her fingers. I slip my nani's ring on and hold her hand tightly. I whisper close to her ear, "I think I'm still dreaming, so I'm never letting go."

Sana squeezes my hand back, and there are tears of joy in her eyes. "Me too."

EPILOGUE

SANA

Scarsdale, New York

This house always felt like ours. I see why Shahida Auntie left it to us. *Us* is such a beautiful word. Daniel and I are an *us* now.

Today is going to be a good day, InshAllah. Is it qismet that we're together? Not all of it. If I hadn't gone after him, we wouldn't be here today. Maybe our fates were determined, but we still had to find a way to each other.

The colors of spring are vivid in our backyard, and the tree with our carved initials is vibrant. A butterfly buzzes on the rose garden that Zia and I have been planting in Shahida's memory. It's a sign. Everything is full of new life. I take in the late-spring air and rub my hands clean of dirt. Soon I won't be able to do this. And the thought of why gives me tingles.

I put away my gardening tools. Daniel's Tesla and Mirchi are both in the garage, which means he's home from work. I tuck an envelope under my arm and head to the kitchen to hide it.

As I put the teakettle on, Daniel's big arms envelop me, and he kisses the nape of my neck. In my eager response to his tenderness, the cup slips from my hands. He releases me in time to catch it. "Salaam, Soni," he whispers in my ear.

His warm breath causes goose bumps. I turn to face him and, standing on my tiptoes, kiss his forehead. "How was your day?"

He loosens his tie and pulls me against his chest. "It'll be better as soon as we head upstairs."

"I thought you would want chai after a long day. I'm being the good desi wife your mother wanted." I smile. "Plus, I thought being your own boss meant less stress."

He grabs milk from the fridge.

I love this about him, that he wants to be with me all the time, even when he's had a long day. But I want to surprise him, so I tell him, "Go change, then let's sit outside and enjoy the rest of the day."

He puts the cups on the table, drops a kiss on my forehead, and leaves. I prepare the tray, setting the envelope behind the teapot, and head to the expansive deck we just built.

Once Daniel's changed into casual clothes, he comes outside and sits on the wicker sofa next to me. I pour his tea.

He catches sight of the white envelope next to the teapot and picks it up. "What's this?"

My heartbeat spikes. I purse my lips to contain my smile.

He opens the envelope and stares in disbelief at the paper. He's still and noticeably quiet.

Ya Allah! Did I misread him? I reach out and squeeze his hand. "Dani?"

A watery film covers the gray pupils of his eyes. His voice is hoarse, as if he's about to break down. "Is this true?"

I nod.

"Holy shit! I'm going to be a father." He holds me tight. "I wish I could tell you how happy this makes me. We are going to have a *family*!"

The last time I saw him cry was when we buried Shahida Auntie next to her father in Islamabad. The only solace I have is that she lived to see us get married.

Our nikah was a small affair. Just our families and Ainee, Haroon, and Reema. Our mothers forgot their differences, at least for the day. Rana had a big part in Ammi agreeing to come to Pakistan. Once she was there, Zahida explained how all the rumors surrounding Daniel's birth were just that—rumors. I think that after I was gone, she really looked at everything through a different lens. Not as a mother who hated her would-be son-in-law, but as a woman who was about to lose her best friend to cancer forever. The entire time she was in Pakistan, she spent most of it with Shahida.

Of course, she and Zahida were still not on the best of terms, but they decided to behave for our sake.

Zia sat next to me as my wakeel, as I said qabool hai to the love of my life.

A week after our honeymoon, Shahida Auntie died peacefully in her sleep. We were all there when she breathed her last.

Soon after, Daniel received a call from AG Shah asking his help with a case. So we moved back here.

Saleem urged us to do so, because he thought a change of scenery could help Daniel with his grief over Shahida Auntie's death. Saleem stayed in Islamabad, promising to visit.

Haroon got another promotion, and he and Ainee moved to Brooklyn, so they didn't need the house after all. Ainee was thrilled to move away from her mother-in-law.

The wind chimes tinkling at a distance bring me back. It has gotten dark. Daniel's gone missing, probably to call his mother.

After a final deep breath filled with the smell of green lawns and flowers, I go inside. He's not in the kitchen, so I call out, "Daniel? Where are you?"

He answers, "In the living room." His voice sounds funny, like he's trying not to laugh.

Curious, I walk to the living room and see my mother and brother sitting with Daniel.

"Salaam, Ammi, I didn't know you were here." I bend over and hug her.

"Daniel called me. He said you need me now."

Daniel says, "Yes, we have some special news." He looks at me. "Do you want to tell them? Or shall I?"

"I will." I stay cuddled in my mother's arms and whisper, "You're going to be a grandmother."

Ammi covers her mouth with her hand, and her eyes widen. Then, when the shock settles, she wipes her eyes and hugs both me and Daniel. "I wish Shahida were alive to see this. We used to joke about how we'd raise our grandkids together."

"Well, there was a time you wanted nothing to do with her, Soofia Auntie," Daniel teases Ammi, a smile breaking at the corner of his lips.

I glare at him, urging him to cut it out.

Ammi takes in a long, fortifying breath. "Uff, mujhey maloom tha yeh baat toh—of course a lawyer like you would want to dig deeper into all that."

Daniel holds her hand in his and smiles. "Only if you're ready to talk about it, Soofia Auntie. I love and respect you regardless."

Ammi shakes her head. "Haan, haan. This conversation needs to happen before my grandchild arrives. It took a mutiny from all my children to make me understand. Sana left for Pakistan, and Rana and Zia too, in their own ways, spoke for you, Daniel. Rana was chatty, but Zia retreated. I could tell he was mad, but he couldn't protest like Rana. That broke my heart."

Zia, hearing his name being mentioned, leaves the game on his iPad and joins us.

Ammi continues. "Shahida and I talked so much while in Pakistan. All this time, maybe I should've let that happen; it's what my heart needed. I missed her as a friend, and I couldn't even properly grieve the end of my friendship with her, or my husband's passing. Her fragility made me realize, life is short. She actually said to me, "'Now that I want to live and see my son marry and have grandkids, I have to leave.'" Ammi's voice breaks when she completes the sentence. "'You love them for me, Soofia.'"

Daniel turns to Ammi and says, "Ammi died with her heart full. I think she was waiting for you to see her. I'm so happy you two were able to settle your differences. Of course, I think the real hero of our story is Zia. He convinced you, in his way, what was best for all of us." Daniel hugs Zia and squeezes his shoulder. "Bud, thank you for convincing your mom. You've made us so happy."

Zia is confused but hugs Daniel back. "Why are there laddus?"

His comment makes us all smile. He is a reprieve from the tense moment.

I run a caressing hand over my belly. "You are going to be Mamu again."

"You too?" Zia's forehead is clouded with furrows. He doesn't like kids too much—not my sisters' kids anyway, because they're messy and noisy.

"I promise you will love this one." Daniel smiles.

Ammi observes us and reaches out to cradle my face. "I'm so sorry I ever doubted you two."

"And I'm glad I didn't listen." I smile and give Daniel a kiss.

ACKNOWLEDGMENTS

Bismillah.

A book is a dream. And the dreamer in me has brought me here. The storyteller in me has pulled me through many disappointments, because the world in my head was always so lively and vivid.

If I could tell my ten-year-old self something, it would be to never give up. And yes, the thousands of rupees I spent on mailing a hard copy of my first book, written at the age of ten, was not a waste. It began a lifelong obsession with dreaming and creating on paper.

When I started writing Sana's story in 2018, it was to amuse myself. Someone wise told me that I have to write to please myself first and not worry about everyone else. So I did. But that was just the beginning of writing, and rewriting, Sana's story. Sana was the name of the protagonist of the story I first wrote when I was ten, so Sana is special to me in more ways than one.

A book is a collaboration of so many people. Writing is solitary, but almost everything after isn't. So first and foremost, I want to thank my agent, Becca Podos, for believing in this story so much.

Through all the revisions, we pulled through; she didn't give up on Sana, even when sometimes I wanted to. You are the calm to my chaos.

To my editor Jess Verdi, who has held my hand and always been patient and so gracious. You are the yin to my yang.

To the entire team at Alcove, thank you for answering all my anxiety-ridden emails.

Even before this was a book, I had my writers group cheering me to the finish line. Thank you to my friends at the Raritan Valley group of writers for always believing in my stories. To my #Pitsquirrels, Amelia, Beck, Janet, Kim, Liv, and Rose, you are my people. Thank you for holding my hand and always being there to lift me up.

To my critique partners, who have always read through multiple crappy drafts. Thank you, Jannat and Nat, for always nudging me back to the meat of the story. My WhatsApp soul sister, Soniya, for those midnight texts through submission and revisions. And Amanda, for loving Daniel as much as I do.

My parents, who are no longer with me, sacrificed so much to get me where I am today; may Allah have mercy on them in the Hereafter. I am truly lucky to have been born into a family where dreams were never discouraged.

To my wonderful family. I am who I am as a writer because you left me alone with my thoughts when I needed to and distracted me when writing life was overwhelming. You are my Ishq, forever.